She'd never made an offer like this to a man

Live dangerously, Serena Davis told herself, as she walked toward the chutes at the Wolverton Rodeo. She rounded a corner in the maze of pens and stalls, and then she stopped, her heart drumming in her chest.

There he stood! Cal McKinney. Crystal Creek's most famous cowboy. Only tonight he didn't look like the man she had heard about. That man was supposed to be too carefree and what-the-heck for his own good. Not sullen and dangerous like this.

Serena's heart beat harder. She kept her eyes fixed on her quarry, noticing a bruise that darkened one cheek and made his jaw swell slightly. And he limped as he walked around the big bay gelding he was currying.

Great, she thought, *he's bruised, he's banged up and he's in a rotten mood. I picked a wonderful time. He looks like he'd just as soon murder a stranger as talk to one.*

Live dangerously, the voice in her head repeated.

Special thanks and acknowledgment to Bethany Campbell for her contribution to the Crystal Creek series.

Special thanks and acknowledgment to Sutton Press Inc. for its contribution to the concept for the Crystal Creek series.

Published May 1993

ISBN 0-373-82515-3

AMARILLO BY MORNING

Printed in U.S.A.

Amarillo by Morning

Bethany Campbell

Harlequin Books

TORONTO • NEW YORK • LONDON
AMSTERDAM • PARIS • SYDNEY • HAMBURG
STOCKHOLM • ATHENS • TOKYO • MILAN
MADRID • WARSAW • BUDAPEST • AUCKLAND

Dear Reader,

Welcome back to Crystal Creek! In the heart of Texas Hill Country, the McKinneys have been ranching, living and loving for generations, but the future promises changes none of these good folks could ever imagine!

Crystal Creek itself is the product of many imaginations, but the stories began to take shape when some of your favorite authors—Barbara Kaye, Margot Dalton, Bethany Campbell, Cara West, Kathy Clark and Sharon Brondos—all got together with me just outside of Austin to explore the Hill Country, and to dream up the kinds of romances such a setting would provide. For several days, we roamed the countryside, where generous Texans opened their historic homes to us, and gave us insights into their lives. We ate barbecue, we visited an ostrich farm and we mapped out our plans to give you the linked stories you love, with a true Texas flavor and all the elements you've come to expect in your romance reading: compelling, contemporary characters caught in conflicts that reflect today's dilemmas.

Author Bethany Campbell wrote AMARILLO BY MORNING because she was fascinated by the character of the rodeo cowboy, Cal McKinney. Cal is a true Western cavalier, free, easy and used to having his way—especially with women. Then he meets a bootmaker, the elusive Serena Davis. A man who seldom thinks of tomorrow, and a woman obsessively focused on the future. Each of these characters has something to learn from the other. And that is precisely what they do.

Next month, Cal's baby sister, Lynn, finds that WHITE LIGHTNING is not only the name of her prized Thoroughbred. It also describes the effect of a certain Austin dentist's brilliant smile....

C'mon down to Crystal Creek—home of sultry Texas drawls, smooth Texas charm and tall, sexy Texans!

Marsha Zinberg
Coordinator
Crystal Creek

A Note from the Author

It seemed inevitable that I grow up fascinated with the West. On both sides of the family, my forebears were pioneers who came westward in covered wagons. One became an Indian trader in Wyoming territory. Another was neighbor to the Dalton boys, of bank-robbing fame.

One of my great-grandfathers homesteaded in Nebraska, and when he plowed, he often turned up arrowheads, reminders that the land he homesteaded had once been hunting grounds to the Sioux. Another called it quits with Anglo civilization and went off to live with the Indians. I have a photograph of him in buckskins, his hair hanging to his shoulders.

To me, Crystal Creek is more than a locale; it is part and parcel of the great myth of the West. It is a country of the heart and all of the heart's charted and uncharted desires.

An elderly poet of the West, John Neihardt, once said he would tell me a secret. All I would ever need to know, he confided, could be summed up in two words.

"What are they?" I asked.

"Courage and love, lady," he replied, "courage and love."

He would have liked Crystal Creek. It is a humble little town and a flawed one, and no one in it is perfect, but its tradition is proud, and courage and love are its guiding spirits. I've loved my sojourn there. I hope that you will, too.

Bethany Campbell

Cast of Characters

AT THE DOUBLE C RANCH

John Travis (J.T.) McKinney	Rancher, owner of the Double C, his family's ranch. A man who knows his own mind.
Cynthia Page McKinney	J.T.'s wife. An ex-Bostonian bank executive learning to do things the Texas way.
Tyler McKinney	J.T.'s eldest son, a graduate of Rice University. Now he wants to grow grapes in his daddy's pasture.
Cal McKinney	J.T.'s second son, a rodeo cowboy who loves 'em and leaves 'em.
Lynn McKinney	J.T.'s only daughter. She bucks the trend by raising Thoroughbreds in quarter-horse country.
Hank Travis	J.T.'s ancient grandfather. Old Hank has seen and done it all.
Ruth Holden	Californian vintner, daughter of Dan Holden, J.T.'s old army buddy. Ruth is visiting the Double C to help Tyler plan his vineyard.
Lettie Mae Reese	Cook. ⎫ Together they know all
Virginia Parks	Housekeeper. ⎬ the household secrets.
Ken Slattery	Foreman at the Double C.

AT THE CIRCLE T RANCH

Carolyn Randolph Townsend	J.T.'s sister-in-law and neighbor.
Beverly Townsend	Carolyn's daughter and a former Miss Texas.
Lori Porter	Carolyn's cousin. Lori lives at the Circle T and keeps the ranch accounts.

AT THE LONGHORN

Dottie Jones	Owner of the Longhorn Motel and Coffee Shop.
Nora Jones	Dottie's son's ex-wife.
Martin Avery	Mayor of Crystal Creek.
Bubba and Mary Gibson	Old friends of J.T.'s.
Nate Purdy	The McKinneys' family physician.
Vernon Trent	Real-estate agent.
Wayne Jackson	Sheriff.

NEWCOMERS TO CRYSTAL CREEK

Serena Davis	Talented bootmaker. Cal's image and body are exactly what she's looking for.
Tracey Cotter	Serena's business partner and closest friend.
Patti Chadron	Serena's sister in Amarillo.

To Bea and Howard,
with love and gratitude, now and forever.

This book could not have been written
without the assistance of the following:
Lee Miller,
bootmaker extraordinaire, of Texas Traditions, Austin, Texas
Jackie Daugherty,
Manager, Boots 'n Brims, Springdale, Arkansas
Bill Carpenter,
former rodeo roper and rider.
And most especially,
to the Huntington's Disease Society of America,
which keeps lighting candles to drive back the darkness.

CHAPTER ONE

SHE WAS NERVOUS. She'd never before made an offer like this to a man. Especially a strange man.

Live dangerously, she thought, and held herself a little straighter as she walked toward the chutes.

The Wolverton Rodeo was glitzy, she brooded as she left the brick pathway. Year-round rodeo still seemed foreign to her. To tell the truth, she wasn't fond of big rodeos, and Wolverton was big, even for Texas. But it had its uses. She intended to use it.

Serena Davis shrugged imperceptibly and pulled her Stetson down to a more determined angle. She was a tall woman of twenty-seven, with long black hair and gray-green eyes. She wore a pale sage-green shirt of Western cut, and darker green denims that hugged her slim hips and long legs.

Of all her clothing, her boots alone called attention to themselves. High-heeled and hand-tooled, they were cream-colored, with dusty-green prickly pear and yucca plants inlaid into them. They were the best pair she had, the best pair she'd ever made.

They might well be the most expensive pair of boots at the rodeo tonight, which, at Wolverton, was saying something. The upscale auditorium had its own Western-wear store, a gift boutique and even a barbecue restaurant with a live band. Its top tier housed fifty-six glassed SkyBoxes with closed-circuit television, bars and a fortune in Western artworks.

Serena, who remembered the old rodeo in Wolverton before it became so showy and oversized five years ago, still felt uncomfortable with its grandeur. At least, she thought, wrinkling her freckled nose with wry pleasure, it still *smelled* like a rodeo. They couldn't take that away.

The rich scents of horse, hay, leather and cattle mingled and grew stronger. The mixture was a pungent one that had bewitched her since childhood. And as usual, the aroma filled her with conflicting impressions. Safety because this had been her grandfather's world, and as a little girl she had felt secure in it. But even back then despite the illusion of safety, she had sensed danger in the air, as well. It had, after all, been rodeo. In rodeo, anything could happen.

Anything could happen.

Live dangerously.

She rounded a corner in the maze of pens and stalls, and then she stopped, her heart drumming a small stampede in her chest.

There he stood. His profile was to her, and he was engrossed in currying a big, ugly bay gelding with a scar that ran from its foreleg up to its chest. The man didn't look happy. The handsome face looked stolid, almost angry.

He *should* look happy, she thought in momentary confusion. She hadn't watched the rodeo tonight, but he always did well. Last week in Brazos he'd won the top money in calf roping, and he'd done admirably in bareback bronc riding as well, tying for third.

His family was rich, he was good-looking, and he was one of the best calf ropers in the business, once champion of the Cheyenne Frontier Days, twice champion of the Texas circuit and three times contender for world champion. He always acquitted himself admirably. What did he have to be unhappy about?

Another cowboy, much smaller and with one badly squinting eye, lounged against the bars of the stall, talking to him, a twisted smile on his face. But the handsome man, the one she had to talk to, wasn't smiling. Not at all.

The short cowboy saw her, looked her up and down and then said something out of the side of his mouth. The handsome man turned, gave her a brief glance and still did not smile. He muttered something and turned his attention back to the horse.

Serena kept her eyes fixed on her quarry, the handsome cowboy, and moved toward him purposefully. He was a tall man, at least six foot two, with dark hair and eyebrows. His black Stetson hung on one of the uprights of the stall, and his worn leather chaps were thrown over a railing.

He had extremely regular features that gave him a deceptively boyish look at first glance. But there was nothing boyish in the ranginess of his body or in his expression. His good looks were temporarily marred by a bruise that darkened one cheek and made that side of his jaw swell slightly.

Her heart beat harder. He wasn't supposed to be like this, sullen and dangerous looking. His reputation was the opposite. His attitude was supposed to be too carefree and what-the-hell for his own good. He was *supposed* to be full of easy charm, not simmering anger.

He moved to the other side of the big horse, still ignoring Serena. She thought she detected a slight limp in his step. Maybe his back injury was acting up, she speculated. And the closer she got, the harsher the bruise on his face looked.

Well, she thought fatefully, *he's bruised, he's banged up and he's in a rotten mood. I picked a wonderful time. He looks like he'd just as soon murder a stranger as talk to one.*

Live dangerously, the voice in her head repeated.

Of course. How else could she live? She had no choice.

She stepped to his side, looked up at his frowning profile and tried to smile. She found she couldn't. Her mouth was suddenly dry.

She refused to allow nervousness to stop her. She thrust out her hand and spoke in a voice so cool and confident it surprised her. "Cal McKinney?" she asked. "I'm Serena Davis. I'd like to take you to supper. Will you go?"

His head snapped up. Her eyes met a pair of blazing hazel ones. They were deep-set, long-lashed and so full of life that their intensity startled her. Caught in their gaze, she had the sudden, dizzying sensation of falling through space.

He smiled, and the fall grew faster.

He took her hand in his. At that moment the fall became so headlong that she couldn't breathe.

Stop it, she told herself in panic. *I can't be attracted to this man. I can't. I can't be attracted to anybody. I'm at risk.*

It seemed such a simple word: risk. Serena, looking at the tall cowboy, knew it wasn't simple at all.

CAL MCKINNEY HAD BEEN in a mood blacker than chuck wagon coffee. He was back on the rodeo circuit. That should have been good, but it felt hollow, without its old joy.

He knew his daddy was unhappy with him for rodeoing again. He'd heard what J.T. had supposedly said about him back in Crystal Creek: "When he wants to grow up and be a real cowboy, he'll come home. In the meantime, he's back in the circus."

The words stung. He'd told his father he'd try to find a different life from rodeo. He had tried many times but there was nothing else he wanted to do.

A few weeks ago Cal had turned thirty. He had done so in Fort Worth and, as if to commemorate the day, a bareback bronc had ignominiously thrown him three seconds out of the chute.

Rodeo made a man superstitious, and Cal had come to believe in omens. The bronc that dusted him was named Fate. Fate had not only sent him crashing into the dirt of the arena so hard it wrenched his back, Fate had also kicked him in the head.

Last week, in Borger, right before Brazos, he'd drawn another rank horse, been thrown at the buzzer and damn near landed under the hooves of the horse

of the pickup man. He'd seen a horseshoe grinding in
the dirt five inches from his eyes, watched as it barely
cleared his head.

Worse, although he made good time roping and tying his calf tonight, the maverick had somehow
knocked him in the jaw with a thrashing foreleg. A
three-hundred-pound calf had a kick that hit a man
harder than a baseball bat. An hour afterward Cal was
still seeing stars and spitting blood and testing his
teeth.

Tonight Shorty, a bull rider from Tucson, was on
Cal's case. Shorty was a squat, snaggletoothed redhead with a bad eye. The bad eye was compliments of
a bull in Cheyenne two years ago.

Shorty had always been a jealous, gibing little coyote, and the eye made him more so. Women hung
around good-looking rodeo riders like bees around
honey. But none ever buzzed around Shorty, and he
resented it like hell.

He resented Cal in particular because Cal usually
drew more than his share of women. Cal'd had a bet
with Shorty tonight about being in the money in calf
roping. Instead he'd been kicked, had ruined his time,
and he'd had to pay off the little son of a bitch. It had
all put him in a mood meaner than a cut snake.

Tonight Shorty had been jawing him because no
women had been coming around for Cal the past two
nights. No women were likely to show up, either,
Shorty needled. Cal had looked like a fool in Borger,
nearly getting himself killed by the pickup man, who
was there to *save* him, for Pete's sake.

Cal had looked like an even bigger fool tonight, nearly getting his brains kicked out by a trussed-up calf. Didn't he know by now how to stay out of a calf's way? Maybe he was in the wrong business.

Besides, Shorty scoffed, no girls were likely to come around Cal now. He walked with a gimp and had a bruise the color of an eggplant ruining that pretty face. No, sirree, Cal wasn't such a pretty boy right now, and where did that leave him? No gals hanging around lately, were there? Someday that pretty face might get stepped on *good,* and then where would Cal be? Nope, no girls would want him then.

Then Shorty had stopped briefly and sworn. "Look at the boots on that girl," he'd said in awe.

Cal had glanced up and seen Serena. She was a long drink of water, and she had the kind of face that could stop a man's heart in its tracks.

"Look at the girl in those boots, fool," he'd muttered to Shorty, then gone back to grooming his horse.

He didn't know who the girl had come to see, but it wouldn't be him. Shorty was right. Cal's back ached, making him carry himself as stiffly as an old man. His knee hurt, making him limp. His jaw was purple and swollen, and it throbbed like the tick of a cheap watch. Somebody might be getting lucky tonight. He wouldn't be the one.

But then, like a woman sent from heaven, that long-stemmed beauty had walked right to his side, introduced herself and offered to buy him supper. Right in front of that jabbering troll, Shorty. Hallelujah!

Cal looked at her again, smiling, and this time he paid attention to what he saw. She was tall, at least five foot ten, he estimated, and slender. Dressed in muted shades of dusty-green, she reminded him of one of the long, graceful leaves of a century plant.

He'd always liked tall women, the more willowy the better. This one, he thought with satisfaction, was as willowy as they got. Shorty was right: her boots were mighty fine. But Cal didn't waste time concentrating on her boots. It was her face that hooked his attention.

When he looked into her gray-green eyes, it jolted him as powerfully as when Fate kicked him in the head. A man could fall into those sea-green eyes and drown with no protest, happy never to resurface.

Her black hair was long and it hung past her shoulders, almost straight with just a hint of a wave. Her jaw was delicately squared, her nose straight and regal, her mouth wide and full, her eyebrows like dark wings. Freckles, a beautiful constellation of them, spilled across her nose and rounded cheekbones.

She was stunning in a way he had never before imagined a woman being stunning. This, he told himself, was no ordinary cowboy groupie. The gods had smiled on him. Belated happy birthday, Cal—have fun. Signed, The Gods.

He grinned at her, even though it hurt his jaw. He glanced out of the corner of his eye at Shorty. He could *feel* the burn of the smaller man's jealousy, almost smell it smolder, almost hear it crackle.

"You want to take me to supper, sugar?" Cal drawled, his voice as teasing as he could make it. "You sure you got the right man? You sure you don't want Shorty here?"

"You're the one I want," she said unsmiling. She'd drawn her hand back quickly. "Cal McKinney, right?"

"The one and only," he said. She had a throaty voice, soft, that vibrated like a purr along his spine.

Numerous thoughts, none of them gallant, swam through his mind. He wished he'd kept his room at the motel neater. He'd taken out part of his bad mood by strewing his clothes and boots and magazines about wildly. He'd left word for the maid to stay out; he hadn't wanted himself or his stuff disturbed. No. The atmosphere was not romantic.

Maybe she was a local girl, had her own place. He tried to imagine it. An apartment? A house? A water bed? Shorty would nag him for every detail. He wouldn't give the little rodent one.

She raised her chin, still unsmiling. She acted as if she were unused to what she was doing. "When will you be ready to go?" The question, even in her quiet cat's-purr voice, sounded curt, almost reluctant.

He tossed the currycomb to Shorty, who automatically caught it, then suppressed a glare of resentment.

"Honey, for you, I'm ready right now. Just let me stop by the boys' room, wash up."

He reached for his black hat and settled it on his head, adjusting the brim to its jauntiest angle. "You want to go in my van, or you got wheels of your own, sweetheart?"

She shook her head almost solemnly, and her long hair swung with the motion. "I'll drive."

He grinned. This was getting better and better. A girl with that kind of boots had to have money. He imagined her in a wicked-looking little sports car, a convertible, with her hair flying. A white Corvette, he thought. That was what a girl like her should have. Yes, indeedy.

He clapped his hand on Shorty's shoulder with false camaraderie. "Shorty, buddy, take my chaps back to the motel for me, will you? I'll pick 'em up later."

Much, much later, he hoped.

But the girl refused to return his smile. She acted as if she were either very serious or scared. Or both. Maybe it was the first time she'd ever picked up a cowboy. He'd do his best to make it an extremely pleasant experience for her.

He took her arm with a courtly air and kept smiling, trying to put her at ease. "Selena?" he asked.

"Serena," she said tonelessly.

Her arm seemed slight, almost fragile against his hard-muscled one. But her hand, he'd noticed, was hardened and marked by small scars. She must be a sportswoman, he thought. A woman with boots like that didn't work for a living.

She seemed uneasy, uncommunicative as he walked her to the parking lot. This both puzzled him and piqued his interest.

"You from around here, darlin'?" he asked, looking her up and down again with appreciation.

"Yes."

"From Wolverton?"

"Yes."

"Been here all your life?"

"No."

Her one-word answers began to grate on his nerves, threatening his sense of triumph. "How long you been here?"

She swallowed with apparent nervousness. "Ten years."

Well, thought Cal, she'd said two words. That was improvement. He tried again. "Where you from? Originally?"

She swallowed again. "Agatha."

"You have much to do with rodeo?"

She shook her head. "My grandfather," she said, as if that explained everything.

He studied her profile, which was regular and perhaps even patrician. She held her head high, whether in pride or determination he couldn't say. Her skin was lightly tanned, but in spite of it she seemed unnaturally pale, which made her freckles stand out.

"Your grandfather *what?*" he asked, half impatient with her aloofness, half intrigued by it. Lord, he thought, she was beautiful, but there was something fascinatingly elusive about her.

"Raised stock," she said shortly.

"A stock contractor?" he asked. Stock contractors supplied rodeos with bucking animals, steers, calves. Most of them had been contestants once themselves.

She nodded.

Honey, this is like pulling teeth, he thought.

He had a sudden bad vibration. Maybe this was one of those rich women who liked to pick up a man, get her kicks on a purely physical level. Snobbery twisted such women; they couldn't resist the lure of sexual slumming, but they wanted no mental or emotional connection.

The thought threw a cold shadow on his ardor. He liked women—in fact, he loved women—but he didn't aim to be some rich girl's toy. Flirtation was half the fun for Cal. He'd tried once to explain it to Ken, the foreman back home: "See, it's no fun makin' love if you can't make *like* first."

"Make *like?*" Ken had asked, his brow creasing without comprehension.

"Yeah. She makes you like her, you make her like you, and then it's all more *friendly* when you get to bed. More fun."

"Boy," Ken had said in his sober way, "you're crazy."

But Cal knew the truth of what he said. Girls had chased him from the time he could walk. He knew he could get almost any of them into bed by merely asking. The only ones who interested him were the playful ones, those who flirted and sported as avidly as he in the elaborate game of wooing.

The girl at his side had come on strong, but now she'd stopped playing. Intellect told him to be suspicious, but instinct whispered that she had might have gone shy on him, nervous at her own boldness. An optimist, he decided to trust instinct.

Besides, he thought, she was pretty enough and different enough for him to expend extra effort. He could imagine those unsmiling lips softening with desire, her mysterious eyes dazed with pleasure and her dark hair spread against the white of a pillow as he bent above her.

He could also imagine her body, which would be long and slender and pale, with a sprinkle of freckles kissing her shoulders. Small breasts, but slim, tight hips, and legs that went on forever. Oh, yes, thought Cal. Oh, *yes*.

"So," he said, determined to play the courting game, "your granddaddy—was he ever *in* the rodeo?"

An odd look crept into her eyes. Her beautiful, ripe mouth kept its stoic set. "Before I was born," she answered. "A bronc rider. He gave it up when he—when he got married."

"Some do."

Their boots crunched on the gravel at the edge of the parking lot. The lot was almost empty now, and a breeze stirred the night air. It tossed Serena's dark hair, making her face dance in the shadows. He had a sudden irrational desire to stop her, lace his fingers in that black mane and tilt her face up toward his.

Then he'd say something to make her smile, and when that first smile began to fade on the outside, he'd lower his lips to hers and kiss her until she smiled inside as well, warm and glowing.

Slow down, he told himself. He didn't usually move that fast. He didn't know if she could smile. Maybe she was some kind of poor little rich girl or something.

"Honey, you're mighty quiet," he said instead. "Don't say much."

"I prefer action to words," she said, pulling her hat down more firmly against the tug of the breeze.

Now what the hell does that mean? Cal wondered in mixed pleasure and frustration. Was it an invitation? A warning that all she wanted was physical?

"Here," she said, stopping. She reached into the pocket of her jeans and pulled out a set of keys. "This is it." She unlocked the door of a battered green Chevrolet sedan.

Cal frowned, pushing his hat back on his head. So much for the new Corvette he'd expected. This car was at least ten years old, dented, scratched, one hubcap missing and the paint rusting out. It made no sense. He'd imagined a coach. She was driving a pumpkin, and the pumpkin had seen better days.

She didn't seem to notice his surprise. Businesslike, without speaking, she got into the car, reached over and unlocked the door on his side.

Darlin', he thought, *I don't know what you have in mind. But I aim to find out.*

He opened the door and got in beside her. He had an odd, unbidden thought. For some unknown reason he remembered a poem from high school. Cal had usually stared out the window, but one poem had snapped him into alertness because it was weird and sexy.

In it, a young knight met a lovely but otherworldly girl in the forest. He took her onto his horse with him, she said she loved him, and they went to an enchanted grove where they made love: "And there I shut her wide, sad eyes / With kisses four..." Was that how it went? They slept, but when he awoke she was gone, and his soul had gone with her. The knight was doomed to search for her forever.

What a thing to recall after all these years, Cal thought. He had no intention of losing his soul, but he didn't mind the idea of shutting Serena's eyes with kisses four. Or more.

She tossed him a brief glance. "Where to?" she asked crisply.

He grinned his laziest grin. "You decide," he said. "I'm all yours, sweet thing."

I'M TERRIBLE at this, Serena thought in growing frustration. *I'm awful at this. I hate this. This is the worst idea anybody ever had.*

No sooner had she asked him out than she'd grown tongue-tied in his presence. He was so outrageously flirtatious that she couldn't deal with it. She simply couldn't.

"Honey," he'd called her. And "darlin'." And "sweetheart" and "sugar" and "sweet thing." He could get the most innocent smile on his mouth, but at the same time his eyes would burn with the delight of sheer sexuality.

There was, in fact, a languid, mischievous sexiness in every line and motion of his lean body. He might walk with a limp and as if his back hurt, his face might be marred by a bruise, but it didn't slow him. He was used to conquest, and he blithely took for granted that she wanted him.

She'd *kill* Tracey, Serena thought. She'd just kill her. "All you have to do is walk up to him and ask him to dinner," Tracey had said. "Tell him you want to talk to him."

"That's not businesslike," Serena had objected. "And this is strictly business. I should write him. I should phone."

"Look," Tracey had argued, her expression determined, "he's a *cowboy*. You don't know where he's staying. You don't know when he'll move on. He's the one we want. He's here. Go get him."

"*You* go get him," Serena had countered, horrified at Tracey's proposal.

In the end they'd flipped a coin to see who would do it. Serena lost.

Now here she was, driving through the Saturday night traffic with cow country's answer to Casanova. He'd obviously taken her invitation to mean she wanted to check him out for her bed, and she didn't begin to know how to disabuse him of *that* idea.

Lord, she fumed, it was her own fault, too. That sort of thing must happen to him regularly. She'd heard of rodeo groupies. She'd never expected to be taken for one.

Setting her jaw, she told herself that despite her own culpability, he was still a conceited so-and-so, thinking she'd asked him out to satisfy her own pleasure. She had to admit, though, that he was handsome, in spite of the bruise and the limp. She even had to admit he was charming.

He was obviously as shallow as a wet-weather creek, yet beneath his superficiality she sensed genuine friendliness, a basic and irresistible amiability. The appreciation that shone in his eyes seemed, without question, to be honest. He was a paradox: perfectly sincere and insincere at the same time.

She didn't know why he'd seemed so ill-tempered when he was talking to the small cowboy. She didn't know why his face had lit up with such brilliant satisfaction when she approached him. She only knew that now that she had him with her, he made her supremely uncomfortable.

She chose a steak house close to the rodeo so the drive would be short. It looked higher priced than she could afford, but she wanted to get him to the dinner table so she could talk business, get things out in the open, over and done.

She tried to rehearse what she would say to him in the restaurant. It was hard with him lazing there next to her with all the comfort of a big cat. He had tipped his hat low over his eyes and was whistling softly.

He picked up a sketchbook she had left lying on the front seat. He paged through it, studying each pencil sketch with surprising thoroughness. He nodded, as in appreciation. Her hobby was drawing flowers, wild ones, garden ones, hothouse ones. But the sketches were always in pencil, so faint they seemed almost ghostly.

"You're good," he said with a sideways look and a lazy smile. "Don't you ever draw people?"

"No," she said shortly, concentrating on parking. "Never. Nothing but flowers."

"Then you do them in ink? Or paint or something?" he asked. The sketches, he decided, were like her: clearly defined yet somehow, at the same time, undefinable.

She shook her head. "No. I work only in pencil."

He cocked his eyebrow, slightly puzzled, slightly amused. "Nothing permanent."

"No," she answered with surprising emphasis. "Nothing permanent. Ever."

A sexual innuendo? he wondered. Or merely a statement of quirky fact? He shrugged, figuring he'd find out soon. He scrutinized the sketchbook and went back to his whistling. The song he whistled was "All the Girls I've Loved Before."

The steak house she had chosen so desperately was new and it had ambience with a vengeance. It kept the lights low; at each table a candle cast a golden, flickering light; soft music floated in the background; and the head waiter had a French accent. The tablecloths and napkins were of snowy-white linen, and the ornate silver glinted expensively.

I should have taken him to some barbecue and beans place, she thought, looking at the forest of potted palms in antique jardinieres. This place was too romantic; it looked even more as if she had seduction on her mind.

The head waiter cast a disapproving eye at their jeans and boots but said nothing. She thought she saw his nostrils curl and realized that Cal, in spite of having washed up, still bore the faint whiff of horse and leather.

"Zeez way," the waiter said in a world-weary voice and led them to a table in the rear of the room.

With ill-concealed reluctance, he pulled out Serena's chair for her, set down silk-covered menus before them, then folded his hands with false unctuousness. "Would ze gentleman care to see ze wine list?"

"The gent'd like a Lone Star beer," Cal said with a wry smile. "But the lady might like wine. Would you, honey?"

The expression on the waiter's face grew more martyred, more pained as he turned to Serena.

"Nothing," she said brusquely. She wanted, above all else, to keep her head clear.

The waiter sighed and swept away, obviously relieved to be free of them. Serena shifted uncomfortably. She hated snobbish waiters because she hated anything snobbish.

Cal had set his black hat at the table's edge. The candlelight played on his features, bronzing them. He grinned at her, a slow, wicked grin that further disarmed her.

"I believe that old boy got to you," he said, nodding in the direction the head waiter had taken.

Serena unwrapped her silverware from her napkin and spread the napkin in her lap. She kept her motions brisk and practical. "I don't like people who make you feel inferior."

"Hell, darlin'," he said, a dimple playing in his unbruised cheek, "nobody can *make* you feel inferior. Not unless you cooperate."

She blinked at him in surprise. She hadn't expected him to spout philosophy. Perhaps it was simply his conceit at work again. "Nobody's ever been able to make you feel inferior, I take it?"

He shrugged one wide shoulder. "No." He paused. "I mean a person might make me feel—bad. But not inferior."

His smile faded. He thought of J.T. back in Crystal Creek. He thought of the ranch, those thousands of rolling acres. His daddy wanted him home and settled. But here he was thirty years old, still on the circuit, battered, bruised and wiling away the night with a picked up woman. It was a somber thought.

He was glad when a waitress interrupted these gloomy reflections by bringing him his Lone Star. He looked across the table at Serena. She might be a pickup, but she was the most amazingly pretty pickup he'd ever had.

By candlelight her fair skin looked duskier, her soft hair darker and her eyes more mysterious and haunting than ever. She was such a pretty enigma that he decided to worry about making peace with J.T. later.

He filled his glass and raised it in salute to her. "To the moment," he said, and his grin returned.

She nodded, her hands folded primly on the table before her. "That's your outlook, isn't it?" she asked. "Live for the moment."

"Yup." He said it without apology. He drank the beer. "How about you? What do you live for?"

The question startled her. She stared at him in surprise, parted her lips to answer but found she had no words.

What did she live for? It struck her suddenly that the man across from her lived completely for the present, but she was different. She lived almost entirely in the future, and what that future might hold terrified her.

She kept her face carefully blank, but he studied her so intently that she feared he could see through her facade. He leaned back against his chair, stroking the beer bottle absently. "So what's your story, little filly? I can't figure you. You're waltzing around in two-thousand-dollar boots, but you drive a car—pardon me for saying so—that's ready for the scrap heap. You carry yourself like a queen, but a waiter with a snooty attitude makes you nervous. Like I say—what's the story?"

"I—I—" she stammered, unsettled. She was saved by the return of the waitress, asking if they were ready to order.

Serena made a frantic choice from the offerings, picking the dinner that was least expensive, ground round steak.

Cal, watching her with disconcerting steadiness, ordered the same thing without hesitation. The only difference in his order was that he flashed the waitress one of his most captivating grins. "Could you make that rare, honey?" he asked. "And bring me another Lone Star when you've got time?"

The waitress, who was old enough to be his mother, smiled breathlessly, simpered and batted her eyelashes. Serena watched ruefully as the woman bustled away.

Cal had an extraordinary effect on women, there was no denying it. His good looks and easy charm were a powerful combination. And dangerous. Serena had been careful so far. She would continue to be careful.

He turned his attention back to her. His dimple flickered in his cheek, and his hair shone golden brown in the dancing light. "Your story?" he repeated, his voice warm and lazy and teasing.

It was time to get down to business, Serena thought, adjusting her napkin. She took a deep breath. "I have fancy boots because I'm a boot maker. I have an old car because I'm a bootmaker who's just starting out. I have a business, La Herencia, here in Wolverton."

He arched one brown brow thoughtfully. "La Herencia. The Heritage."

She nodded, keeping her face carefully blank. La Herencia was a name loaded with significance for her, more than she would ever wish him to know.

She went on in the same no-nonsense tone. "I have a partner, Tracey Cotter. We hire mainly Mexican craftspeople. We have ambitions. We want to expand. To have boot shops across this state. What we don't have is a spokesperson. That's why I asked you here tonight."

His eyebrow descended, became part of a frown. "A which-what? You asked me here *why,* darlin'?"

She tossed her head slightly, pushed her hair back from her shoulder. "A spokesperson. We need an endorsement. We'll pay for it. We can't pay you in money. But we can give you a pair of custom-made boots. And keep you in supply if the—the relationship works out."

Cal's ego, which had been dismally down, then euphorically up, came smashing down again. He frowned harder. "You brought me here on account of *boots?*" he said in disbelief.

Serena nipped nervously at the corner of her lip. She hadn't meant to offend him, but obviously she had.

"Custom-made boots," she emphasized. "Top of the line. You said mine looked like two-thousand-dollar boots. We'd see that you got the same quality."

He looked at her for a long, simmering moment. Then he sat back in his chair, looked up at the ceiling and laughed. His eyes met hers once more as his brow arched up evilly, and he smiled again.

"Honey," he said, drawling out the words, "I didn't come here with you tonight for *boots*. I got a friend who runs a boot factory. Boots are one thing I don't need. Not at all."

Sensual challenge flickered in his gaze, and Serena looked away. "They're all I have to offer. We're a good company, but we're small. We need recognition. You're well-known. You could get it for us."

He lounged farther back in his chair, but Serena could sense the tautness underlying his apparent carelessness.

"I'm well-known?" he said sarcastically. "Me? Come on, honey. There's better-known cowboys than me. You want a name? Get a big one. Get yourself a world champion."

The waitress appeared, setting a second beer in front of Cal. He interrupted his wryly dour mood long enough to flash her a smile. "Thank you, sweetheart," he said, beaming up at her. "You're a real angel, that's what."

"Oh—you!" said the waitress, plucking with pleasure at the ruffles on her organdy apron. "I'll get your salads."

His smile died as soon as the woman left the table. He stared at Serena with a disgusted quirk to his mouth.

"We can't afford a bigger name," she said earnestly. *Damn!* she thought. *I always say the wrong thing to him. Always.*

"I mean," she amended, "you're known across the state. You're kind of—a local celebrity. We don't plan to expand beyond Texas. Not for a long time. Maybe not ever. You're—you're perfectly adequate for us right now."

His lip curled a fraction of an inch more unpleasantly. He laughed. "You mean I'm small-time enough for you. You think I should be cheap enough, too."

Serena gritted her teeth in frustration. Somehow she'd managed to make things worse. His grin was back, but it was crooked and self-mocking.

"I didn't mean it the way it sounded," she apologized, plunging on. "Look, you've done well. So have a lot of riders. But you've got—a certain, well—charisma. And you've done publicity work before. You photograph well. You can handle yourself on television. You did all those ads for the Exceptional Rodeo promotion."

He gave another snort of mirthless laughter. "Listen, sugar," he said, shaking his head. "I didn't take money to do those ads. And I sure as hell didn't take *boots.*" He packed an eloquent amount of contempt into the word. "I did it for the kids. I'm a cowboy. And I'm *not* for sale."

"I'm sorry," Serena said with all the sincerity she could, but she was frustrated. He'd done wonderful magazine and television and radio ads as the Texas spokesperson for the Exceptional Rodeo program. It was a program for children with physical and mental disabilities, and he'd been nothing short of sensational. That was when Tracey had gotten that inspired gleam in her eye and said, "There's our man."

Serena looked at him beseechingly, and he looked at her with disgusted accusation. Then the waitress swirled up and set their salads before them. Cal changed his persona in a split second, and smiled his dazzling smile at the older woman. "Thank you, angel," he said.

The waitress fluttered off, and he glared again at Serena.

"Listen," Serena said. "Don't be insulted. Everybody thought you did an excellent job on those ads—"

He rolled his eyes as if asking heaven for patience. "People got crazy over those dumb ads. I'm not an actor. I'm not—for God's sake—a *model*. You know what they make a model do? They make him wear *makeup*."

He picked up his salad fork and speared a piece of lettuce with impressive ferocity. He frowned again as he ate it. After he did the ads last year, embarrassing things had happened. Strange women had written asking him for his picture. Giggling teenage girls had phoned the ranch until J.T. had lost patience and gotten a private number. A modeling agency in Dallas had tracked him down in Houston and phoned him at his hotel, asking him if he'd like to model tuxedos in a spread for *Texas Monthly*. Tuxedos! He'd been appalled. Shorty had laughed his fool head off when he heard. "They want you in a penguin suit? That I gotta see. Ha—see the cowboy in the penguin suit."

Worse, some mincing, effeminate small-time talent scout from Hollywood had come after him in Galveston, following him, nudging him in the ribs and talking seductively about screen tests. Soon every rider in the rodeo knew about it. Cal had never before been as embarrassed or depressed. Shorty liked to parade up to him in front of other people and say, "Excuse me, Mr. Movie Star, may I have your autograph?"

No, Cal thought darkly. No more ads. He had vowed it: never again. Now here she was, as desirable a woman as he'd ever seen, and what did she want from him? *Ads*. For a pair of boots.

"If people went a little crazy over the promotion," Serena reasoned, "that just proves you're good at it. What's wrong with that? I'm not asking you to do anything wrong. Or for free."

"But, darlin'," he said with irony, "I want to do something wrong with you. And for free."

Serena sat back as if slapped. "No," she said. "No. Don't even think it. I never had anything like that in mind."

"Didn't you?" he challenged. "You acted like it. You come sashaying in there, all dolled up and giving me the eye—"

"I *wasn't* giving you the eye," she objected.

"Look," he said with spirit. "Trust me. I know when a woman's giving me the eye. You ask me to dinner. You bring me to this place that's all candlelight and froufrous. You lead me on—"

"You jumped to a conclusion. I did *not* lead you on—"

"You led me on," he said inexorably, "now you sit there and tell me all you want is some free advertising and you'll give me some damn *boots?*"

"I didn't lead you on," she repeated with indignation. She kept her voice low to avoid making a scene. "I didn't ask for free advertising. They're not 'damn boots'; they're fine, custom-made—"

"Honey," he interrupted, his eyes flashing and his smile dangerous, "if I wanted your boots, I'd buy 'em. I can afford it. You want to talk business? I got better things to do. You want to talk pleasure? Pleasure interests me. Now you decide. Are we going to talk? 'Cause if we do, we talk pleasure. Or not at all."

It was Serena's turn to bristle. "I'm not interested in your idea of pleasure. I'm a craftsperson and a businesswoman—not some…groupie. You came here of your own free will. You heard my proposition. Either we talk business, or we talk nothing."

He pushed back his chair and rose, taking his hat. He put it on, pulling down the brim with a gesture of finality. "Then we talk *nothing,* sweetheart," he said.

He dug into his pocket and pulled out a crumpled wad of paper money. He unfolded a hundred-dollar bill and threw it on the table. "I'm going somewhere and get a real steak," he said between his teeth. "But I'm paying for this. Give the change to the waitress. She's a nice lady."

He turned on his heel and walked away, his limp and stiff back giving an odd swing—a sort of John Wayne gait—to his wide shoulders and slim hips.

Serena's face burned. "Go rustle a pig," she practically snarled under her breath.

Yet when he disappeared out the door, something exciting and vibrant seemed to die within her. She was angry, but she felt strangely hurt and empty, as well. Her heart began to beat at a normal speed for the first time since she'd seen him. It beat regularly, but its cadence seemed mournful to her.

"Too bad," it seemed to say. "Too bad. Too bad."

"Good riddance," she whispered to herself. He was no good. He was vain, shallow, self-centered and shamelessly pleasure-loving. He was no loss at all. She and Tracey were better off without him.

But then, unexpectedly, she remembered his effortless smile and her heart switched cadence. It changed so fast that it left her breathless and perplexed.

Now, for no logical reason in the world, it said, "Get him back. Get him back. Back. Back. Back."

CHAPTER TWO

CAL LEFT THE RESTAURANT, pain shooting up his leg at every step. As he left, he caught a reflection of himself in the window. He saw the bruised side of his face, and the dark glass distorted his reflection so the swollen jaw made him look like Quasimodo.

Hell, he thought, Shorty was right. What good-looking, high-class woman would come after anybody as gimped up, black and blue, and back-cracked as he was? All the girl had wanted was some two-bit local celebrity she thought was cheap enough to buy off with a pair of boots.

He hobbled down the street toward the rodeo, too mad to hail a cab. Walking might get the kinks out of his back and his soul, but it played the devil with his leg. Well, let it hurt. He was in a dark enough mood to take grim satisfaction in discomfort.

For the first time, he noticed his shoulder hurt, too. He must have pulled a muscle roping tonight. The woman had kept that latest injury from registering. Too bad the green-eyed lady had only business in mind.

The night was dark, the street lamps cast little light, and the gloom suited his self-deprecating mood. He remembered once more his daddy's warnings.

"You may have a lot of flirty girls chasin' you, boy. But what're you going to do when you want a *respectable* woman?"

Cal had only grinned. "Daddy, I can't say I ever particularly thought of wanting a respectable woman."

J.T. hadn't been amused. "You're almost thirty. What's your future? Cal, a rancher can go on ranching damn near forever. But a rodeo cowboy's an old man at forty. What do you aim to have at forty—besides every bone in your body broken?"

Cal limped on through the darkness, his hat pulled low on his forehead. Until he turned thirty, forty had been too far away to think of. Hell, until he turned thirty, *thirty* had been too far away to think of.

He'd made decent money for a rodeo cowboy; he'd been Cheyenne Frontier Days All Around Champion, and Texas Circuit champion, but he'd never quite made the true big time. He'd think he was on his way for a world championship, but something had always happened.

He'd broken an arm. He'd broken a leg, the same one, twice. He'd broken his collarbone six times. He'd stopped counting broken ribs. He'd sprained his back five times. He'd broken his foot. He'd broken fingers eight times. Pulled more muscles than he could remember. Five hairline fractures, two concussions, a dislocated shoulder, and a crushed disc.

By some miracle he'd never broken his nose, and he still had all his teeth. But parts of him were patched and parts were wired together, and every year more of him got patched and wired. His daddy was right. He didn't have the most promising of futures.

But, Lord, how Cal loved the life. J.T. couldn't understand it. None of the family could, except maybe his younger sister, Lynn.

By now he'd made his way almost halfway back to the rodeo arena. A neon sign with a bucking horse blinked off and on above the door of a brick building. Bronco's, it said. It was a hangout for some of the rodeo riders. And the girls who always followed them.

Cal looked up at the shimmering outline of the rearing horse. Outside the streets were nearly empty, the night dark. Inside he could hear honky-tonk music and laughter. He didn't think twice. He opened the door and went in.

He recognized several faces—cowboys who were competing at Wolverton.

A lanky, stoop-shouldered man of about thirty-seven in faded jeans and a gray Resistol hat ambled up to the bar beside Cal. Rayburn Wallace was a kind-faced man, who'd been out of luck and out of the money lately because of tendon injuries. Cal figured Rayburn must have just blown into town tonight.

"Cal," he said in his easy, mournful voice. "Didn't expect to see you tonight. Shorty said you'd gone off with a big, lanky freckledy gal."

Cal's mouth took on a disgusted angle. He noticed that Rayburn had nursed his beer down to the last inch and guessed the man probably couldn't afford another. He signaled the bartender for two long necks.

"I'll buy," he said, leaning his elbow on the bar. "She wasn't any 'big, lanky freckledy gal.' She was tall and beautiful."

"Well," Rayburn said with a slow smile, "most everybody looks big and lanky to Shorty. What happened to her?"

Cal put his foot on the brass rail and pushed his hat back carelessly. "She was just some businesswoman with a cockamamy deal. I got better things to do."

"Yeah?" Rayburn asked amiably, leaning against the bar. "Like what?"

"Like having a beer, seeing a few friends, maybe meeting a girl who wants some fun. Better things."

Rayburn shook his head. He turned just long enough to pick up his beer, then leaned back, facing out to look over the smoky dimness of the room. He shook his head again. "Gets old," he said.

Cal was studying his indistinct reflection in the mirror that ran behind the bar and hardly heard him. The bruise, he thought, made him look like some cheap street fighter. No wonder the woman had found him so easy to resist. What would she, a beautiful woman who drew flowers, see in someone who looked like a bum? And why, he wondered, did she do her lovely drawings only in pencil? She had an air about her of something undiscovered, perhaps undiscoverable. Something inexplicable about her baffled and haunted him.

"What?" he said absently.

"Gets old," Rayburn repeated and sipped his beer. "I'm gettin' out."

"What?" Cal turned to face him, his eyebrow cocked in disbelief. "You mean quitting?" Rayburn had been a fixture of the rodeo circuit ever since Cal started. Rayburn couldn't just up and *quit*. It would mean Cal's own time was running short.

Rayburn nodded laconically. "Every year I make less money, break somethin' new or break it again. I been through two wives, and a third one ain't never goin' to want me if I keep on like this. I'm tired of the kind of woman hangs around bars and prowls around the chutes. Yep. It gets old."

Cal gave him a dubious smile that made his jaw hurt. "Hell, Rayburn, it's in your blood. You can't walk away."

Rayburn didn't smile back. "Might be in my blood. But it's plumb been knocked out of my joints and everythin' else. Doc says I've got the arthritis. If I break this ol' elbow once more, it's goin' to quit on me for good."

The cloud that had been living in the back of Cal's mind grew somewhat larger, somewhat darker. "What you aim on doing?"

"Go back to Crockett. Start of next week. I got me a cousin there with a spread. Needs an assistant foreman. I'm almost thirty-eight. Time I got sensible." Rayburn nodded to himself, looking resigned. His lined face was slightly sad, but peaceful.

Cal frowned. Part of his mind resented this change in his familiar world and wanted Rayburn to go on rodeoing, like old times. But another part said, "He's right. It's past time. He's an old man for this sport. It's got no future for him."

Cal took a long pull of his beer and stuck his thumb in the belt of his jeans. "Hell, Rayburn," he said as casually as he could. "I'll miss you. I wish you luck."

"Same to you," Rayburn answered, staring straight ahead. Neither man looked at the other. It was as emotional as they would allow themselves to get.

Later Rayburn drifted off, hitching a ride back to his motel with a saddle bronc rider from Dumas. Cal stayed standing at the bar because his back felt better when he stood. He nursed his beer because he didn't want to go back to his room yet.

"You look lonesome, cowboy," a woman's voice said beside him. "Cowboy as good-lookin' as you should never be lonesome."

He glanced to his left. A short woman stood by his elbow. She had artificially blond hair and a T-shirt that said See Anything You Like? across the chest. The shirt, he noted with clinical interest was tight, but that wasn't as intriguing as it might have been because the woman was overweight. It looked as if she had tires piled inside that T-shirt.

He smiled, although once more it hurt his jaw.

"I know you," the woman said. "You're Cal McKinney."

He nodded.

For a woman so heavy, she had a high, little voice. Her yellow hair was frizzy, and her lipstick looked black in the dim light of the bar.

She reached up and touched his bruised cheek with her plump forefinger. "You done got yourself hurt, sugar. You want me to kiss it and make it well?"

Cal smiled without sincerity, shook his head and turned his attention back to his beer. For once in his life, he realized, he'd rather be alone than with a woman. There'd been a little redhead over in the corner—more attractive and younger than the blonde—who'd been giving him the eye since he walked in.

But tonight he wasn't interested. Not in the redhead. Not in the blonde. Which was odd, he reflected, because for the first time that he could recall, he felt downright out-and-out stony lonesome. His insides ached with an eerie, unpleasant emptiness he didn't understand or like.

"What's the matter, cowboy?" the blonde asked softly, her arm brushing his. "You look sad. Unhappy love affair?"

He looked at her again, pulling down his hat so that it shaded his eyes. If he looked sad, he wouldn't let anybody see it.

"Sweetheart," he said flippantly, "in my book there's no such thing as an unhappy love affair." But somehow, although he said it, his heart wasn't in it.

She giggled. "Buy me a beer?"

"Sure," he said without enthusiasm and gestured for the bartender to bring her a long neck.

He kept seeing another face floating, phantomlike, in the dark air. It was Serena Davis's strangely beautiful face, the long hair flowing, the green eyes full of mystery. It was the face of the one woman in Wolverton who *didn't* seem to want him.

He tried to eject the vision of her from his mind. Stubbornly, it stayed. He remembered her coming to his side, all solemn and nervous, while he was grooming his horse. He remembered how her expression had tantalized him, and how her freckles had seemed more beautiful to him than the markings on any butterfly's wings.

The way she walked came back to him, her hips so slim and her legs so long that they made his groin tingle. The shape of her mouth, sensuous yet carefully controlled, came back to him, as well. He'd wondered immediately how that mouth would taste. He was still wondering.

The blonde snuggled closer to him. She wore enough perfume to choke a horse, Cal thought miserably. She was so short he had to look way down to see her, not like Serena Davis, who was so tall she could almost look him in the eye.

Irritably, he glanced around the room. Hell, there wasn't a woman in the bar that was a patch on the one he'd walked away from tonight. He'd visualized having her in bed, her long, cool body easy and generous beneath his. He'd imagined her lying there afterward staring up at him, her hands on his face and her lips finally smiling.

Instead he was standing in this stinking bar killing the night with a bunch of other drifters and steer scalders and loop tossers like himself. At his side wasn't an intriguingly aloof brunette, but an all-too-eager blonde.

"So where you stayin', cowboy?" the woman beside him asked, looking up and batting her eyelashes. She wore so much mascara, he thought uncharitably, that she looked like a raccoon in a yellow wig.

But he didn't want to hurt her feelings. "With my grandma, sweet thing. She's waitin' up for me. She'll skin me live if I don't get there. I'll catch you another time—when I don't have a grandma to worry about."

He bent and kissed her on the tip of her pug nose, then faced back toward the bar, while she looked after him with an expression of both triumph and sorrow.

He walked down the street alone. He had one more night left in this miserable place, then it was on to Albuquerque. After Albuquerque, Taos. After Taos, out to California. The prospect, usually pleasurable, suddenly seemed bleak.

Hell, he thought, his daddy was right. It was time he settled down. Got married. Raised kids.

Married? he thought, genuinely startled at the foreign idea. J.T. had never suggested that. The idea had bloomed, just now, without a hint of foreshadowing. *Kids?* What in God's name put *that* into his mind?

And what would he do if he didn't rodeo? That had always been the jackpot question. Working on J.T.'s ranch had somehow never seemed enough to Cal. He liked ranch work, but he wanted something of his own, something he'd built without J.T.'s help, something with his own name on it. Like a business, maybe.

That was it. A business. Like the green-eyed woman had. A nice business to build. He even knew something about the boot business, from his friend in Amarillo. He knew a lot, in fact. Yeah, a business.

And get married. And raise kids.

A whole passel of kids.

The thought gave him unaccountable pleasure. It was true he'd been good at publicity. He didn't want to be anybody else's spokesman again, but a man might do a bit of dignified publicity work for his own business, a family business. He could permit himself that. That wouldn't be bad.

He smiled to himself and limped on into the night, not minding the pain so much.

"YOU'VE GOT TO TRY again," said Tracey. "That's all." She shrugged with finality and bit into her peanut butter sandwich. The noon sun fell through the window, making her short hair gleam around her face like a dark halo.

"No." Serena's jaw had its most stubborn set. "Once is enough. He walked out and left me sitting there. I'm not a masochist. I don't court humiliation."

She stared without appetite at her own sandwich. The two women sat at a small, cluttered table in the back room of La Herencia. The shop's air was warm and redolent of the scent of leather.

It was Sunday, and their three employees, Jesus, Estaban and Estaban's wife, Dolores, who worked part-time, had the day off.

So, technically, did Tracey and Serena, but like many people starting a business, they found one slave-driving word dominating their lives: overtime.

They came into the shop early, they stayed late, they worked weekends and holidays. They worried overtime, too. The business was doing well enough, but to do better, they needed to expand. To expand, they needed more craftsmen. To pay more craftsmen, they needed more money. To earn more money, they needed more commissions.

Tracey reached into the brown paper bag that held her lunch and took out a pale green Granny Smith apple. She pushed an awl and a scrap of ostrich-skin leather out of the way and set down the apple.

"Serena," she said, quietly but firmly, "we've *got* to have more business. Estaban's brother and Mickey Sanchez are both willing to work for us. But we can't offer them jobs. Besides that, Dolores would like to work full-time. We need more customers."

Serena toyed uninterestedly with a corn chip. "I know," she said. She pushed away a stray tendril of her dark hair, which she had pinned back today with a leather clip.

"So go back and ask McKinney again," Tracey said calmly. "He's the best man for the job. You know the response he got on those Exceptional Rodeo ads."

"I know," Serena repeated without enthusiasm. She slipped Tracey a furtive glance. Her partner was also her friend, and had been since high school. But sometimes Tracey's outlook on the world seemed too simple, at least to Serena.

To Tracey, right was right, wrong was wrong, and she would fight to the last ounce of her strength to further a cause or aid an underdog. The idea of quitting anything simply never occurred to her.

It was she who handled the sales and business end of the shop, and she who had settled on Cal McKinney as the best person to be spokesman for La Herencia. Serena suspected that Tracey's enthusiasm for him, typically, stemmed from his volunteering for a good cause.

Tracey should have been the one to approach Cal, Serena thought bleakly. He might not have walked out on Tracey. Tracey was petite and elfin, with wide amber eyes that announced to the world, I believe in truth and justice and equality and hard work. Nobody, thought Serena, would ever look into those visionary eyes and mistake Tracey for a groupie.

That idealism shone out of Tracey's face now even as she sat at the littered table holding her half-eaten peanut butter sandwich. She stared into the middle distance as if she could see a future where dreams came true.

"Serena," she said softly, "he's our man. I *know* it. You've got to try again. Appeal to his better self."

"Me?" Serena cried. "Why me? If you want him, you go after him. I botched it. Besides, he hasn't got a better self."

"Everybody's got a better self," Tracey said. "Besides, it's mostly your business. You own seventy percent. You're the one who *should* talk to him."

"It's impossible." Serena moodily pushed away from the table. She moved to a bench and began sorting through a pile of colored inlay leathers. She had a pair of child's boots to work on this afternoon, pale blue with rainbows and pink and white clouds inlaid in the sides.

"I don't know what's got into you," Tracey said from the table. "You're usually aggressive about business. You wouldn't have got *this* far if you weren't aggressive." She paused.

A certain delicate awkwardness vibrated in the pause. "Serena?" Tracey asked. "Why does he—bother you so much? Is there something you're not telling me?"

Serena felt the muscles in her shoulders stiffen nervously. She had given Tracey only the sketchiest account of her disastrous evening, leaving out much. What she had most deliberately left out was her inexplicable attraction to Cal McKinney. She didn't *want* to be deeply attracted to any man. Especially one like McKinney.

She continued sorting the leathers. "It was an unpleasant experience," she said. "That's all."

Another pause tingled in the air between them. "Serena?" Tracey said again, her voice gentle.

Serena didn't look up. *She's known me too long,* she thought in frustration. *She knows me too well.*

"Does it have to do with—you know?" Tracey asked. "I—I don't mean to pry, but you always swore that—you know—it wouldn't affect the business as long as you could help it. I thought this was a business matter. But if you felt something more between you and Cal McKinney—"

"I felt *nothing* for him," Serena lied with spirit. "He's not appealing in the least. He hasn't got a serious bone in his body."

"Because," Tracey went on, "if he attracted you, well, then I'd understand. You'd have a conflict. I wouldn't push your going after him. I mean, I think he's the best man for the job, but I respect your feelings—"

Serena's head snapped up and her normally soft eyes flashed. Tracey was her best friend, but Serena's patience, sorely stretched by last night's events, broke. "I don't *have* feelings about him. He doesn't *attract* me, for God's sake. I don't *have* any conflict."

Regret swept over Tracey's face. The wide golden-brown eyes blinked apology. "I'm sorry," she said. "I didn't mean—I had no intention—"

"Don't you have billing to do?" Serena asked, her voice brisk. "Don't you have orders to send? Weren't you going to work on the mailing list today?"

"Right," Tracey sighed. She tucked her sandwich crusts into the paper bag, tossed it into the wastebasket, picked up her apple and stood.

Serena turned her back until Tracey left for the front of the shop. Unaccountably, for she never cried, she felt tears sting her eyes. She blinked them back fiercely.

What was wrong with her? she wondered. She'd been edgy and off-center all morning, and now she'd snapped at the woman who was both her best friend and business partner.

She'd treated Tracey like a meddler when Tracey had only shown sensitivity to Serena's problem. But Tracey had actually put Serena's worst fear into words. The fear that she might be able to care for Cal.

Care for him. Fall in love with him. It was unspeakable to Serena. It was unthinkable. That, she reminded herself coldly, was right. It *was* unthinkable. It was foolish for her ever to contemplate falling in love. That was how she made her life tolerable, by not thinking about things like falling in love.

She reached for an skiving knife and accidentally scratched her hand. Blood welled out of the tiny cut, a round drop of incongruously cheerful red.

Serena stared at it as if hypnotized. *Blood,* she thought. *It looks like everybody else's but it's not. There might be a taint in my blood.*

Oh, how stupid and overdramatic, she thought, the unwanted tears burning her eyes again at the sting from the cut. But it was true. She might have inherited a genetic disorder, Huntington's Disease, that could make her a young invalid, then slowly kill her.

She was what physicians termed "a person at risk." There was no way for her to determine if or when the disease would strike her, and there was no cure for it if it did.

She had long ago decided she must never marry. She must never have children. She must never even take the chance of having children.

If she had inherited Huntington's disease, it would kill her, it was that simple. And if she had inherited it, each child she bore had a fifty-percent chance of inheriting it. She had lived with the burden of the risk herself, and she wouldn't inflict it on any child.

She had seen the disease unexpectedly seize first her grandfather, then her father, weakening and wasting them to death. It was a ghastly disease, stealing not only strength and health, but independence and dignity and even sanity.

Now its threat hovered over her. She was twenty-seven. The insidious thing about Huntington's was that it hid in the system secretly, not showing itself until a person had reached thirty or so.

The irony, of course, was that she might be safe. But she wouldn't know for years. The disease was treacherous. It might lurk in her system, waiting until she was fifty before it seized her.

It had struck her family unexpectedly and had wrought such chaos that Serena could hardly stand to remember it. She could not forget when her older sister, Patti, had run off and got married at eighteen. Serena had been thirteen. Patti, it turned out, was pregnant.

It was the only time Serena ever saw her mother's iron control break. "My *God,*" her mother had cried in anguish, "she's bringing another one into the world. Doesn't she know she can get this thing? So can you. Now a baby? Another generation? I can't stand it—doesn't it ever stop?"

Then she had turned and looked into Serena's frightened eyes and said the unforgettable thing: "I wish I'd never had children. Every day I look at you and Patti and wonder if you'll die of it, too. Do you know what that feels like? Don't you ever *dare* put another human being through what your father has done to me—don't you dare do this to another family." She had seized Serena's arm and shaken it so hard that Serena had involuntarily cried out.

The cry made her mother's carefully controlled mask fall back in place. She dropped Serena's arm, apologized brusquely, turned away and never mentioned the incident again. But her words had burned into Serena's memory, marking her forever. She would never be like Patti.

She wouldn't marry. She could not bear the thought of becoming an afflicted stranger to her husband, a burden of enormous medical bills and suffering.

She had vowed never to fall in love because she didn't want the pain of renouncing it. Her family had shown her the joy love could give as well as the pain it could inflict. She was a woman who took vows seriously. This one she intended to keep.

She put her finger to her mouth, sucking it to take away the sharpness of the sting. She had understood her situation for a long time, ever since her father had been stricken when she was eleven. He had inherited it from his father. She stood every chance to inherit it from them. She didn't feel sorry for herself. She had simply faced facts.

One fact was that Cal McKinney must never mean anything to her beyond business. He couldn't and he wouldn't. That was that.

THAT NIGHT, the gods of rodeo were more fickle than usual.

In bareback bronc riding, Cal had drawn a horse that had worried him for the past two days. Nobody'd yet ridden the damn thing. The bronc's name was Judas, and he lived up to it. He was as treacherous a little horse as ever struck arena dirt.

Cal climbed into the chute and settled onto the bronc's restless back, grasping the handhold and muttering his ritual phrase under his breath: "Luck, be a lady."

Aloud he said, "Let 'im buck," and the chute door flew open.

Luck wasn't listening. Judas must have been in an especially nasty mood. Five seconds out of the chute, he threatened to sunfish, which meant he bucked so crazily he was going to flip, landing on his back, crushing Cal beneath him. Cal had no choice but to bail out. He and Judas hit the ground at the same time, but at least Cal fell clear of him. The fall shook his spine so hard that Cal limped off numb, hardly hearing the crowd's applause of consolation.

Rayburn made his ride until a second before the buzzer, then ate dirt. As he picked himself up and made his way shakily back to the chutes, a sympathetic crowd gave him a round of applause.

"Too bad hand-clappin' don't buy no groceries or gas," Rayburn said to Cal.

"You land on your bad elbow?" Cal asked, eyeing Rayburn's dirt-smeared shirt.

"Hell, no," Rayburn said with a bitter smile. "I landed on the good one, and I ain't sure that ain't worse."

Shorty, on the other hand, drew a rank bull named Bends, gave it the ride of his life and became a candidate to be several thousand dollars richer by the night's end. There was, obviously, no justice.

Cal wasn't roping that night, but he'd loaned his horse to Rayburn, who'd taken on two events in hopes of making extra money to help him get back to Crockett. But Rayburn drew a scrambled-brained calf that ran along the wall, making it impossible to settle a loop. Worse, Cal's horse, Grumpy, threw a shoe, and Cal could tell by the animal's gait when Rayburn rode him back that this time out it was Grumpy who'd garnered the injury.

Running his hand down the horse's hind leg, he felt the bulge and heat of a sprained muscle near the hock. *Damn!* he thought blackly. Grumpy, with his scarred foreleg and chest, was no beauty, but he was the best roping horse Cal had ever had. A good horse was half of roping. His backup horse, Sneezy, was home at the Double C, with a badly split hoof that Cal's sister, Lynn, was tending to. He swore inwardly.

Rayburn was downcast about the horse's injury, and tried to stay stoic about his own. He kept his teeth gritted because he'd done something to his bad elbow when he threw the rope. He was obviously in pain.

"I tell you I'm glad to be gettin' off this suicide circuit," Rayburn said from between clenched teeth. "That's a fact."

There were two rounds of bull riding at Wolverton, and in the second, Shorty drew another mean one, stuck to it like a cocklebur and took the night's purse. The last bull rider, a boy from Oklahoma who was little more than a kid, wrecked badly when the bull tossed him, then slammed him sideways against the fence and tried to gore him.

The clowns lured the bull away, but the kid just lay there, curled into a skinny, motionless knot of pain. People gathered around him, but nobody tried to move him. A doctor came and, at last, ambulance attendants. The rumor spread that he had a couple of broken ribs, a concussion and maybe a punctured lung.

The kid's injury cast a pall over the evening. Cal led Grumpy—man and horse both limping—behind the chutes to the trucks and Grumpy's temporary stall.

Normally he didn't let a cowboy getting hurt bother him. Things like that happened. But tonight the memory of the kid lying there gnawed at him. It was as if everything lately was conspiring to tell him to quit—and quit soon.

Get a business, get married, and raise some kids, said the voice in his head. For no reason at all, a picture of the green-eyed woman in the green and white cowboy boots drifted into his consciousness and took command of it. All day long it had been like that; she haunted him like a song that wouldn't leave his brain. No woman had ever done such a thing to him before.

Get out of my head, he silently ordered her. But the image he had of her wouldn't smile and it wouldn't leave.

He told himself the only reason he wanted her was because he couldn't have her. Her single source of appeal was that she was unattainable. Well, he was never one to moon after what he couldn't have, and if she should show up again, she'd lose her counterfeit charm in a second. He wouldn't look at her twice. She'd bore him crazy out of his mind. He'd see there wasn't one damn thing special about her. He'd see she was ordinary as dishwater.

He reminded himself of that several times as he took off Grumpy's saddle and blanket and began to rub down the horse.

Shorty came scuttling up on his wishbone legs. He grinned so widely that his bad eye squinted more than usual. He leaned against Cal's van, well satisfied with himself.

"See me out there tonight?" he asked, tilting his hat up. "I couldn't do no wrong."

"Congratulations," Cal said with resignation.

"Going out tonight?" Shorty asked. "Got a gal? I heard that long-legged one last night wouldn't have nothin' to do with you. Heard she walked out on you."

"You heard wrong," Cal muttered, brushing Grumpy's flank. "I walked out."

"Well, I heard you come back early. And alone," Shorty said with satisfaction. "Me, I got lucky. Met this bea-u-tiful blonde. Shape on her like a movie star. T-shirt so tight I thought it'd pop. Right across the front it says, See Anything You Like? Man, you wouldn't believe it. I'm seein' her again tonight. And you ain't got nobody? That's a switch."

"Have a good time, Shorty," Cal muttered, suppressing a sigh. "Don't spend all your money."

"Not havin' much of a night, are you?" gibed Shorty. "No girl, no points, no money. And it looks like Rayburn screwed up your horse."

"I'll live."

He was glad when Shorty finally swaggered off in search of his blonde. He looked down in disgust at his shirt, which was covered with arena dirt and ripped at the shoulder. He took it off and threw it over the top bar of the stall. The night air was cold, but he didn't give a damn. He checked the tape on his ribs and saw it was holding and somehow amazingly clean. He'd probably be taped for at least another three days.

He got down to the business of tending Grumpy.
Out of his duffel bag he drew a jar of Lynn's all-
purpose remedy, rubbed the ointment on the horse's
pulled muscle and bandaged it. Mentally he swore
again. Grumpy shouldn't be ridden for at least a week.
He'd either have to borrow horses when he moved on
or turn out—not compete at all. He stood, his back
aching, as usual.

He saw a tall, slender woman standing a few yards
away between two trucks. His eyes met hers. *Serena,*
he thought, a strange sense of wonder filling him.
She's come back.

All the better to ignore her, said the cynical part of
his brain. But he didn't listen to the cynicism. All he
could do was stare at her.

Something crazy seemed to be happening inside
him, something he had never suspected could happen
to a man like him. He was stunned, astonished. It was
as if after being blind all his life, he suddenly saw. He
looked into her mysterious green eyes and felt as
transformed as if he'd been struck by lightning.

"I CAME BACK," she said simply. She was wearing her
gray twill Western slacks and a gray shirt with red
piping on the collar and cuffs. Her boots were dark red
and so was her suede jacket. She had no hat. Her hair
fell past her shoulders, free.

She supposed that she had come here for Tracey's
sake—loyal, dependable, warmhearted Tracey—who
thought Cal was the best man for the job. It was Serena's way of making the ultimate apology to Tracey
for her own snappishness. And to prove to Tracey and

herself that she was immune to any of this cowboy's questionable charm.

This time she had come knowing what to expect. She wore her emotional armor and was prepared for the man.

But she was not prepared for the look he gave her. His hazel eyes had locked on hers with an expression she could not read. It might have been joy, it might have been ferocity, it might simply have been intense surprise.

He still moved as if his back hurt him. She had watched in fear tonight when he was wrenched and tossed in the bareback bronc riding. It had to have been terribly painful for him, she thought, and wondered why he put himself through it.

The bruise on his jaw had faded slightly and the swelling had gone down. Even with it still shadowing his face, she could see he was an extraordinarily handsome man.

His body was whipcord lean, his chest wide, well muscled and smooth. His skin gleamed like copper next to the white of the tape patching his ribs. Except for the tape, his body was near to perfect: Michelangelo's David, in live bronze rather than cold marble. She found its naked masculine power somehow embarrassing, too sexual to be on casual display.

And he kept giving her that disturbing, electric *look*. She tossed her head nervously and licked her lips.

"Listen," she said, burying her hands in the pockets of her jacket, "I wasn't very professional last night. To tell the truth I'd never done anything like that before. I'd like to try again. Could I buy you a drink—or something to eat—and talk business with you?''

"Business?" he said with a slow, lopsided grin. "I thought maybe you came back for pleasure. No?"

"Business is supposed to come before pleasure," she said. She glanced away, off into the night, not wanting to risk the things his smile made her feel.

"Maybe we could compromise. I'm an accommodating sort of guy."

She glanced at him almost shyly. "You weren't last night."

"Aw," he said, "I was a jerk last night." He shrugged his bare shoulder with self-deprecation, making his muscles ripple.

She turned from the sight, blinked with surprise at his words. She hadn't expected humility in any form from him.

"I shouldn't have walked out on you like that." He shook his head, his smile rueful. "I wasn't too nice. I'll give you another chance if you'll give me one."

Serena's heart felt giddy, as if it had taken flight.

He held his hand out to her. "Deal?" he asked.

Slowly, hesitantly, she grasped his hand. It was strong, lean, hard and surprisingly warm in the cool night air. "It's a deal," she said solemnly. She didn't want to look into his vivid hazel eyes, for she had an irrational fear she might lose her soul in them.

"I just need a clean shirt," he said with the same wry grin. "I got dusted tonight."

"I saw," she said, glad when he released her hand. She thrust it, tingling, back into her pocket.

"Wasn't too impressive, was I?"

"Not bad," she said. "Nobody's ridden that horse yet. I don't like his looks. He's got a genuine mean streak. He'll hurt somebody."

"That he will," Cal agreed. He reached into his van and pulled a clean shirt off a hanger. Serena was profoundly relieved when he slipped it on and buttoned it up, covering the coppery, sculpted sweep of his chest, the intriguing musculature of his arms and shoulders.

The shirt was blue plaid, and it brought out the brown of his hair and made his hazel eyes seem almost golden. He reached into the van again, took out a denim jacket and drew it on, too.

"What about you?" Serena asked, watching him adjust the brim of his hat. "Did he hurt you?"

He looked at her from beneath the hat's shadow and grinned his wicked grin. "Naw. You want me to drive or you?"

"I will," she said. She would feel more in control of the evening if she drove. The idea of a van made her nervous. Some cowboys had beds in them. It implied more intimacy than she wanted.

"Fine," he said. They started to stroll toward the parking lot. "But I buy supper. To make up for last night."

She shook her head and started to protest that this was a business meeting, and it was her place to pay.

He reached out and took her arm firmly, just above the elbow. "I mean it. If we're going to talk, we have to compromise, like I said. This is part of the compromise, sugar. You let me pay."

Oh, Serena thought in frustration, it was far worse when he was gentlemanly than when he was obnoxious. How easy it would be to fall under his smiling spell, his effortless charm, his physical magnetism. She drew away from him.

"All right," was all she said. She kept her head down and neither of them spoke until they reached the parking lot. Her arm tickled and burned where he had touched her, as if she had been brushed by a magic fire.

I shouldn't have come back, she thought. *This is a mistake. What I'm feeling has nothing to do with business.*

"One more thing," he said, taking her arm again and stopping her at the lot's edge.

A ripple of apprehension mixed with forbidden excitement eddied through her. She looked up into his shadowy face. He raised his other hand and gently tilted her chin up to him. He looked down into her eyes.

She felt hypnotized, incapable of moving away from him or objecting to his touch.

"What I have to know," he said softly, "is can you smile? You never smile. Can you? Will you?"

She was suddenly frightened. She didn't want to care for this man or desire him. She must not. And she couldn't smile. She remembered for the thousandth time that she wasn't like other women. She could not live or love as other women did.

But neither could she draw back from Cal. She stood staring up at him, all too conscious of his hand on her arm, his lean fingers resting with such surprising gentleness against her face.

"You never, never smile," he breathed. "Are your lips frozen? Let me warm them."

He bent his head and kissed her. He kissed her until she saw galaxies of stars swimming behind her eyes, although the real night was starless. He kissed her until a strange, foreign happiness surged through her, making her feel as if her private stars were filling her with light that grew more and more dazzling.

He took her face between his hands and kissed her more deeply still. An irrational and wildly intense joy swept over her. Beneath his lips, her own curved in a trembling and reluctant smile.

"That's right," he whispered, his mouth still against hers. "Oh, yes, that's right." And he kissed her again.

CHAPTER THREE

CAL HADN'T PLANNED on kissing her, at least not so soon. But he hadn't kissed her from mere impulse. Impulse was something he could resist if he wanted to. No, he had kissed her because he'd *had* to. He'd had no choice.

When her lips curved with pleasure beneath his, his heart started bucking like the craziest bronco in the world. For a moment he felt her give herself to him, and he was drunk with the triumph of it and the delight of shared desire.

But then she drew back, and he knew he had frightened her. Hell, he had frightened *himself*.

He wasn't used to such intensity of feeling and it bewildered him as much as it bewitched him. He knew he must move quickly to keep her from bolting in fear.

"I'm sorry," he said simply. His hands fell reluctantly away from her face. "I shouldn't have done that."

Serena watched him warily, her breathing shallow. Her heart drummed, and she forced herself not to tremble, even though she was chilled by something far deeper than the February cold.

"No," she said, her voice strained. "You shouldn't have." *And I shouldn't have let you,* she thought with dismay. *But I did. Why?*

She should have stepped back, put more distance between them, but she didn't move and neither did he. They remained perilously close.

"Couldn't seem to help myself." His voice was low, earnest and apologetic. "It was sort of like a fire I couldn't put out. Sorry."

The sincerity of his tone confused Serena. She couldn't see his face; it was hidden by the shadow of the Stetson. Her lips still prickled from the touch and taste of his. Her flesh, where his fingers had touched her, throbbed with a poignant, pleasurable ache.

She turned her face away and stared off into the darkness, too perturbed to speak. The scent of him, leather and hay and horse and soap, made her oddly faint.

"I only wanted to make you smile," he said.

She took a deep breath, trying to calm herself.

"You make me want to make you smile," he breathed. "To smile all over."

He could do it, she thought, hating herself for realizing it. *He could make me smile all over. He could make every atom of my body dance with pleasure.*

"Don't talk like that," she said shortly, still not looking at him.

"Why not? It's only sweet talk, darlin'."

"I don't want sweet talk, and don't call me 'darling.' I'm not your 'darling.'"

"Shouldn't I be the judge of that—darlin'?"

"Oh," Serena said with a furious shrug, "you're impossible. All I want is to talk business. Why do you have to keep trying to make things personal?"

He reached out as if to take a strand of her hair, then stopped himself, his hand falling restlessly to his side. He stood with one hip cocked, one shoulder raised in determination. "Sweetheart, you have no idea how possible I am. I may be the most possible man you ever met. But if business is all you'll talk to me, I'll talk business. I just happen to talk it *personal*, is all."

She shook her head in frustration. "Look, can we just get in the car?"

"In my most businesslike manner," he drawled, nodding. "I'll be the very model of a modern major-general of business. In a personal way, of course."

She glanced at him and smiled in perplexity. A cowboy who could quote Gilbert and Sullivan? He *was* impossible, there was no question.

"Ahh," he murmured with satisfaction. "You smiled. That's good. You ought to always do business with a smile. Who could resist you?"

"Come on," she said, her face going grim. She started across the parking lot.

He followed, limping slightly and whistling. The song he whistled was "I Am the Very Model of a Modern Major-General." He whistled more beautifully and with more finesse than anyone she'd ever heard.

Impossible, she thought again, shaking her head. *Just impossible.*

* * *

THEY CHOSE a more comfortable restaurant this evening, a homey place with red-and-white-checkered
cloths on the tables and barbecued ribs as the specialty of the house. Serena tried to remain aloof and a
little stern with Cal, but she couldn't.

"Just tell me one thing," she said. "How do you
know Gilbert and Sullivan well enough to whistle it by
heart? It's a very...uncowboylike thing to do."

"My mama," he said easily. "She loved it. She
played it on the piano. Sang it, too." He smiled as if
remembering with genuine fondness.

Serena hesitated. "You—you used the past tense.
She's gone? Your mother?"

His smile faded. "Yeah. But my daddy's still alive.
And he's got himself a new wife. She's a nice lady. Of
course, they don't exactly approve of me. I was ever
the gray sheep of the family."

"Gray sheep?"

"Hell, darlin', I love 'em too much to be an out-
and-out black sheep. To tell the truth, that's one reason I'm willing to talk business. In my personal way,
of course."

Serena set down her fork and stared at him with
perplexed puzzlement. He was cheerfully eating
spareribs. "What do you mean?"

He wiped his mouth with a napkin and grinned his
most beguiling grin. "Well, I thought about what you
said. About me being a good spokesman. The thing is,
I can't see hiring myself out for it. Now I've got a
cousin Beverly—she's a beauty queen, and there's
nothing she likes better than sashaying around in front

of people and showing off just for the fun of it. Not me. I find that demeaning. But if I was to speak on my own behalf—for my own purpose—well, that's different."

She frowned slightly. "Your own behalf? What are you talking about?"

"I'm talking about throwing in with you, sugar. Becoming a partner."

He said it with such geniality and sincerity that at first she did not comprehend what he meant. Then the words registered and her jaw dropped.

"You *what?*" she asked. "You can't—I already *have* a partner."

"There's no law says you can't have two," he said amiably and picked up another sparerib.

"I don't *need* two," Serena said, aghast.

He shrugged. "I believe you do. As a cowboy, I could say, 'You ain't got no money.' But strictly as a businessman, I'd say you've got insufficient capital. You didn't even offer me a fee or a percentage or residuals or anything contractual to endorse you. Nothing. Except a pair of boots."

She sat, simply staring at him, her lips slightly parted. She was amazed that he could use words such as "insufficient capital" and "residuals" and "contractual."

"We happen to make very *good* boots," she managed to say at last.

"I've seen that," he said with an approving nod. "But you talked about expansion. To expand you've got to have more than just a spokesman, honey.

You've got to have money. I happen to have a little set aside."

Serena's eyes narrowed in disbelief. "Are you saying you'd invest . . . ?"

"I'm saying I'd think about it." He smiled. "Now I don't particularly relish being a spokesman, but if I was properly *motivated,* well, that's a different story, isn't it, darlin'?"

He could not have surprised her more if he had announced he was a Martian, about to sweep her into space in his flying saucer. She toyed distractedly with her napkin. "If," she repeated tonelessly, "you were properly motivated."

"And being a partner would motivate me all right and proper. So what do you think?"

He wiped his fingers on the napkin, set it beside his empty plate and settled back in his chair, smiling his unique smile that, as usual, managed to suggest both innocence and wickedness.

That smile, she thought desperately, should be outlawed. It should be internationally banned, like a secret weapon—too devastating for civilized use.

"I wouldn't think about it at all," she said, her heart beginning to hammer insanely in her chest. "It's our company. We built it from nothing. Last night you wouldn't even talk to me. Tonight you want to be partners—it's crazy."

"Not so crazy," he said with an indolent shrug. "Since last night I've thought it out."

In truth, the scheme crystallized full-blown and beautiful, only a short time ago, as he sat beside Serena in her battered and rusting green car. But it had been floating, half-formed in his consciousness since the night before. When it struck him, it seemed so perfect, so complete, so undeniably right, it was like a gift of the gods. Cal believed in such gifts, and he believed absolutely in this one.

"I understand business," he said, arching one brow and causing the dimple to play in his cheek. "My daddy's a cattleman and a businessman. Even a rodeo cowboy is a businessman. There's good ones and bad ones. I'm a good one."

That was true, and he knew it, in spite of his father's opinion. Except for a few hard times, he'd made good money rodeoing, and unlike some cowboys, he usually came out ahead. Besides, he had his trust fund money from his mother. He'd been meaning for a couple of years to figure out exactly what to do with it. Now he knew.

"Our business isn't for sale," Serena said flatly. "No part of it's for sale." Besides, she thought rather desperately, if he were a partner, who knew how often he might be around? She didn't want to think about that; the prospect filled her with a trembling, heightened sensation she supposed was fear.

He only smiled with more wicked innocence. "Sweet thing, think about it. You need more money and more business. I can get you both."

She shook her head so her dark hair swung intriguingly against her shoulders. He decided that, more than anything, he wanted to see it swing against her shoulders when she was naked in his bed. He wanted it so much he ached. But first, he must talk business, talk it well and fast.

"Both?" she asked dubiously.

"Both," he guaranteed. "I told you I have a friend that runs a boot company. Amarillo Tex boots."

"Amarillo Tex makes *factory* boots," she said scornfully, green eyes flashing. "They've got nothing to do with what we do."

He shook his head in good-natured disagreement. "You're right. Tex just sells stock boots right now. The kind you buy off the shelf. But he's thinking about offering made-up boots, too. You know. Putting out a catalog and letting people pick their own designs and colors and such. I talked to him not very long ago. Trouble is, he doesn't have anybody to do that specialty work for him. Not yet."

Serena's face went a shade paler, making the dusting of her freckles stand out. For a moment her eyes looked almost fearful. "You're saying—"

"I'm saying, custom-making boots is a good business. But if you really want to expand, you'd best start thinking big. Why, sure, keep your own company. But to take up slack, take on Amarillo Tex's make-up business. Do well at that, and you can take on other company's make-up business. You can expand to your sweet heart's content."

Serena's mind whirled drunkenly even though she had sipped nothing except iced water. Cal had taken her so by surprise that she could sort out neither her thoughts nor her emotions.

What he was suggesting was outrageous—and yet it made a bizarre sense. She and Tracey wanted to hire Estaban's brother and Mickey Sanchez, but they couldn't afford to. Neither could they afford to use

Dolores full-time. But if the shop fulfilled Amarillo Tex's specialty needs—then they could put both men to work. And with Cal's endorsement, and his investment money as well, who knew how far they might go?

"I—" she stammered, "I—" She couldn't finish the sentence. La Herencia was, figuratively, her baby, the only thing close to a child she would ever allow herself to have. Ever since she had conceived the idea, it had grown close to her heart. It would take care of her, and if need be, her sister, and her sister's children, too. It was not only the heritage of a great tradition, but her own heritage, her source of independence and her way of taking care of those she loved.

"I'd be your spokesperson because I'd be my own, too. 'Cal McKinney Boots.' How's that sound to you?"

Serena was horrified. "It sounds terrible," she said passionately, throwing down her crumpled napkin for emphasis. "Our name is La Herencia—the heritage. It has—special meaning for us."

"Okay," he said with an amiable shrug. "Cal McKinney's La Herencia Boots. Like I said, I'm accommodating. I'll accommodate."

"What—what—what is this?" she sputtered. "Some insane—whim? Did you land on your head tonight when that horse threw you? I can't let you walk into my business—into my whole *life*—just like that. I won't."

"Honey, I've already done walked into your life. And I don't choose to walk out."

"I—I—now what's *that* supposed to mean?" she asked, disconcerted. Her face had been pale before. Now she felt her cheeks burn as the blood flared into them.

The smile faded from his face. His eyes took on that odd light of intensity they'd had when he first saw her tonight. "It means," he said slowly, "I want part of the business. But all of you."

Her cheeks blazed more hotly. "That's not possible," she said, her voice choked. "And that's not how I do business. No."

He shook his head, still not smiling. "I'm not asking *if* it'll happen. I'm warning you it's *going* to happen. And I believe we both know that's true. I've been thinking about you all day. I don't usually do anything like that. You must be special. This must have been meant to happen."

In Serena's universe, nothing was meant to happen. Life was a series of accidents, and you tried to control those accidents and keep from getting hurt as best as possible. This man threatened to be one of the worst accidents to ever befall her. She had a sudden and irresistible desire to escape him.

She pushed her chair away from the table and stood up. "Come on," she ordered coldly. "I'm driving you home. This conversation's gone far enough. I'm not interested in your offers. Not any of them. Not business. And not personal."

"We'll see," he said, his jaw set. He stood, keeping his eyes locked on hers. Then he smiled again. Again she had the nervous, slightly crazed feeling that his smile ought to be outlawed.

"I like you," he said with what seemed total sincerity. Frank admiration shone on his handsome face, the expression of a man mightily pleased with what he saw.

Once again, though her feet were on solid ground, she had the powerful sensation of falling. Odd feelings swarmed through her, making her skin prickle and her knees shaky.

Dear God, she thought desperately. *This can't be happening. Not to me. And not with him. Oh, especially not with him. Please, God, no.*

She willed her body and spirit to grow stiff and cold. She turned and headed for the door, not waiting to see if he followed. But follow he did, so she tried to fight her feelings by not talking to him.

She didn't speak as she drove him back to the rodeo grounds as fast and furiously as she could without breaking the speed limit. He seemed unaffected by her mood. He thumbed through her sketchbook once more although the flashing light of the street lamps made it difficult to see.

"How come you always draw just flowers?" he asked. "Never people?"

She didn't answer. When they reached the rodeo grounds, she hit the brakes so hard that the car screeched to a lurching stop in the parking lot.

She turned to him, her back straight and her eyes hostile. "Get out," she ordered, hands tight on the wheel.

He ignored the fury in her glance. He set her sketchbook on the dashboard. "Think about what I said." This time his smile struck her as being as insolent as it was charming.

He leaned over and kissed her, warmly and briefly on the lips. She was too surprised to resist, and when the kiss stopped, she was oddly disappointed. It had been all too warm, all to brief, and it had shaken her to the center of her being.

"I'll be back," he promised. "Once I get something in my head, I'm not one to quit." He opened the door, then turned to look at her again.

"I believe you're going to be the mama of my children," he said with maddening confidence and cheer.

He could not have stunned her more if he had struck her, but she let no emotion register on her face or body. None. He unfolded his long form and got out, limping off into the darkness.

This kiss, like the first one, jolted her. For the first time in a long while she felt fully alive. But his words pierced her heart like a spear.

I'll be back, he'd said. *I want all of you,* he'd said. *It will happen. I'm not one to quit.*

But that wasn't the worst thing he had said. The worst he had said was, *I believe you're going to be the mama of my children.* If he'd searched for centuries, he could have found no crueler thing to say.

Yet she realized, sinking, that for all her vows and for all her years of discipline and denial, she wanted him, too. All of him. She wanted him for every second of all the good time she had left on earth.

But it shouldn't happen. It couldn't happen. She wouldn't let him into her life. She would let no one in.

Although she had lived with the knowledge of her risk of disease for years, for the first time its full reality hit her with sickening and very personal pain. She was stricken by all the things she would not allow herself to have: marriage, family, children, lifelong love.

Before tonight, such things had seemed abstractions, losses she could take. But now the abstraction had Cal McKinney's face, his drawling voice, his wide shoulders and brave rodeo limp. It was marriage to him she wouldn't have, his family, his children, his love.

Don't be ridiculous, she told herself with ferocity. A man like that, the last thing he would ever want was a home, children. His kind never settled down. Never. He didn't want anything from her except the simple thrill of sexual conquest. He probably told every woman he met that he wanted her to be the mother of his children.

But that only made her situation more ironic. He made her yearn and tremble for all the things she could not have, even though he would never really want to give them to her.

How stupid, she thought wretchedly, remembering how his kiss had riven her through like a lightning bolt. *How stupid.*

There, alone in the parking lot, she laid her forehead against the steering wheel and for the first time in years wept, long, silently and hopelessly.

AS FOR CAL, he made his way back to his van, whistling. The song he whistled was Dwight Yoakam's "You're the One."

She was, he'd decided. She was the one. The moment he'd seen her again, after thinking of her all day, he'd had a gut-level certainty of it, and that was that. He had found his fate, or it had found him. He had never figured out which way it worked, but it didn't matter. She was the one.

It wasn't just her face and body, although they were lovely. It wasn't just her air, although she had such a quiet elegance that his blood quickened to fire in her presence. It was more: something elusive, almost magical about her that challenged him to the depths of his soul.

He was a man who had gone for years without making a major decision because he'd known, unconsciously, the time, the circumstances, were not right for deciding.

Tonight he had made two decisions with lightning swiftness. He would buy into Serena Davis's business and work to make it a success. And he would marry Serena. He wanted her, and he wanted her to be the mother of his children.

He could already see those children, lined up like stair steps in his mind's eye, at least two boys and a girl, just like the family he grew up in. Perhaps two or three more, just for the fun of it. They would be tall, a bit rangy, like both him and Serena. They would probably have his brown hair, his McKinney grin and athletic ability.

But he hoped they would have their mother's freckles and certainly that they would have her lovely green eyes. He smiled as he saw the kids standing there, waiting for him in the future. He nodded to himself. Yes, they'd have her green eyes. And they'd be tall, strong and healthy. Perfect.

She might resist him now temporarily, but he was a man used to winning. Stubborn as hell, his daddy had always said, dead set on not giving in until he got his own way, smiling all the while.

Cal grinned, feeling like the master of his fate again, a champion once more. He wanted the woman, and he would have her. He had made up his mind, and he could not imagine anything thwarting his neat and happy plans.

"You," his Grandpa Hank had once said in disgust. "You ain't never figured out that life is serious business. It's gonna have to kick you in the head harder than any horse to teach you just how serious it is."

I'll be bringing home a bride, Grandpa, he thought. *You might be holding that great-great-grandchild you want so bad in your arms yet. Even before your hundredth birthday. And it'll be mine and hers.*

CHAPTER FOUR

STUBBORNNESS WAS ONE THING there was plenty of in the McKinney household. It was often debated who was more stubborn, Cal or Grandpa Hank, J.T.'s maternal grandfather.

Cal's stubbornness was deceptive because he was so genuinely good-natured and persuasive he could beguile people into forgetting that he was also as hard-headed as hell.

Grandpa Hank, on the other hand, had given up being congenial when he was ninety, claiming it took too much effort, and like all good citizens, he intended to conserve energy—his.

If he felt cantankerous, he acted cantankerous, and enjoyed his own ill-humor so immensely it often put him in good humor. And while Cal was stubborn mostly about deeds and going his own way, Grandpa Hank was too tired for many deeds these days. Instead, he had become stubborn about opinions. In his old age he had taken to collecting more and more opinions to be stubborn about.

Grandpa Hank was ninety-nine, and his firmest opinion was that he would undoubtedly live to see his hundredth birthday because he deserved to. He did not intend to die before he reached one hundred even if somebody whomped him spang on the head with a shovel or shot him point-blank.

This morning was atypically warm for February, and Hank sat in the rocker on the porch of his house, drinking his coffee, staring out at the sunlight falling on the brown hills and enjoying the sight profoundly.

He liked to sit there, fondly remembering the old days and thinking grumpy thoughts about the new-fangled ones and what these crazy times were doing to his family.

J.T. seemed to finally have got himself settled down again, and Hank grudgingly admitted that he had learned to tolerate Cynthia, J.T.'s new wife, even if she was a blue blood and from Boston, of all places. Hank had never seen Boston and he never wanted to. He imagined that its entire populace did nothing except eat baked beans and codfish and attend Harvard. It sounded like a good place to be from, and Cynthia was lucky to have escaped to the heaven of Texas. Hank supposed he was even a bit fond of her.

In his crotchety way, he was also fond of his three great-grandchildren, but he firmly believed that they were all going to hell in a hand basket unless they mended their ways and began to think more like him.

Not one of them seemed dedicated to carrying on the old ways, the old values. Not one of them was married yet or producing great-great-grandchildren for him to enjoy and gloat over, as was their sacred duty.

Cal drifted through life grinning and with no thought of tomorrow, and J.T. was worried to distraction that the boy would get his fool head kicked off by some bronc somewhere someday, and end up as a

vegetable tucked between hospital sheets. Grandpa
Hank opined that if Cal got kicked in the head often
enough, some sense might get knocked into him, and
he'd come home where he belonged.

Cal's older brother, Tyler, had stayed on the ranch,
but from somewhere he'd got the crackbrained notion of growing grapes and starting a goddamn *vine-
yard* on the family land. Wine, thought Grandpa
Hank with disgust. Real men drank good sippin'
whiskey, and Hank enjoyed a shot glass of it every
day, the way a real man should. He enjoyed more than
a glass if his hip was giving him trouble.

Wine was for ladies and invalids and foreigners who
talked funny languages. But at least Tyler seemed to
be settling down at last with a good woman, and that
was something. It was also about time.

Hank had opinions about the youngest of his great-
grandchildren, too. He liked little Lynn—he supposed, oh, hell, he loved her—but she'd taken it into
her head to fool with Thoroughbred racehorses. Here,
in the heart of cattle and quarter horse country, she
was wasting her time and money on those long-legged
nervous, wild-eyed, overbred, useless blue-blooded
hay burners that wore saddles that looked like burned
pancakes and were ridden by people dressed like
clowns.

Lynn herself was jockeying and wore one of those
silly silk suits, and it put Hank in a sour mood every
time he thought of it. Why couldn't she put on her
cowgirl hat and ride a good quarter horse or Appa-
loosa, the way God had meant women to do?

It was, however, Grandpa Hank's strong opinion that as misguided as Lynn was, at least she thought for herself, and she wasn't as bad as her bubble-headed cousin, Beverly. Among Hank's blessings, he counted as one of the greatest the fact that he was no actual blood kin to Beverly. He thought a sillier, more useless girl had never existed.

Lynn had a serious streak, and J.T. always said she was "sensitive." Hank supposed she was, and it made him feel grumpily protective of her. But whatever she saw in Beverly that had made them friends all these years was beyond Hank's comprehension and always had been.

Lynn was full of real and deep emotions, but Beverly wouldn't recognize a deep emotion if it came up and bit her on her beauty-queen butt. Lynn had the guts to go her own way and was dedicated—even if it was to something as asinine as racehorses. Beverly drifted through life as brainless as a balloon.

Sometimes people compared Beverly to Cal, and said it was too bad the two of them were cousins because they'd make a perfect match, both flirtatious, both with no thought for tomorrow.

Whenever anybody was impolitic enough to say this, it made Hank hotter than Satan in long johns. Cal, at least, had some damn *character*. He was friendly, he was good-natured, he was generous to a fault. He had drive, and lots of it, even though it was misdirected on his fool roping and bronc busting.

Cal just might grow up someday, and Hank hoped he lived to see it. He felt, deep down in his old bones, it might even be getting close for the boy. Beverly?—

never. She'd been a beauty queen and thought she still
was one. She went through life smiling mindlessly and
never entertaining one genuine idea in her pretty head.

That was one of the things that irked him most
about Beverly. His great-grandchildren were flawed
individuals, but at least they were individuals who had
opinions that he could enjoy disagreeing with. Beverly had never had a real opinion in her life. He
doubted, darkly, if he'd ever see that one grow up even
if he lived to be *two* hundred.

"WELL?" Lynn asked pointedly as she began to rub
down Lightning after his workout. "Do you still think
I'm crazy? To get involved with racehorses?"

Beverly's beautiful blue eyes widened, but her face
went blank. "Lynn," she said solemnly, "I never
thought you were crazy. I just frankly don't know one
thing about racehorses. I only want you to be happy."

Lynn looked across Lightning's sleek back at her
beautiful cousin. She smiled in spite of herself. Beverly had won so many beauty contests that Lynn
couldn't keep track of them, and had once been Miss
Texas and third runner-up for Miss America.

The problem was that Beverly had trained so long
and worked so hard at pleasing people that she seldom uttered anything other than the safest and
blandest of statements.

Sometimes it puzzled Lynn that she and Beverly
were best friends. On the surface, they had little in
common. Even as children they had been different.
Lynn had been a tomboy and something of a loner;
Beverly, even then, had been a creature of ruffles and

eager smiles, anxious to please the world and be admired by it.

But friends they were, and good ones. They were held together by a thousand bonds, large and small. Their mothers had been sisters and had been close. Lynn and Beverly were the only girls in the family, had in early years often found themselves allied against the boys, who were older and, with typical masculine disdain, didn't like them hanging about.

So Lynn and Beverly formed one of those childhood nations of two and did everything together. They rode their ponies together, they played with their Barbie dolls under the mesquite trees behind Aunt Carolyn's kitchen although Lynn usually brought G.I. Joe, whom she preferred. She'd begged and begged Cal for the soldier doll, and softhearted as ever, he had finally yielded it to her, although it had been one of his favorite toys.

They went to grade school together, where Lynn was quiet and got good grades and Beverly was so pretty that all the boys liked her, but few of the girls did. High school was exactly the same, except that Beverly started winning local beauty titles. This meant the boys grew awed by her, frightened by her as a celebrity.

The more things change, the more they remain the same. A French philosopher had said that, and Lynn had read it in college. She and Beverly both started University of Texas the same year, and in a sense, they went separate ways. Beverly joined a sorority, was crowned queen of this and that and enrolled in dramatics, although her success as a serious actress was minimal.

Lynn lived at home, studied hard and spent her spare time working with her horses. But somehow Lynn and Beverly remained close and grew closer still.

Beverly didn't mind Lynn's shy ways, her seriousness or her single-minded commitment. Lynn was one of the few girls who was not jealous of either Beverly's beauty or growing fame. They had known each other forever, it seemed; the same threads were woven through the fabric of their lives, and each knew well the vulnerable personality that hid behind the other's facade.

"Daddy thinks I'm crazy, spending all this time with Thoroughbreds," Lynn said, hanging up Lightning's bridle. "He says this state will never take to Thoroughbred racing."

"Well," Beverly said demurely, "you *do* work awfully hard. All work and no play's not good for you. That's why I came over. To see if you wanted to go shopping in Austin. There's a new shop at the Galleria."

Lynn adjusted her dusty jeans. Beverly looked perfect, as usual. The gold suede suit she wore so prettily was Neiman-Marcus's best, and her long blond hair cascaded down her back in an artfully arranged tumble.

Lynn's clothing consisted of Wrangler jeans, battered boots and one of Cal's old cowboy shirts, comfortably baggy and worn. Her auburn hair was inelegantly swept into a schoolmarmish knot atop her head, and she had a dusty smudge around one bright brown eye.

She laughed, holding her arms out from her sides so Beverly could better evaluate her wardrobe. "Shopping? What do you mean 'shopping'? You're not hinting I need new clothes?"

"All women need new clothes on a regular basis," Beverly said with a rare tone of conviction. "It keeps us mentally stable and emotionally healthy. When's the last time you went shopping for yourself?"

Lynn shrugged, a bit guiltily. "Cynthia bought me a dress for her and Daddy's wedding."

"Well, that's not really shopping *yourself*, honey," Beverly said. "And besides that was months ago. Nearly."

"I can't," Lynn said. "I have too much work to do."

"You always have too much work," Beverly said with a pretty little pout. "I don't want to go alone. I hate doing things alone. And you're my best friend. I hardly see you anymore. And I want to talk." Suddenly tears welled in Beverly's eyes, threatening to spoil her mascara. "I still miss my daddy," she said softly.

Lynn, whose heart was almost as easily touched as Cal's, gave in immediately. Her own mother had died five years ago, and her father had just remarried. Although she considered herself a person of strong inner resources, life since her mother's death had seemed a period of constant and painful adjustment.

During that period, she had turned repeatedly to her Aunt Carolyn and Beverly, the only women left in the family. Three years later Beverly's adored father, Frank, had died, and she was having even greater trouble with her grief than Lynn had had. Sorrow, real and bone-deep, had never touched Beverly so closely before, and life had not prepared her for it.

"Sure," Lynn said a bit gruffly. "You're right. I work too much and my clothes are a scandal. We'll shop till we drop."

Beverly's tears vanished as if by magic, and she smiled her beautiful smile. "We'll shop, but not till we drop. I want you to stop by the hospital with me on the way home. The children's party's today. I'm supposed to help from three till four. I'm taking Dinky."

Lynn diplomatically suppressed a sigh. Beverly did charity work now all the time, which was good. But Dinky was Beverly's ventriloquist's puppet, and, unknown to her, the source of many a wicked joke at her expense.

To compete in the talent section of beauty contests, Beverly had originally tried dramatic readings, but her wide-eyed Southern belle's version of Cleopatra killing herself with an asp was not successful. "Only a man with a heart of stone could keep from laughing when she dies," had been Tyler's sarcastic remark.

So after advice from her drama instructor, Beverly had switched her allegiance from the muse of tragedy to that of comedy, and Dinky, rolling eyes and all, came into her life. Her father, Frank, had paid a Dallas comedian to write her a few short acts, and Beverly learned to talk in a high, squeaky voice without moving her lips.

She was better at playing Dinky than Cleopatra. Indeed, she was skilled enough to become Miss Texas and go on to the finals of the Miss America contest. Frank had almost busted his buttons with pride.

So it wasn't that Beverly wasn't good with Dinky, Lynn thought glumly. She was surprisingly good. The trouble was that people who were envious of Beverly made fun of her and Dinky.

They made snide remarks like, "Which one's the dummy?" or "Hey—who's going to watch her *mouth?*" or "Guess which one's head is made of wood."

Nobody ever said these things to Beverly's face, of course, and she would have been wounded and crushed if they had. Beverly was, in truth, not stupid, but people assumed she was because she was a beauty queen.

Beverly also didn't help her own case. Through naïveté or innocent vanity or some deep inner shyness, she carried her public persona into her personal life. Frank had paid a good deal of money so that she could study at a famous school that trained beauty contestants. There she had mastered the art of perpetually smiling, perpetually pretending to be congenial and perpetually refraining from controversial opinions.

And, Lynn knew as well, there were any number of people who were simply jealous of Beverly. She had wealth, status, beauty and not one real responsibility in the world. Few people besides Lynn and Beverly's mother, Carolyn, knew how sweet-natured, caring and passionately loyal Beverly was.

But now Beverly was at it again: going off looking gorgeous and expensive and bubble-headed and doing her act with the dummy.

"A party with Dinky," Lynn said. "Oh, boy. Beverly, you're twenty-five. Don't you think you ought to give up Dinky? He doesn't exactly exalt the image of you as a mature and responsible woman."

Beverly looked stricken, but then managed to pull her face back to a smiling, neutral blandness. "I know you've seen the act a hundred times," she said sweetly. "And I'm as tired of it as you are. But this is the children's party, and the children haven't seen Dinky. Children *always* like Dinky."

That's right, Beverly. Children love Dinky. But we're adults now. It's time to change.

But Lynn felt guilty for thinking such thoughts and she could never bring herself to be unkind to Beverly, not ever. "Okay," she said as gently as she could. "We'll shop till we almost drop, and then we'll go do the Dinky. You'll wow 'em. They'll love you."

"I hope so," Beverly said, her pretty eyes clouding over. It pained her to realize that some people wouldn't like her even when she tried with all her might to be as likable as possible. Not to be liked— that was the most terrible thing in the world that she could think of.

LYNN SAT in the children's ward of the Crystal Creek Community Hospital. She sat at a table with balloons and pieces of cake on brightly flowered paper plates, watching Beverly do her routine with Dinky.

Beverly had been right. Most of the children seemed to love Dinky—and the beautiful blond lady who made Dinky tell his silly jokes.

And Lynn had to admit that Beverly did something else very well. She kept her perfect, cheerful smile in place with all the children. Beauty-queen school had trained her well.

Lynn's own heart had clenched at the sight of so many children in casts and bandages, with crutches or wheelchairs or IVs. Her face had grown stony with tension, and tears had stung her eyes. She tried to smile as naturally and brightly as Beverly, but the best she could do was force a weak, slightly smirky slant to her mouth.

Beverly finished her routine and had Dinky take his comically awkward bow. Dinky was a particularly smug-looking dummy, with sleek, painted-on black hair and a permanently self-satisfied grin. He wore a little powder-blue cowboy-style tuxedo and tiny cowboy boots complete with silver spurs.

Lynn and Beverly passed out presents. "There," Beverly whispered when they had finished. "Come on. We can go now. The nurses'll close the party down."

She stepped out of the ward, drawing Lynn with her. Lynn was surprised to see Dr. Nate Purdy standing there, as if waiting for them. He was a foxlike little man with gray hair and bushy gray eyebrows. Lynn was so used to seeing the man bustling about, it was a slight shock to see him standing still for once.

"I want to thank all the volunteers who made this party possible," Dr. Purdy said in his fast, scratchy voice. "But I want especially to thank you, Beverly.

You're gifted at this, you know. But I wish you'd give us more of your time."

"Me?" Beverly asked brightly, with her best beauty-queen smile. "Why, they just like that silly ol' puppet, you know. And I brought my cousin. They all think she's just so romantic with her horses and her brother in rodeo and all."

Dr. Purdy didn't smile. He arched one bushy brow in something resembling a frown. "I said *you're* gifted. And I wish you'd give us more time."

"Well, I *love* to do what I can," Beverly said, beaming, "and I'd love to work on a regular schedule, but these days I just seem so busy I can't see straight. But when things smooth out a bit, why, I'd just be happy as could be to think of doing more."

Beverly was turning on her charm full force, but Dr. Purdy still refused to smile. In fact, he seemed irritated. "I'm not a pageant judge, Beverly. Don't bat your eyelashes at *me*. I've known you from the day you were born. I smacked your bottom before it got so all-fired royal. I've said I need you. You want to give me an answer or you want to give me another runaround?"

"Why—I—" Beverly stammered, for she was not used to being spoken to sharply. "Why—I—didn't give you any runaround, Dr. Purdy. I just told you the very truth. How's your lovely wife, Rose? I thought we'd see her here. My, but she does such fabulous work here. I hope she's well?"

Beverly glanced at her gold watch without waiting for an answer. "Oh, bless—look what time it's getting to be. And I haven't put a decent cup of coffee into Lynn yet. She'll die, poor thing.''

She grabbed Lynn's wrist and half walked, half dashed away from Dr. Purdy. "Bye," she called cheerfully over her shoulder. "You tell Rose hello from me. I love seeing you. Thanks for having us.''

"What was *that* all about?'' Lynn demanded when they reached the lobby. Beverly was almost panting, still gripping Lynn by the wrist and carrying Dinky in his powder blue suitcase, in her other hand.

"Oh, he *always* does that to me,'' Beverly said unhappily. "He flatters me and says he wishes I'd do more work, but he always says it so sharp, it's like I'm guilty or something. Well, I have other things to do, as I tell him and tell him and tell him. And I don't think it's gallant for him to mention my bottom. He looked at me like he'd like to smack it again.''

Lynn looked up at her glamorous cousin in puzzlement. Dr. Purdy seemed to have struck a nerve in Beverly, but Lynn did not understand how or why.

"The children love Dinky, that's all,'' Beverly said, almost to herself. Then she turned to Lynn and absently released her wrist. "I'm sorry,'' she said. "I just wanted to escape him, you know? Let's go to Dottie's and eat.''

Lynn shrugged in agreement. From childhood, the one sure cure for Beverly's distress was lemon pie, and nobody made lemon pie the way Dottie Jones did at the Longhorn coffee shop.

Beverly was driving her dark gold Cadillac, and all the way to the coffee shop she chattered about the morning's shopping and purchases. "Maybe I should've bought the dove gray shoes instead of the slate gray ones," she mused. "I've got that dove gray cocktail dress, but of course I can always wear my silver shoes with that, but that means my silver jewelry, which is *certainly* not my favorite...."

Lynn stared out the window, barely listening to her cousin's meaningless babble. She wondered if Beverly herself was listening, or was simply talking trivia so they couldn't talk about anything important.

The coffee shop was full, despite the lateness of the afternoon. Lynn saw at least half a dozen familiar faces, most of whom she and Beverly had known from childhood. Martin Avery, J.T.'s lawyer and mayor of Crystal Creek, sat at a table with Vernon Trent and Wayne Jackson, and behind the counter both Dottie Jones and her divorced daughter-in-law, Nora, were working.

"Look," Beverly whispered, "there's Bubba Gibson with that ol' Billie Jo Dumont. If I was his wife, I'd *kill* him, I swear. How can he be so mean?"

Beverly's statement was surprisingly vehement for her. Lynn looked at the couple in question and shrugged helplessly. Bubba Gibson was fifty-eight years old and J.T had known him since the two were boys. But now Bubba was openly cheating on his sweet wife, Mary, with Billie Jo Dumont, a strawberry blonde little older than Lynn and Beverly. In fact, Bubba and Mary had a daughter living in Connecticut who was thirty, actually ten years *older* than Billie Jo. It was all a terrible scandal, and Lynn didn't know how Mary Gibson bore it with the dignity that she did.

"I'd like to snatch him bald," Lynn said between her teeth. "Except he's going that way already. Poor Mary."

"Oh, it's too unpleasant to think of. Let's talk about something else," Beverly said, even though she had brought up the topic.

Lynn shrugged again, feeling oddly impatient with her cousin. "Beverly, you can't spend your life avoiding the unpleasant. It isn't good for you, and it isn't right."

Beverly straightened her back and tossed her long hair prettily. "I know I have numerous faults," she said with a mixture of pride and humility, "but I do not think it wholesome to *dwell* on the darker side of things. Now, you may not agree with that, but everyone has a right to his—or her—opinion. That's one of the blessings of America and why it's great."

"Nobody asked you to dwell on the dark side, for God's sake," Lynn said in exasperation. "I was just trying to suggest—gently—that you have a tendency to avoid unpleasantness."

"Well, my goodness, who doesn't?" Beverly asked in surprise.

Dottie Jones appeared at their table, and Beverly beamed up her beauty-queen smile. "Dottie," Beverly said, "if I don't have some of your lemon pie, I believe I will die. It is surely the best pie in the whole world. Please bring me a piece and a glass of milk."

"You're full of banana oil," Dottie said, a wry smile on her wrinkled face. "But I like you well enough not to kick you out. What'll you have, Lynn? The usual?"

Lynn nodded. Her usual was a buttermilk doughnut and a cup of Dottie's strong but excellent coffee. Dottie scribbled a brief notation on her pad and sped away, moving with remarkable rapidity for a woman of her age and weight.

"Now," Lynn said, "let's talk. That's why I came with you today. You said you were still having trouble. About your father."

"Oh," Beverly said, waving her hand ineffectually. "Yes. But we don't have to talk about it. Not really."

"Beverly," Lynn persisted with exaggerated patience, "you wanted to talk. You've been funny ever since we left the hospital. Ever since Nate Purdy spoke to you. What's wrong with you?"

Suddenly tears welled again in Beverly's lovely eyes, once more threatening the artistry of her makeup. "Oh," she said, shaking her head, "never mind. I shouldn't brood on my problems. It's negative thinking. A successful person is always positive."

Lynn picked up her water glass and took a fortifying swallow. "Bull," she said bluntly. "That's beauty-queen school talking. Nobody can always be positive. If you have a problem—face it. First you said you needed to talk, and now you say you don't. If you're going to be that wishy-washy, I'll never take a day off to go with you again."

Beverly stared vaguely out the café's big picture window. "Lynn," she said with simplicity, "I miss my daddy. Every day, I miss him." The tears glistened more brightly.

Impulsively, Lynn reached out and put her hand over her cousin's, squeezing it. Frank had been dead almost two years. The anniversary of his death was swiftly approaching. Such anniversaries could be traumatic, she knew from experience.

"Bevvy," she said fondly, "I know. I miss my mother, too. It takes time to get over. It's nothing to be ashamed of."

Beverly bit her perfectly made-up lip. "But I get so confused. Everything gets mixed together. That's another reason I asked you to come with me today. I used to *like* visiting the hospital. I used to *like* working with the children. Now—because of Daddy—it's different."

Lynn didn't understand and raised her eyebrows questioningly. But she squeezed Beverly's hand, urging her to go on.

"Before Daddy," Beverly said, still worrying her lower lip, "I always tried to think positively. I tried to think optimistically when he had his heart attack. But it didn't work. Nothing worked. Not even praying worked."

A tear spilled onto Beverly's lightly powdered cheek, and with a quick, discreet movement, she wiped it away. Lynn swallowed hard again, still clutching her cousin's hand. "I know, Bevvy," she said earnestly. "I went through it, too. With Mama."

Beverly nodded and forced her tears back by what seemed an enormous effort of will. "I understand that now," she said. "I didn't when your mama died. I guess I wasn't a very good friend for not understanding how bad it was. Sometimes lately, I think I'm not a very good person."

"Oh, poot," Lynn said, giving Beverly's hand a friendly spank. "Don't talk like that. You're a perfectly lovely person—you just don't let people really know you, is all."

"No," Beverly said unhappily, shaking her head so that her long, golden hair swung and gleamed. "I'm not good. Dr. Purdy's been after me almost a year to work more at the hospital. But I don't *want* to. It's wrong, but I don't."

Lynn looked at her cousin in perplexity. "What do you mean? Why? He's right, you know. You *are* good with those kids. They loved you."

"Well," Beverly said in a shaky voice, squeezing Lynn's hand in return, "I went to the hospital every day when Daddy was sick. But now I hate going there. It's just too hard to make friends with people who are not going to get well."

"Oh," Lynn said, stabbed with compassion. They sat for a moment, two young women with linked hands and linked lives. "It's true," Lynn said at last. "Not everybody gets well. But everybody can use someone kind to talk to them. And you could do that. Be kind. I know you are."

Beverly swallowed and tried to maintain her composure. She was an expert at maintaining her composure, a professional, in fact, but today her emotions were apparently particularly hard to subdue. "I hate thinking of bad things," she said. "The worst thing of all is something happening to somebody you've come

to love. So maybe—and I know this is wrong of me—
it's better not to love anybody at all. If I start working with those kids, I'll get all torn up inside, worse
than I am now."

Dottie appeared and looked at them curiously as she
set down their plates and drinks. Beverly drew her
hand away from Lynn's and gave Dottie her most
charming smile. "Pie," she said with great enthusiasm. "I declare, Dottie, you have saved my life. What
would I do without you? Surely I'd perish."

Dottie gave her a long, odd look. "Surely not, kid,"
she said at last. She rumpled Beverly's beautiful hair
affectionately. She left them.

"Poot," Beverly said, picking up her fork and
avoiding meeting Lynn's eyes. "I shouldn't put all
these negative feelings on you. But sometimes I just—
just don't hardly know what to think. Like—like your
father got married again. I honestly don't know how
you can *stand* it. I think of Mama married to somebody besides Daddy, and my blood runs cold. Just
cold."

Lynn shrugged philosophically. She had fought her
own private battles, fierce and deep down, about her
father's remarriage. "They have a right to live, too,"
she said. "They have a right to happiness. They can't
just stop living. You have to learn to accept it."

"I couldn't," Beverly returned with surprising passion. "My mama is still a beautiful woman. I see men
giving her the eye. Even *him,*" she said, nodding toward the table where the three men sat. "Old Vernon
Trent."

Lynn was surprised by the amount of emotion Beverly allowed to show. "There's nothing wrong with Vernon Trent," she answered mildly. "He's a nice enough man."

"He's *overweight*," Beverly said with contempt. "My daddy believed in keeping up appearances, and he always did. What would I do with an overweight stepdaddy? What would I do with any stepdaddy at all?"

Lynn shrugged again, this time in frustration. "I don't know," she said. "Cope, that's all. The one thing I know is that I don't ever want to *be* a stepparent. I don't ever want to make some poor child feel the things you and I have felt."

"Amen," said Beverly. "But on the other hand, whatever *will* we be? Here we are, twenty-five years old, both of us. Together that's fifty years. But we both still live at home, and nothing's different from five years ago, or even ten, to tell the truth. You never find a man you think is good enough, and I never find one that's brave enough to put up with me. I declare, we're both going to be spinsters and never do anything at all with our lives."

Lynn stiffened in resentment. "I'm doing something with my life. I'm training horses. I know hardly anybody believes in it, but I'm doing it anyway—"

"Oh, hush," Beverly soothed. "I didn't mean to insult your precious horses. But that's just it. You're still doing what you always did, and so am I." She sighed unhappily. "Daddy loved me being a beauty queen," she said pensively. "He just truly loved it. The problem is, what do you do for a second act? I don't know. And he isn't here to tell me. You tell me. What's to become of us?''

Beverly looked so taut and earnest, so anxious for an answer, that Lynn was unsettled. "I don't know," she said, trying to keep her voice steady. "I guess we'll find out."

She and Beverly were privileged, and she knew it. They had come from loving families, well-to-do and secure. Both had been valued and taught to value themselves. They should be happy and carefree as butterflies in a summer meadow.

But if they were butterflies, they were twenty-five-year-old ones, and Beverly had hit upon a truth that even Lynn didn't want to face. Their outward existence *hadn't* changed that much in the passing years.

Suddenly Lynn was envious of Cal, always so at ease in the world, going so many places, taking so many chances, seeing so many different things, never knowing—or caring much—what tomorrow might bring.

"The trouble is," Beverly said, with true perplexity clouding her pretty face, "life is so much more complicated than anybody ever tells you. I'd *like* to work at the hospital. I'd *like* to help the children. But after what I've seen, I don't want to ever feel hurt like that again. I don't want to take chances. I *hate* taking chances.''

Lynn squared her shoulders. Once again she thought of Cal, who lived on luck, day in, day out, and always kept smiling. How could he face such gambles, ones concerning life and death, all the time, while she fretted so over her smaller ones? Suddenly she wished he would come home to cheer her up, give her an infusion of courage and confidence.

"That's all life's made up of," she said, trying to sound wise and strong. "Taking chances."

But even as she said the words, they frightened her: *taking chances*.

CHAPTER FIVE

CAL PHONED HOME that evening. His calls were always irregular and unexpected, and Lynn felt lucky that it was she who answered, for she'd been thinking of him and missing him.

She politely shooed Virginia, the housekeeper, from the den and settled down to monopolize her big brother's attention for a few selfish minutes.

"Tell me the truth," Lynn said, settling into the corner of the couch, her legs crossed, "am I crazy to want to race Thoroughbreds?"

"You're askin' *me?*" Cal laughed. "Daddy doesn't think I've got the sense of a common-size gnat. You must be desperate, asking me."

"Cal, be serious. It's just that everybody else's lack of confidence—well—*gets* to me."

"I got confidence in you. You're little, but you're mean. I've got the scars to prove it. You'd never give up even with *both* me and Tyler sitting on you. If you fought us, honey, you shouldn't be a bit shy at taking on the rest of the world."

"Cal," Lynn said in exasperation, "being told how *mean* I am isn't what I had in mind. Couldn't you say something nice about Thoroughbreds?"

There was a moment of silence, designed to madden her, she was sure. She expected him to say something flippant, such as he liked long legs better on women than horses, or some such nonsense.

"Well, honey—" he spoke gently, but there was a smile in his voice "—I reckon the nicest thing about 'em is that you like 'em. Do you believe in what you're doing—in your head and heart?"

Lynn swallowed. "Yes."

"Then you're doing the right thing," he told her. "What if you did something everybody approved of, but you didn't like it?"

"I'd go crazy," Lynn answered with passion.

"Then there you are, baby Sis. Do what you've got to do."

Oh, Cal, Lynn thought fondly. *You could always drive me crazy, but when I was sad, nobody could make me stop crying faster or smile sooner. I love you.*

"I'm sorry for being a wimp," she said. "I'm not usually like this."

"I know. I find it downright *amazing.*"

She shrugged. "I don't know what got into me. I just got kind of depressed. I was out with Beverly today, and—"

"Beverly? Lord, who wouldn't be depressed? She didn't have that dummy, did she? Doo-Doo, or whatever his name is?"

"Dinky," Lynn corrected, immediately defensive. Trust Cal to keep a sentimental moment short. "And yes, as a matter of fact, she did have him. We went to the children's ward at the hospital for a party. Beverly's very depressed. She doesn't know what to do with her life."

"Lord, I thought *that* was settled. She'd spend it in front of a mirror. Tell her she can't be depressed—it's not allowed in the Beauty Queen's Manual. Good night, nurse, an afternoon with Doo-Doo? That could make anybody doubt the universe was meaningful."

"Cal-*vin*!"

"Listen, half-pint, I didn't call to talk about Beverly. I got a serious problem. A horse with a sprained tendon."

"Grumpy's hurt? Oh, no!" The conversation departed into more familiar territory: horses and their afflictions.

"So you're staying in Wolverton?" Lynn asked at last. "Until Grumpy's better?"

"Might as well. He's the half of the act with the talent."

She thought she heard something different in his usual carefree tone, something almost serious. "Cal—you're not hurt again, are you? You haven't banged yourself up again, have you?"

"I'm fine," he said blithely.

She suspected he was lying. "Cal," she said, "if you're hurt again—don't take any chances, please? Promise me that, will you?"

"Hey," he said without a beat of pause, "don't worry about me. Take care of yourself. Tell everybody hello. I'd talk to 'em, but I have to go see a lady. I don't want to be late."

"A lady?" Lynn asked, narrowing her eyes speculatively. "Is that why you're hanging around Wolverton? You've got a woman? Well, I mean, of *course* you've got a woman. It wouldn't be somebody special, would it?''

She was surprised by a moment of silence. Then his voice came, slow and lazy. "Could be."

Lynn was taken aback. Cal never talked that way. He must be joking. Cal and one woman? It was impossible.

CAL HAD SPENT most of the day badgering Serena at her shop by phone, trying to make her see him again. At first she wouldn't talk to him. He'd get either a woman who he assumed was her partner or one of the Mexican craftsmen.

The partner's name, he'd learned, was Tracey, and he promptly set about trying to charm her into putting Serena on the line.

He could bewitch her just to the point where she was agreeable, then she would go ask Serena and come back with a resolve that sounded renewed: Serena said *no*.

The craftsman who sometimes answered the phone was named Estaban. He sounded sympathetic, but hopeless. "She is a woman. She will not talk. What can I tell you? If a woman, she will not talk—what can you do?"

Cal was nothing if not hardheaded. He sent flowers not once, but twice. First a dozen long-stemmed white roses because the florist said white roses meant respect. Then two dozen long-stemmed red roses, because the florist said red roses meant passion. Respect and passion, he thought with wonder. It was a hell of a combination to feel for a woman. It made him pleasantly crazy.

In the meantime, he kept calling every half hour. He'd talk to Tracey, who always wavered, or Esta-ban, who sounded more dolorous each time.

At last, after he estimated the second batch of flowers had had time to arrive, Serena agreed to speak to him.

"Hello, sweet thing," he said, grinning to hear her voice. "How've you been?"

"Are you crazy?" Serena demanded.

"Only since I met you. I believe you better take pity on me. It's my only hope."

"Then you have no hope," she answered flatly. "And stop sending flowers. It's a waste of good money. We don't have any vases. We had to put them in boots."

"How many boots you got, darlin'? I'll fill 'em all with roses if it makes you happy."

"It *doesn't* make me happy. Stop it. And stop call-ing. I told you last night—I don't have any interest in your propositions. Any of them."

"You're ignoring an excellent business opportu-nity. Have you told your partner about my offer?"

"No, because it's ridiculous," Serena said with heat.

"It's not ridiculous. Maybe I should tell her my-self—get a fair hearing."

"Don't you *dare,*" Serena ordered. "And if you show up around here, I'll whop you upside the head with a bootful of flowers."

"Is that a promise, sweet thing?"

"Don't 'sweet thing' me. I'm going to hang up—now."

"Darlin'," he said with determined patience, "it won't do a *bit* of good. I'll just keep calling. Until you say you'll see me tonight."

"No." She hung up.

Cal put the telephone receiver back in its cradle. He groaned slightly as he lay back on his motel bed. His back still hurt, and this was the most elusive woman he'd ever pursued. Sometimes he had the fleeting, sinking feeling she could no more be possessed than a rainbow or a moment of starlight, yet it only spurred his yearning to possess her. If he didn't have the crazy conviction that she was worth every iota of the effort, he'd have cheerfully given up and moved on.

Well, when they made up their minds, McKinneys didn't quit, and Cal was sure he had less *quit* in his system than any of them. Gritting his teeth, he rose on his elbow, picked up the phone and dialed the florist again. He'd call Serena herself again in another half hour.

The familiar pang cracked through his ribs, and he wondered how many colors of roses there were to send a woman. He'd find her green ones and blue ones if he had to.

TRACEY, IN THE MEANTIME, had cornered Serena in the back room. Serena, obviously upset, didn't want to talk.

"This is the problem, isn't it?" Tracey demanded, looking up at her friend. "This man's fallen for you—hard. And you don't know how to deal with it. Oh,

Serena, you could have *told* me. He sounds so sincere. The least you can do is talk with him. He sounds as if he really cares about you."

Serena knew Tracey meant well but it made no difference to her. "He's not sincere. How could he care for me? He hardly knows me. No—he's got an ego as big as—as the Astrodome, and he doesn't like to take no for an answer."

"Serena, that's not what he sounds like. I mean I've always considered myself a good judge of character, and even Estaban seems to be rooting for him—"

"Estaban!" Serena said, throwing her hands out in frustration. "*That* great man of the world—he's been married since he was eighteen. I'm a good enough judge of character myself, thanks. And I don't want to be involved with *anybody*. That's my decision, it always has been, you've always known about it, and don't you dare disagree with me *now*."

Furious and ashamed, she felt tears glinting in her eyes again. Tracey took a step back in the little room, disconcerted. "Oh, Serena," she said, her amber eyes alight with understanding. "I didn't mean it that way. I just mean—if he cares for you—and he really sounds as if he does—"

"He *doesn't*," Serena insisted, shaking her head passionately. "He's just making all these insane offers and propositions because he's got one thing in mind. I won't even think of splitting the business with him. And I'm not climbing into his bed even if he sends every rose in Texas."

Tracey looked puzzled. "Offers? Propositions? Split the business? I don't know what you mean. You said he didn't want to go in with us—"

Angrily Serena wiped away the tears welling in her eyes. "I said he wouldn't accept our terms. That's the truth. He's got some crazy scheme—"

"Scheme?"

Serena wiped her eyes again, more in rancor than sorrow. Tersely, she told Tracey about Cal's business proposition, that he become the third partner in La Herencia.

"Oh, wow," Tracey said softly, looking slightly stunned. She sat down on a tiny bench with a thump and ran her fingers through her short hair. She looked up at Serena in disbelief. "Oh, wow."

"Get that look off your face," Serena ordered, her voice taut with obstinacy. "I know what you're thinking—it's too good to be true. That's right, it is. He's not going to put any money in this place. He's not going to introduce us to Amarillo Tex or anybody else. And he's not going to be our spokesman. It's all—bullfeathers, that's all."

Tracey shook her head dazedly and stared into the shadows of a corner. She rubbed her blue-jeaned thigh meditatively. "Well, I'll say this for him. When he sets out a deal, he really sets one out. Wow."

"This is no *deal*," Serena said in contempt. "He doesn't mean it. He'll say anything that comes into his head if he thinks it'll get him what he wants. He's *used* to getting what he wants. I just don't know why he has to pick on me. Why me, dammit?"

She wheeled and faced the small window, putting her elbow on the sill and her chin defiantly on her fist. She stared out at the narrow gray street, bleak in the cold February afternoon. Errol, a neighbor's handsome young yellow tomcat, was swaggering down the sidewalk with easy grace, looking for new worlds to conquer.

That's all Cal is, Serena thought, watching Errol's confident, languid gait, *just a tomcat, catting around. Let him sit on somebody else's fence. Howl at somebody else's window. Not mine.* She steeled her jaw in determination.

She could feel Tracey watching her.

"Serena?" Tracey said it hesitantly, but there was kindness in her voice. "You—like him, don't you?"

Serena took a deep breath to deny it. She let it out again, too tired to dissemble. "I suppose. Who wouldn't?" She felt the tears bite at her eyes again and blinked them back.

An awkward pause filled the little room. "Well," Tracey finally said, with the same hesitation, "what if he really means all these things he's saying—?"

"He doesn't," Serena snapped and kept her back to the other woman. "He couldn't."

There was another silence. Tracey broke it. "How can you be sure?"

Serena took another deep breath and sighed. She gnawed unhappily at her thumbnail. "I can prove it," she said and turned to face Tracey.

Tracey looked up at her friend, her expression concerned. "But how can you *know?*"

Serena straightened her shoulders, tossed her hair back over her shoulders. She made her face as blank as it would go. "Easy," she said with a coldness she didn't feel. "I'll tell him the truth. About me. Watch how fast he'll bolt then."

Tracey looked stricken, because she knew in all likelihood, what Serena said was true.

"YOU CAN PICK ME UP at the shop at seven," she told Cal bluntly the next time he called. "I'm not dressing up. I'll just have on my work clothes. And I don't want to eat. We'll just have coffee."

"Fine," he said with a triumphant grin. Then, just to while away the time until he'd see her, he told himself, he called home and talked to Lynn.

Deep down, he knew there was a more important reason to call home. He was, in a sense, saying goodbye. He was not the same man who had left home a few weeks before. His home would never again truly be on the Double C.

Maybe that was why he told Lynn there might indeed be a special woman; it was a way of telling her, of telling them all, that his life was changing. Everything was becoming different now.

AT PRECISELY ONE MINUTE to seven, Cal stood on the tiny porch of the boot shop. It was a small building, longer than it was wide, with cedar shake siding. Above the door hung a wooden sign with a boot and the words *La Herencia* carved into it. It swung slightly in the brisk evening breeze. A lilac bush grew next to the porch, its branches winter-bare.

The sky was already dark, and the light from the
shop's windows gleamed warm and gold. The only car
in the driveway besides Cal's van was Serena's battered green Chevrolet. He raised his fist and knocked
at the door, then shoved his hands into his pockets and
waited, shifting from foot to foot in the cold.

She swung the door open and stood in a rectangle of
golden light. He drew in his breath with pleasure. A
strange, giddy joy flooded through him at the sight of
her, a joy so sharp it ached. She wore tight, faded
jeans that emphasized the sweep of her lovely long legs
and the kind of simple unornamented boots he always found most elegant.

Her shirt was blue chambray, its sleeves rolled up to
her elbows, and she had a dark blue bandanna knot-
ted around her neck. Her beautiful black hair was
pulled back, but a few dark tendrils escaped. He had
the immediate desire to reach out and smooth them,
so he thrust his hands more deeply into his pockets.

She pushed open the storm door without smiling.
"Come in," she said. Her smoky-green eyes looked
him up and down warily.

"Hello, darlin'," he said huskily.

She looked away without answering. He was a tall
man, but not so tall that he should suddenly make the
shop seem uncomfortably small, yet he did. His dark
jeans were ironed to a sharp crease, beneath them the
pointed tips of his boots were polished till they
gleamed, and his black Stetson was pulled to its most
rakish angle over his eyes.

He wore a weathered leather jacket with a sheep-
skin lining, the collar turned up. His well-sculpted

cheekbones were burnished by the cold, and his smile was somehow too intimate, his gaze too full of undisguised desire.

"So this is your place," he said in his lazy drawl. "Mighty nice."

Serena shrugged. She really had set his flowers about in various old boots that people had left behind to be copied. The shop smelled of leather and warmth, a comforting scent that always made her feel at home. But now it smelled of roses, too, and with Cal there, she suddenly felt off balance, a stranger in her own territory.

"Lordy," he said, looking up at the ceiling. It was nearly covered by hanging cobbler's lasts, made of both wood and white plastic. The lasts were custom-made replicas of customers' feet, and the boots were literally built around them. Serena kept them hanging from the ceiling with names and numbers, so new boots could be made for the same customers.

"You got feet all over your ceiling," Cal smiled. "I feel like I'm standing under a convention of marionettes, all these wooden feet. You've got this many customers?"

"They go back for years. I bought this business from the man who taught me. Juan Sanchez."

He stepped to a shelf displaying various styles and designs of boots. "You do all these?"

She nodded, still not smiling. "I work on the uppers, the fancy work. Jesus and Estaban do the bottom parts. Estaban and I both measure and make lasts."

"Nice work." He nodded in approval, then turned to capture her gaze with his own. "Beautiful," he said, looking into her eyes. "Purely beautiful."

A quiver ran through her, sheer and dazzling. She drew in her breath sharply. The muscles in her thighs seemed to melt like warmed wax, and she tingled with awareness of him. A strange, yearning loneliness filled her, stretching out toward him as emptily as a prairie.

"I'll get my jacket," she murmured and ducked into the back room. She snatched up her navy wool jacket and her white hat. She shrugged into the jacket and pulled the hat brim low over her eyes as if it could protect her.

When she stepped again into the front of the shop, Cal still seemed to dominate its space, all wide leather-covered shoulders and long, muscular legs that tapered to the boots' gleaming tips.

A slow, teasing smile curved his lips. "I thought you said you weren't going to dress up."

"I—I didn't." She zipped up her jacket almost defensively and drew on her leather gloves.

"Then how do you look so blamed gorgeous?"

"Don't *talk* like that," she ordered irritably. "Come on. If we're going to have coffee, let's do it. I've had a long day."

He nodded amiably and opened the door for her. "You always work this late?"

"Usually later," she said, stepping into the cold and shuddering involuntarily against its bite. "You don't build a business by knocking off early. Where do you want to go? I'll meet you there. I want to be able to leave from there."

"You are frostier than this February wind. And you're a workaholic. Do you ever let yourself have fun?"

"Life," she said tightly, "is about more than having *fun.*"

"Could have fooled me," he said with a grin, watching her unlock her car door. "There's a little Mexican restaurant about two blocks up the street. How about you meet me there? And you know—I believe you could have fun—if you worked at it."

"I believe you'd only work if you could have fun at it," she retorted crisply, getting into her car.

He only laughed, his breath a frosty plume on the air. "You remind me of a rainbow," he said with a grin.

She didn't even know what he meant, but the words made her heart tighten with a pleasure so sharp and strange it took her breath away.

The Mexican restaurant was called Premio Gordo, a brightly decorated, homey, hole-in-the-wall sort of place with sombreros and serapes and velvet paintings on its stuccoed walls and its warm air fragrant with spices.

Serena had arrived first and was already seated in a booth upholstered with patched red vinyl by the time Cal entered. She'd taken off her hat and set it on the seat beside her, so Cal would be forced to sit not next to her, but across from her. She'd unbuttoned her jacket but not taken it off; she meant to signal that she didn't intend to stay long.

Still, her blood quickened and the excited tingling swarmed through her when Cal strolled in. He touched his hat brim in salute to the middle-aged Mexican woman who was waiting tables, and he gave her his most winning smile. The woman brightened and smiled back widely. She tossed Serena a look that mingled conspiracy with happy approval, as if to say, "Ah! Aren't you the lucky girl? He's something, this one."

Serena bit her lip unhappily. Cal shucked off his jacket and hung it on a coat tree next to the booth. He hung his hat beside the jacket.

He'd dressed up, Serena noticed with distraction. His Western-cut shirt was snowy-white and pressed to formidable crispness. It stretched across his muscled chest and hugged his narrow waist. He had a large silver belt buckle set with nuggets of rough turquoise. The belt itself was leather hand-tooled in an abstract design, expensive without being gaudy.

"Want me to hang up your jacket?" he asked.

She shook her head.

He sat down and grinned at her, folding his hands in front of him on the table. "Now you can't sit there and smell these wonderful smells and not order a bowl of chili, can you? You aren't so hard on yourself you'd deny yourself that small pleasure. You must be hungry. Come on. One bowl of chili?"

She hesitated. Her stomach growled slightly. Maybe that was why she felt so dazed, almost faint, she thought; she'd eaten no lunch. "No," she said, determined to be Spartan. "Just coffee."

He leaned his chin on his fist and stared at her. "Then I won't, either. But—a bowl of good chili and a beautiful girl. That's probably what heaven's like."

"Well," Serena said, still trying to sound stern, "you might as well imagine whatever kind of heaven you want. At the rate you're going, you'll never actually get there."

"Sugar, I'm there now."

"*Don't* talk like that."

"I can't help it. It's like a bird singing to celebrate spring. I look at you, and I got to talk sweet. It's an impulse that won't be denied."

"Some impulses should be denied."

The waitress came and took their orders. She beamed, her eyes crinkling with merriment when Cal teased her with questions about the hotness of the salsa.

Again Serena watched him with conflicting emotions. He seemed genuinely friendly, as if it was his pleasure to make people smile. She had been in the restaurant three times before for lunch and had learned nothing about the plump waitress. Cal, in contrast, was there for five minutes and knew the woman's name was Rosalita, she came from San Antonio and had four children, one in medical school.

Serena shook her head when the waitress finally left. He was such a free spirit, so different from her. She wished suddenly, achingly, that she were more like him. She could learn much from such a man.

"What's wrong?" he asked.

"Nothing."

"You look sad," he said, real concern in his voice. "Why? Sometimes you do. I don't want to make you sad."

She shook her head again, wondering why she had agreed to come. It would have been easier, she decided in despair, not to have seen him again at all. She squared her shoulders, tried to look him in the eye, but couldn't. "First," she said, alternately wrinkling and smoothing the napkin, "I'm telling you no, once and for all. I'm not selling any of La Herencia. It's my— security. I started with nothing, and I've built it this far. I'm not interested in another partner."

"Honey," he said, not smiling, "I can make your security more secure. That's a fact. I'm talking sense, and you know it. You don't trust me? I'll work to *make* you trust me. I guarantee you'll never regret it."

"I already regret it," she said wearily.

"Sugar, don't shut me out. I want what's best for you. What's best for us. I truly do."

"Oh, there is no *us,*" she said with impatience. "And that's another thing—why would I ever get emotionally involved with somebody and go into business with him at the same time? It's…ridiculous. It's a bad way to run business. What if we had—had a fling and ended up hating each other? And then we were still tangled together by business. It'd be chaos. No."

"There *is* an us," he said quietly. "You know it, and I know it. Even *she* knows it." He nodded toward Rosalita, who was bringing them two mugs of coffee and a basket of corn chips with salsa. The woman smiled at them, and Serena was shocked to realize it was the kind of smile people reserve for young lovers. Disturbed, she stared down at the crumpled napkin.

"All right," Cal said when Rosalita left, intensity vibrating in his voice. "Listen. When I looked up and saw you standing there again last night, something inside me said, 'She's the one.' I heard it—clear as I'm talking to you now. 'She's the one.' I knew it. And I have a feeling you know it, too. Look me in the face and tell me I'm wrong."

She didn't raise her eyes. "You're wrong."

"Serena," he said, "look me in the face and say it. You can't. Something happened last night. The earth moved. Everything changed."

She shook her head helplessly, her face still turned from his. "I'm not the one," she said, her voice tight. "I don't get involved—that way. So don't even pretend to be serious about this."

He leaned across the table, his voice low. "I'm not pretending to be serious. I *am* serious."

"Drink your coffee," she said. "You'll hurt Rosalita's feelings."

"Eat some chips. You look hungry. You work too hard."

The silence hung heavily between them. Serena nibbled at the chips without appetite, and although the salsa was burning, she barely tasted it. Hotter, stranger fires seemed to be coursing through her.

The longer the silence grew, the more determined Cal's face became. She had seen that look before on the faces of rodeo cowboys. It meant they were in a state of severe concentration, psyching themselves up for some particularly difficult or dangerous event.

At last he nodded, almost to himself. "All right," he said, staring moodily at his coffee cup. He shifted his wide shoulders uncomfortably. He frowned. "All right. I suppose I should just come out and say it. I love you, all right?"

Serena was so astounded that she broke her rule of not looking at him. She stared. The frown line next to his eyebrow deepened, and the muscles of his jaw were tensed. He wasn't looking at her. He thinned his lips and shook his head thoughtfully. "I never said that to another woman," he murmured broodingly. "Seems funny to say it. But it's right. It even sounds right. I love you."

He glanced up and his flashing hazel eyes caught and held her green ones. "I guess I'll have to get used to saying it—I love you."

Her mouth dropped open slightly. "You can't love me. You don't even know me."

He shrugged as if in irritation, the line of his mouth more intent than before. "In this case, that comes later. My great-grandpa says that's how it happened to him. Except he took only one look at her and knew. He said he knew he was gonna marry her before he even knew her name. That's the way it happens sometimes. Not often, but sometimes."

"I—I—" Serena stammered, unable to finish the sentence. She kept gazing into his eyes as if hypnotized. He had beautiful eyes, deep set, an intriguingly clear golden hazel, with dark lashes.

"So being as I love you and intend to marry you, I might as well put my money in your business, and I can't see what the argument is." His voice was impatient, almost angry. "Now maybe a chili parlor isn't the best place to tell you this, but at least you can see

I've got no ulterior motive. It's not like I'm making rash promises in the midst of passion. It's not like I expect you to surrender yourself right here amongst the enchiladas. No, I'm telling you outright here in a public place to show I'm not afraid to say it in front of God and everybody."

He nodded in conviction, the frown line deepening even more. Having said what he had to say, he finished his coffee in a workmanlike way. He seemed to concentrate all his attention on it, as if he'd said no more to her than, "Nice night, isn't it?"

If Serena hadn't known better, she would have thought he was experiencing something close to shyness or embarrassment. She watched the emotions cross his face, her heart thudding like a hammer against her breastbone. Certainly he couldn't be serious—could he? Was this simply how a master flirt and seducer worked, always by surprise, by playing the unexpected card?

And yet when he looked at her the way he had, something inside her trembled and she felt fatefully bound to him, as if under a spell. As he'd said, it had been that way from the first—as if the earth had moved.

He pushed his mug away, drained. "Now I guess I've gone and declared myself to you. Maybe I should have done it in a different way, but I've never done it before. I'll buy you a ring if you want, or maybe you'd rather come with me to pick it. You're going to have to live with it a long time."

He shook his head and put his hand to his forehead, frowning again. "Lord, you'd think I'd do a better job of this. Me, of all people. Lord. I did that with hardly any style at all. I don't know what's wrong with me. I guess it's you.''

He shifted in his seat and folded his hands in front of him again. Serena noticed how tense his hands were, how atypically serious his handsome face.

"I—can't," she breathed.

He stared at her, a muscle jumping in his jaw. The intensity in his face rocked her, leaving behind an aftershock of pain, a tremor of emptiness.

"I can't," she repeated. "I won't marry anybody. I can't."

"Why? You're not married. You're not seeing anyone. I know—I pried it out of Estaban. He's a good old boy. *He* said you ought to get married."

"I can't," Serena said again. Her voice threatened to choke in her throat. "I won't ever get married. I won't ever have children. I'm what doctors call a person at risk. A disease runs in my family. I may be carrying it. I have no way of knowing. If I am, it'll kill me. If I have children, they could have it, too. I'll never take that chance."

This time when she spoke, she looked him in the face. She kept her head high. The set of his mouth had gone grim and his hands clenched more tightly together. She could tell her words had stunned him and that he did not yet fully comprehend her. He looked at her in disbelief.

"My father died of Huntington's chorea," she said relentlessly. "So did his father. I have a fifty-fifty chance of having it, too. It usually doesn't set in until after a person's thirty. That's only three years away. It may wait even longer, clear to fifty. If I get it, I'll slowly lose control of my body. I'll jerk around like a broken puppet. Eventually I'll be bedridden. But that's not the worst. The worst is it destroys the mind as completely as it destroys the body. There's no prevention. And there's no cure.''

He said nothing. His face was strained, incredulous. *Yes,* Serena thought bitterly, *that's the way men always look when you tell them. A mixture of sickness and sympathy. And then they pull themselves together and try to make the all the right noises of condolence, and then they go away and stay away. And who can blame them?*

She took a deep breath. Telling about it was like going on a journey from which no return was possible. He would never again see her the same way. He would never again feel the same way toward her. But there was no turning back now, so she forged ahead, telling him in words as stark as possible, words designed to shake him and drive him away.

''I want you to understand completely,'' she said. ''You say you think I'm beautiful. I won't stay beautiful. You say you think I'm 'the one.''' Her mouth crooked cynically. ''Don't you see? Even if I *were* the most perfect person in the world for you, I might not stay that way. I might—change. I can't even tell you what I'd change into. It'd be like those science fiction movies—another being would come live in what was left of my body. I wouldn't be *me* any longer.''

''My God, Serena,'' he said and reached for her hand. She drew it back and hid it in her lap.

"I still haven't told you everything," she said, holding her chin higher. "This happens slowly. It wouldn't be over in six months. Or even six years. It took my grandfather seven years to die of it. Nobody could tell us what was wrong—until the end. My grandmother lost the ranch, trying to keep up with the doctor bills. I saw what it did to her. To all of us."

She shook her head and squared her jaw. Her green eyes seemed to see a distant and terrible scene. "No sooner was he dead, than it got my father, and I watched the same thing happen again. For five years my mother tried to stay sane in the face of it. It took all the money, it wore her out, it made her old too soon, it made her die before her time. I won't take a chance on doing the same thing to somebody else. I won't."

"My God," he said again.

Her voice took on a bitter edge. "Last night you said I was going to be the mother of your children. Tonight you see that's not possible. Unless you'd like to take a chance that your children could die the same way. I won't be the mother of anybody's children. So thanks for the romantic thoughts, but I'm sure you'll want to rethink them. I'm not what you thought. I'm not what you want. Where I go, cowboy, I go alone. Whatever happens."

"Give me your hand," he said fiercely. His eyes flashed dangerously.

She shook her head and kept her hands clamped together in her lap.

"Give it to me," he demanded with such force that she responded almost against her will. She brought it up and let it rest against the table's edge. He reached and took it in his so hard that she felt her bones grind together painfully.

"You say you've got a fifty-fifty chance," he said, his gaze locked with hers. "So you might be denying yourself all these things—husband, children—for nothing. You might be fine." He squeezed her hand harder.

"I might." She tossed her head rebelliously. "But any gambler will tell you that fifty-fifty odds are lousy. And I'll never know for sure until it's too late for children."

He kept staring at her, dark emotions crossing and recrossing his face.

"It's like Russian roulette," she said from between her teeth, "only there are three bullets in the chamber instead of one. The gun is aimed at my head. And somebody else decides when to pull the trigger."

His upper lip turned down in sick disbelief. "And there's no way you can *know?*" he demanded. "You mean with everything doctors can do, they can't tell what's going to happen to you?"

She tried to draw her hand away, but he wouldn't let her. "There's a test," she said without optimism. "Relatively new. They'd have to have blood samples from at least three members of my family—two with the disease and one without. They'd check their blood against mine for what they call genetic markers. If I don't have the markers, I don't have the disease. But

I don't have two people left alive that have it. So I *can't* know. I take what fate deals out. I don't even know if I'd want to know—if the news was bad.''

His hold on her hand gentled. He swallowed. ''Serena, let's get out of here. Someplace where we can be alone. We've got to figure things out, to talk.''

''We *have* talked, and I've already figured things out,'' she said. ''I'm already alone. I decided years ago that's how I want it, and I intend to keep it that way.''

This time when she pulled her hand away, reluctantly he let it go. She placed her crumpled napkin on the table, pulled the lapels of her coat together and picked up her hat. ''Thanks for the attention. It was flattering. But I'm really not interested. You shouldn't be, either. So long. It's been good to know you.''

She slid from the booth and stood up. He was on his feet almost as swiftly as she. She headed for the door. He threw a bill on the table, grabbed his jacket and Stetson and followed her into the cold darkness of the parking lot. He jammed the hat on his head and threw the jacket over his shoulder, not bothering to take the time to put it on.

He caught up to her at the edge of the lot and seized her arm. ''Where do you think you're going?'' he demanded, glaring down at her, his lip curling in passion.

''Home.'' She pulled her hat brim down and tried to wrench away from him.

''Where?'' he asked again, holding her tighter, not letting her escape. ''Where?''

"Home," she repeated with vehemence. "I'm going *home.*"

"Then come here," he said, "because this is where home is."

Pulling her to him, he kissed her with devouring hunger.

CHAPTER SIX

HE HAD DROPPED his jacket onto the gravel of the parking lot. The night wind was still high and cold, but he didn't notice. He pulled Serena against his ribs so hard it hurt him, but he didn't care about that, either.

His hat brim knocked against hers, and her hat joined his jacket in the gravel. He could feel the long, loose strands of her hair blowing against his cold cheekbones, feel the soft warmth of her lips yielding beneath his own questing ones.

Wonderingly, almost against his will, he raised one hand to smooth the fluttering silk of her hair, to touch the smooth line of her jaw, the curve of her throat, then to lace his fingers through the rippling wealth of her hair. Cradling her head, he guided her face upward, so that his lips could play more ardently against hers.

Once again he had the headlong, reckless feeling that he was kissing her because he had to: there simply wasn't any choice for him. He hadn't anticipated what she might do in return and supposed, unhappily, she would resist.

When instead her arms wound around his neck, it was as if she filled him full of bright flames, all hun-

gry and blazing with want for her. He drew her against
him so tightly that once again it hurt his ribs, and he
involuntarily gasped against her mouth, her deli-
cious, trembling, intoxicating mouth.

She gasped, too, a sound like a small sob. The sound
shook his heart and made him crazy with love for her.
The flames inside him danced higher and brighter and
cleaner, obliterating everything except his desire for
her.

Her lips opened beneath his, inviting his tongue,
and he let it enter, exploring the loveliness of such intimacy, the moistness, the warmth of her. He ex-
plored it fully, as if it were the only thing in the world
worth exploring.

Serena strained against him, not knowing if it was
the night's cold or Cal's heat that made her shiver. She
had meant to walk off and leave him, breaking it off
neatly and cleanly. But now she was tasting him and
savoring him like some sweet, forbidden wine that
drove all reason away.

He had drawn her back to him as if by some un-
breakable silken thread. But, oh, she thought faintly,
his lips were so hot and sweet and maddening as they
moved against hers. His arms held her faster than any
arms had ever done. She felt as if she could lose all her
doubts, all her fears in the dizzying pleasure of such
kisses, in the reassuring strength of such arms.

He pulled away from her slightly, and his breath
against her face was uneven and hot. "I think we'd
better get out of this parking lot," he said from between his teeth. "And Serena, please don't *ever* just up
and walk out on me that way again. Oh, Jesus, don't."

He pulled her against him so that her face was pressed against his chest. "Don't," he repeated, squeezing her tightly and kissing the top of her head. "Don't."

She closed her eyes, feeling the crispness of his shirt beneath her cheek, the hardness of his muscled chest and the dependable beat of his heart. She felt weak with desire, storm-tossed and wearied by it.

He had his fingers laced in her hair again, and her hair had come loose from its barrette. He stroked it sensuously, hypnotically, his voice low and hot in her ear. She squeezed her eyes more tightly.

"And don't think I'd just walk off and leave you," he said against her hair. "I wouldn't. I couldn't. I told you I love you. Maybe I didn't tell you in the right way, but I'll make up for that. I'll tell you every way in the world till I get it right. I love you. I love you."

Suddenly the real world came crashing back into Serena's consciousness. The real world seemed like a bad accident to her, a messy one she would have to spend her whole life cleaning up.

"Don't say that," she murmured, pushing away from his chest. "You don't know. I do. You don't even begin to know what you're getting into. There are other things I haven't told you. I have a sister. I might have to be responsible for her someday. And she has kids. There are her *kids* to think about, too."

Her voice almost broke when she mentioned her sister. Patti was five years older than Serena. Patti was as emotional as Serena was self-controlled. Headlong and trusting her luck, the eighteen-year-old Patti hadn't told her husband, who was no older than she, about the Huntington's. She'd waited until after her two daughters were born. He hadn't been able to cope with the news. He'd left her. Now she made her way working at the telephone company. But if illness struck her or if the children needed help, Serena was the only person to whom they could turn. Serena, as always, had to be the sensible one, stoic, planning ahead.

Her mind hardened and cooled, and her body, so warm and yearning a moment before, grew tense. She felt desolate and empty.

"It doesn't matter what I get into as long as I'm in it with you," he said, trying to kiss her again. "We'll take it one step at a time, one day at a time—"

"No," she protested, dodging and drawing back. "You're *not* listening. You're trying to be—noble or something. And you don't have the foggiest notion of what you're being noble about. Fools rush in. You may be willing to be a fool. I'm not."

"I'm not being noble, dammit, I'm just being me. If I'm a fool, you'd better figure out what to do with me, because I'm your fool. And I don't plan on being anybody else's."

She stepped away from him, striking his hands from her body, erecting all the old fortifications in her mind. "And I told you," she said with contempt, "you don't know what you're talking about." The contempt was as much for herself as him, for having gone so willingly, so desperately to his arms.

She looked at the gravel and kicked at it angrily, a small, frustrated kick. "Now where's my hat? And there's your jacket—just lying there. Oh, damn, here I am, carrying on like some randy teenager in a parking lot, and my best *hat* blows away."

He picked up his jacket and slung it over his shoulder. He shifted his weight so that one hip was cocked. He stared at her from under the brim of his Stetson. "We're not teenagers. I'll buy you a new hat. I don't know why you're worried about a hat. We've got more important things to discuss."

"We've got nothing to discuss," she said shortly. She tried to smooth her hair, which was tossed from the wind and his caresses. It wouldn't be smoothed. It remained as tangled as her deepest emotions. For the thousandth time in her life, she remembered her mother's bitter words: *Don't you ever dare do to another human being what your father's done to me. Don't you dare.*

Hurriedly, she turned from Cal, dug into her pocket and took out her car keys. She started to unlock the door of her car.

"Serena," he said, a dangerous edge in his voice. He put his hand on her arm.

She wheeled and glared up at him. "Don't touch me again. I told you—we've got no future. You never think about the future, do you? You've never had to. Well, with me gone, you still won't have to, and consider yourself lucky. I told you once, I'll tell you again—goodbye."

"Serena," he said in the same warning tone. "You never did look me in the face and say you didn't care. You don't, because you can't, dammit."

For a heart-sinking moment she studied his face, which was both angry and troubled. His white shirt gleamed blue in the dim light, and his breath, like hers, rose in a fragile, silvery cloud. The now familiar feeling for him came haunting her again, the excited yearning mixed with the emptiness.

"All right," she said softly, staring into his taut, handsome face. "I feel—an attraction to you. It's just biological, that's all. Nothing more. That's your specialty, isn't it, after all? Love 'em and leave 'em—just biology—would you settle for that? A couple of nights. We get each other out of our systems. Then you move on. And so do I. We don't look back."

Her own suggestion shocked her, yet she could not help making it. It was impossible for her to have him for a lifetime, impossible for him to promise to stay with her—even if he could not yet understand that. But they might have each other for a little while. That would hurt nothing. A little while was better than no time at all.

His face went more rigid. He shook his head. "No. I won't settle for that. I want more."

The cold of the night seemed to penetrate her, become one with her. She had made a dangerous and foolish offer. She didn't know whether to be hurt or relieved that he'd refused it. In shame, she sensed a deeper honor in him than she'd given him credit for.

But she showed him no shame. She drew herself up as proudly as she could. "Then I've got nothing left to give you. Sorry, cowboy."

She got into her car, slamming the door behind her. She jabbed the keys into the ignition, started the motor.

He stood in the same spot, motionless, just watching her. Oh, Lord, she thought miserably, she would always remember him standing there in the cold moonlight, just watching her, that look on his face. She would remember it for the rest of her life, however long that might be.

She put the car into gear and pulled away, the gravel grinding beneath her tires. Even after she turned the corner, she could still see him in her mind's eye: a tall, broad-shouldered young man, standing with his hip cocked and his jacket thrown over his shoulder, his eyes stubbornly following her.

She thought of a song. Something about coming with the dust, and going with the wind.

Go, she thought. *Go, Cal, with the wind where you belong. Before you break my heart. My grandfather broke it. My father broke it. Go before you leave it so broken it can't be fixed again.*

CAL STOOD STARING after her into the darkness. The wind whipped more cruelly and a few flakes of snow, small and hard, whirled down around him.

Snow, he thought numbly. *It's not supposed to snow here.* But more flakes came spiraling from the heavens, and then more still, in a cold swarm.

He didn't put on his jacket. He'd forgotten he had it. He stood like a statue, looking at the corner where her taillights had disappeared.

It's not supposed to snow in Wolverton, and pretty women aren't supposed to live under death threats. None of it is supposed to happen this way—none of it.

Cal, the sunniest of the McKinneys, looked up at the darkness and the falling snow and wondered if the sun had gone out forever, and that was why it was so ungodly cold. Maybe it would stay cold forever.

He hadn't felt as dazed since his birthday in Fort Worth, when the bronc named Fate kicked him in the head.

Now it seemed Fate had kicked him in the head again, but this time it wasn't as easy to dust himself off and walk away, acting as if it hadn't hurt. It hurt, all right. It hurt more than any break or sprain or slash he'd ever known.

That night she reappeared at the Wolverton Rodeo, he'd felt a dizzy, swooping, beautiful certainty that she was the woman for him, and he'd fallen in love with her on the spot. He'd been both awed and tickled; he'd never experienced anything like it before in his lifetime. He was certain he never would again.

He'd been just as certain that destiny had a hand in it. She needed help with her boot company. He needed a new career. He had money, he knew Amarillo Tex, he knew a thing or three about business, and if she needed a spokesman, hell, he could speak. He would speak for her as if his tongue were made of gold.

He'd always been lucky, always. And he'd always believed if he waited long enough, his problems, magically, would solve themselves. His family was sick of his rodeoing, and so, deep in his heart, was he. But he hadn't known what he was going to do with his life.

Then *she'd* been there. All of a sudden, he'd known. It had all come together, made sense, felt right at last.

He'd found the right girl, so all he'd had to do was go get her. Easy. He'd always gotten any woman he wanted. It had seemed a natural, inviolable law, like gravity.

How wrong he'd been. How vain, shortsighted and completely wrong.

"Pride goeth before destruction, and an haughty spirit before a fall." He could almost hear the voice of his mother, Pauline, quoting the Bible. "Boast not thyself of tomorrow; for thou knowest not what a day may bring forth."

Boast not thyself of tomorrow. Amen.

Never had he wanted a woman as much as he wanted Serena. It was more than desire; it was a want and need that buried itself deep in his vitals, like a spear, piercing and aching.

But she would not have him.

He looked up at the sky again and swallowed. He could have handled it if she'd simply rejected him. She might have loved someone else, or turned from him for a hundred different reasons. He'd have handled it.

But God, not this reason, he thought, shaking his head. Not because of some damned disease that was going to wreck her life whether she had it or not. She didn't want to have children. Her children *might* be strong and healthy and fine. They might be the most wonderful children in the history of the world. But she didn't dare have them and take the chance.

She was beautiful and smart and courageous and talented, but she didn't want to marry. In a few years the disease might start robbing her of all loveliness, inner and outer. She didn't want to burden anyone with what would become of her.

But, and he had to smile bitterly, she *might* be fine. It was possible that she might be married for fifty marvelous years to someone. Someone such as him-

self. But she would not take the chance. She was afraid
of what she might become.

He turned and drew his hand back, then slammed
his fist into the door of his van as hard as he could.
For a moment physical pain dazzled him, blinded his
mind to everything else, and he was grateful.

Then he swore and flexed his fingers, wondering if
he'd broken something; it felt like it. So he hit the door
again, harder still. He swore again, this time at his
own stupidity and his aching hand.

He blinked and set his teeth against the pain. The
worst thing, the most rotten thing, the one that made
him sick to his stomach, was that she was in danger.

He loved her, she was in danger, and there was
nothing he could do. Cal was not used to a sense of
helplessness. It nauseated him, making him feel like a
man on a sinking ship that was tossing and pitching as
the waters overwhelmed it.

It wasn't fair, he raged. He couldn't lose her. He
couldn't watch anything happen to her. He'd just
found her.

He set his jaw. Well, he'd find her again. He'd find
her again if he had to do it every day of his life. He'd
make her talk and he'd make her listen. She cared for
him. He was certain. She was just so damned proud,
determined to go it alone.

A fifty-fifty chance was better than no chance. He'd
make her see that. He was a man used to taking
chances. He'd spent his life doing it. He'd teach her
that she could do it, too.

* * *

SERENA HAD a small apartment, bright, warm and
cozy, on the edge of Wolverton. She entered it grate-
fully, as if it were a sanctuary where trouble might not
pursue her. But tonight trouble followed her in the
door, dogged her steps, tagged along behind her into
her bedroom as if it intended to make itself at home.

She didn't intend to stay and let trouble keep her
company. She didn't usually run from problems, but
this one was an exception. She would run until she'd
outrun it completely.

Flinging open the closet door, she jerked out her
suitcase, threw it on the bed and opened it. She yanked
open her dresser drawers and began piling clothes into
the yawning suitcase. She didn't consider it cowardly
to flee. She considered it a matter of survival.

She truly didn't want to see Cal again. He made
conflict and doubt and longing tear her apart. That he
would try to see her again, she had no doubt. She
could tell from the rebellious way his eyes had flashed
when she told him goodbye, from his stubborn stance
as he stood looking after her in the night, as if already planning to come after her.

Well, she thought, as determined as he, let him
come looking. She wouldn't be there. She had no place
to go except to Patti in Amarillo, but that was fine.
Perhaps a dose of Patti's life-style was just what Serena needed to get her back on track and keep her
there.

She'd *order* Tracey not to let Cal know where she'd
gone or when she'd be back. Cal's horse was injured,
but that couldn't keep him in town for more than a few

days. He couldn't wait forever for her. He had commitments down the road. They would force him on, and she'd be safe. Until then, Tracey could run La Herencia.

Serena sighed and glanced down at her boots, gleaming in the lamplight. They were her favorite pair. She and Estaban had made them in the shop this time last year.

Her memories tried to drag her into deeper turmoil. She kept packing. *La Herencia,* she thought, grief and confusion tumbling through her mind. *The heritage.*

Old Juan had taught her boot making. That was his heritage, for he'd learned it from his father. She'd been seventeen when she started, just out of high school. Her own father was dying. He was only forty-three, a ruin in both body and mind. That was her heritage.

"How steady your hands are," Juan had said at the beginning, watching her cut fine leather. That was one reason he had taken her on as a disciple. He approved of the sureness and steadiness of her hands.

The other reason was her imagination. "A great boot is first made in here," Juan had said, tapping his temple knowingly. She had a creative imagination, and she could send it ranging over the problems and challenges of design: inventive, triumphant, joyous in its own strength.

She remembered her father, the last time she had seen him, trying to light a cigarette. He could barely control the shaking of his hands. It had taken him forever to get the light to his mouth. His hands had once been as steady as hers.

He'd once had a wry, fanciful imagination. Then it had slowly shattered, and he became obsessed by one illogical fragment after another, trapped in its disintegration. *Heritages*.

Angry, unwanted tears blurred her vision. She held out her hand and studied it the way she did every day: in spite of her emotion, it was steady; she was still in control. Completely.

Furiously she scrubbed the tears away and kept packing, taking her suit bag from the closet and grabbing hangers of clothing to fill it. She had trained herself long ago not to cry over what she couldn't change. She had learned to take charge of her life and fate as best she could.

Serena believed in hardheaded planning, not luck. She had, thanks to Tracey's help, the best and most comprehensive of insurance plans. She had her life mapped out, no matter what fate dealt her. La Herencia was part of her course of action. She wanted it to be profitable enough to take care of herself and Patti and Patti's children, if necessary. It was their security, the best heritage she knew how to give them.

If her health failed, she had made the best arrangements she could with her doctor, her lawyer and Tracey as her business partner. If her health proved fine after all, she would have had a long and meaningful life without having put anyone else through the doubt, the fear, the suspense, the ungodly waiting.

Patti ignored the threat to their lives; Serena looked it squarely in the eye. In the meantime, she lived happily enough, caught up in her work, her ambitions, her friends.

Happily enough, that was, until now. Until she had let a tall cowboy with a reckless smile and long-lashed eyes come limping into her orderly existence. The moment he'd appeared, she'd been stricken by the doubt that what she had thought of as living sensibly, perhaps wasn't really living at all.

She zipped closed her suit bag and looked around her cheerful bedroom. Suddenly its cheer seemed artificial, forced. There were pictures of flowers scattered everywhere, but none of people she had loved. None of people at all.

A taste like ashes prickled her tongue when she contemplated her Spartan, logical life. Like the room, it suddenly seemed sterile, its careful confines imprisoning and hateful.

She searched desperately for her makeup case, found it and packed it. Makeup, she thought unhappily. Putting on a false face. Was she false all the way through? Had she made herself into some creature little better than a robot? Oh, how had Cal put her in this torment of self-doubt, and why had she allowed it?

She gritted her teeth, packing the makeup and snapping shut the suitcase. She hated and feared what Cal had done to her, yet paradoxically, she yearned for it, too.

She packed a few more things into her smallest suitcase, then paused, staring down at her boots again. She bit her lip. She had offered to have sex with Cal. He had refused, wanting more.

She could not give more.

Perhaps sex was all she really wanted from him—was that it? She had carefully tried sex a few times and found it overrated. It was, she decided, a complication she could easily remove from her list of necessities, and she had done so. Sex with Cal should be no different from with her former partners; the same awkward and unsatisfying experience. Yet it *would* be different, she knew.

He claimed he loved her. She'd never allowed herself to believe in love. It was a snare and a delusion, she'd told herself, a foolish rumor that only fools believed in. Someone as practical as she would never fall into such a silly trap.

But Cal could talk of love and look at her with such intensity that her whole being trembled, and she *wanted* to believe him. She wanted to lose herself in his vital hazel eyes, those eyes more full of life than any she'd ever seen. And when he touched her—she shuddered, not daring to think of when he touched her.

No, no, no, she told herself sternly, closing the valise. He couldn't love her, and she couldn't love him. For some reason, they were infatuated with each other, that was all. Perhaps it was simply because they were so impossibly different.

Wearily, she turned and faced her dresser, catching sight of herself in the mirror. Her cheeks were flushed, her eyes too bright and her hair tousled.

She remembered his fingers lacing through her hair, making her heart leap against his. She remembered his lips and the heat of him against her in the cold night. She remembered and couldn't stop remembering.

I don't love him, she told her pale image in the mirror. *I don't.*

CAL STARTED PHONING the shop at nine. He phoned again at nine-thirty, ten, ten-thirty and eleven. At eleven-thirty he appeared in person. The woman—it had to be Tracey—looked up from her desk and seemed to recognize him, perhaps from his pictures. Her face paled. She was a pretty little thing, he thought abstractedly, but nothing like Serena.

He leaned on the desk, putting his weight on his fists, looking into her eyes. "Tracey, darlin'," he said, his voice low and earnest. "Tell me where she is."

Tracey swallowed. "I can't. I really—can't. I'm sorry—but I promised."

Cal's gaze grew more intent, as if he could hypnotize the answers out of the woman by sheer willpower. "Then tell me when she's coming back."

Tracey's mouth turned to a thin, unhappy line. "I can't. Look, I'd *like* to help you, but—"

He cut her off, bringing his face lower so it was almost level with hers. "Why'd she leave?"

Tracey shook her head, looking unhappier than before. "I can't say."

A forked vein in his temple began to twitch. He leaned harder on his fists, so the knuckles turned white. "Is it 'cause she doesn't want to see me?"

"Listen, Mr. McKinney, she *asked* me not to say anything to you."

"How good friends are you?" he demanded. "Do you know what all this is about? Has she told you—about her family and all?"

Tracey fell suspiciously silent, her eyes wary. She was, Cal realized, a woman not used to lying, and withholding information pained her. She knew, all right; he could tell from her face. He didn't think the two Mexican men knew. They looked at him furtively from the workshop, puzzled disapproval on their faces.

"You do know," Cal accused, pointing a finger at her. "Will you at least talk to me, for God's sake? For her sake. I just want to help her. I'd never try to hurt her. Lord, that's the last thing I'd do."

The older of the two men stepped from the workshop. He was a stout, darkly handsome man of about thirty. He spoke to Tracey in Spanish, at the same time eyeing Cal with unfriendliness. "Is this man bothering you?" was what Cal thought he said.

Cal exhaled in exasperation, standing straight. He recognized the man's voice. It was Estaban who stood before him, trying his level best to look threatening. Yesterday, on the phone, the man had been friendly enough. "Estaban, right?" Cal said from between clenched teeth. *"Yo soy Cal McKinney. ¿Donde está la mujer? ¿Donde está, amigo?"*

The man's black eyebrows went up in displeased surprise. Tracey said something to Estaban in such rapid Spanish that Cal couldn't follow. He caught his own name, and Serena's, but little else.

In frustration, Cal dropped any attempt to communicate in Spanish. "I'm not here to make trouble," he said, looking Estaban in the eye. "I want to find her, that's all."

Estaban glanced at Tracey's troubled face, then back at Cal. The two men's eyes locked as they took each other's measure. Cal thought he saw a flicker of reluctant sympathy under Estaban's stern facade. But the man shook his head. "She doesn't want to be found."

Cal straightened, shifted his shoulders restlessly and tried again. "When's she coming back? Just tell me that."

Estaban asked Tracey in Spanish when Serena would return. Tracey replied with the same rapid-fire as before.

Estaban blinked solemnly. He shook his head. "She will not come back while you are here. I'm sorry, Señor McKinney. *Adiós—y salud y pesetas.*"

Estaban crossed his arms, and Tracey looked as if she was on the verge of crying. Cal nodded in frustration. He was doing no good here. He was only harassing people who loved Serena enough to protect her.

"Would you give her a message?" he asked, his eyes meeting Tracey's, trying to force her to hold his gaze. "Would you do that much?"

Tracey shook her head and looked down at the papers on her desk, as if unable to meet the challenge in Cal's face. "Sorry. She said not to take any messages."

Estaban's face remained rigidly controlled.

Cal managed an unamused smile. "I see. The thorough type, isn't she? Well, thanks, honey." He nodded to Estaban. "You, too, friend. I know you'd help if you could. So long. *Salud y pesetas.*"

He turned and walked out the door into the weak noon sunshine. The cement thudded emptily under the impact of his boot heels. The day stretched before him like a vacant plain.

"Wait!"

He turned, looking back at the shop's small front porch. Tracey, coatless, stood there, under the La Herencia sign. She looked cold as she clutched a book to her chest.

"Cal?"

He stared at her, surprised she had used his Christian name. Perhaps she was more on his side than he had imagined.

He quickly moved back to the porch and up its stairs. He looked down at her. Her amber eyes seemed full of grief and regret.

Tracey shivered against the February breeze. "She said—she said if you came by, to give you this. I—I had her copy." She held the book more tightly against her chest, shaking her head. "I didn't want to. It's an old book. Things have changed. I—I personally don't think things are this bad anymore."

She shivered again and held the book to him. "I don't think she keeps up with—with science and medicine and things like that the way she should. She doesn't want it to obsess her. Or want to get her hopes up, maybe. I think she's always tried to prepare for the worst, just in case."

Cal took the book as Tracey watched him. She stood, her arms rigid at her sides with nervousness, her fists clenched. "I think she just wants you to know how bad it could be. . . . I'm sorry, Cal. I really am."

He studied the book, perplexed. It was thick and heavy, with a battered green cover and fading title: *Lonesome Traveler: The Story Of Woody Guthrie.*

Something, instinct perhaps, twisted sinisterly through his innards. "Woody Guthrie. He was a folksinger or something." Once again he riveted Tracey with a questioning gaze. What did some old folksinger have to do with Serena and him?

Tracey took a deep breath and clenched her fists more tightly than before. "Woody Guthrie died of it— the same thing Serena might get. So did his mother. So did his daughter."

He stared down numbly at the book, suddenly not liking the heft or feel of it. The ominous knot in his stomach jerked tighter and harder.

"I'm sorry," Tracey repeated. Her mouth worked as if she might say something else. Instead she suddenly turned and fled back into the shop, pulling the door shut tightly behind her.

Cal stood outside in the cold, holding the book. Over his head, creaking in the wind, hung the sign that read La Herencia.

THAT NIGHT Patti and Serena stood side by side in Patti's small, disorganized kitchen, doing dishes. The dishwasher was broken. At Patti's house, something was always broken.

An ugly cat with one bent ear kept weaving between Serena's feet, rubbing and mewing for attention. Patti had found it somewhere and dragged it home. It was one of four stray cats she'd taken in and harbored.

"All right," Patti said wryly, "now tell me *really* to what I owe this honor. You just didn't take off work and come calling on impulse. Something's wrong if you came to this madhouse for refuge. What's the matter? It couldn't be a man, could it?"

Serena stiffened. Cal haunted her thoughts, a presence so powerful it could be felt even in Patti's houseful of confusion and distraction.

"Nothing's the matter. I just needed to get away. What's *wrong* with this cat? Why's it keep rubbing? What's wrong with its ear? Can a cat break its ear?"

Patti ignored the questions. "I noticed you got antsy at supper. You looked absolutely *stricken* whenever the girls started giggling over the Garcia boys. Don't tell me somebody's finally made you giggly yourself."

Serena tensed more than before. Her nieces, Dovey and Hope, were thirteen and twelve and giggled incessantly. Mostly they giggled over the boys across the street, Dave and Tony Garcia.

Serena, led by her excited nieces, had actually been privileged enough to glimpse the famous Garcia brothers from a window, and had had to admit that yes, they were, indeed, most handsome.

Biology, Serena thought darkly. The girls were falling under its dizzy power with a vengeance. And she was no better off than they were. She was simply having her adolescence at twenty-seven rather than twelve. She hated it, but she was possessed by Cal's face with its lazy smile and vigilant eyes.

"Well?" Patti asked archly. "*Did* you meet somebody who got past your defenses?" She waited for an answer, got none and laughed. "No. What am I, dreaming? You? That'll be the day. Ha."

Patti scooped up the new cat. She put her nose against its nose and cooed, "Wuzza, wuzza, wuzza, her's a pussycat and needs love, doesn't her? Somebody so mean to throw you out. Just because you're gonna have little pussycats. Wuzza, wuzza, wuzza."

Serena threw down the dish towel and stared at her sister in disbelief. "Good grief, Patti, that cat isn't *pregnant,* is it? You already have four. They'll eat you out of house and home. You should get it fixed."

"It's a little late to get it fixed," Patti said, nuzzling the cat. "The blessed event's due any day."

"I'd hardly call it blessed," Serena muttered, watching her sister. She was worried about her. Patti's hands seemed a bit shaky. At supper, Serena had seen her sister's shoulder give a small, convulsive twitch. Her own blood had run cold at the thought of what it might mean.

Patti was five years older than Serena, smaller, shorter and even more slender. She always lopped off her thick black hair with the sewing scissors into an uneven Dutch bob, and she didn't stay out of the sun, so she was covered with freckles, her face, arms, hands, legs, even in winter.

Patti stopped fondling the cat. Her eyes were blue, unlike Serena's, and suddenly they looked defensive. "Why are you staring at me like that?" Patti asked. "I suppose you think *I* should have got fixed, too. Well, I've told you a dozen times. It was a little late for me, too, when I got married. Dovey was already on the way. Honestly, Serena, can you be that cold? Do you wish I *hadn't* had the girls? I *love* them."

Serena quickly put her hand on Patti's thin shoulder. "Of course not! You know that. I love them, too. It's just that—I worry about them. And you. All of us."

Patti met her stare defiantly, without wavering. She held the purring cat closer. "Nothing's going to happen to us. Any of us."

Then Patti's shoulder gave another of its small, jerky jumps beneath Serena's hand, and the two women's gazes locked more intently. A multitude of fears surged through Serena like a crazed mob. Did the shakes and jerks mean *it* was starting for Patti? Was *it* coming out of the shadows at last, to drag her away?

Patti looked shaken but more defiant still. "It's nothing," she said, nodding at her shoulder. "I spent all weekend repainting the bedrooms. I've got a crick in my muscles. A normal spasm. That's *all*. *Nothing's* going to happen to us—any of us. How many times do I have to tell you?"

Serena turned to lean on the counter, staring out the window into the night and shaking her head to herself. How could Patti live the way she did? she wondered in despair. She had hardly any money in savings, her insurance was in shambles, she had two daughters to raise, and a house that threatened to fall down if not propped up every minute.

Then Patti went out of her way to burden herself with even more responsibilities: four cats and more on the way. In the backyard lived Corky, a shambling old mongrel with arthritis and allergies. Serena knew Patti spent a fortune on Corky's shots, money that should be put away for the future.

"I know you don't approve," Patti said, the same defensiveness in her voice, "but I can't live like you. I won't deny myself everything because something *might* go wrong. I want to live my life, not just watch it trickle away."

Serena nodded unhappily. She kept staring into the darkness. She, too, tried to live life. Her way was different, that was all. "I know, Patti. I understand."

"Besides," Patti said, her combative edge suddenly gone, "they might cure it. They might. Anytime now. They found the gene markers, didn't they? If they find the gene, then they can find the cure. And they can treat it much better now than they used to—"

"I know," Serena repeated. But she took no comfort from cures that hadn't been invented, miracles that hadn't been found.

An awkward silence settled between the sisters and made the cluttered little kitchen uncomfortable. Serena was grateful that through the kitchen door came the muted sound of MTV and, as always, the girls giggling. Patti set down the cat. Serena was almost glad when it began to mew and cry for attention again. The silence between her and Patti seemed less strained.

"Serena," Patti said abruptly, "I've been seeing a man. He works for the telephone company. He's divorced, too."

Serena's fingers tightened on the counter. Her heart beat faster. She tried not to think of herself and Cal.

But she did, and her heart ached as if a fist clenched it.

Last night she had kissed him with a hunger born of despair, and when he had held her so tightly, for once she had felt safe. It was foolish to feel safe; he could protect her from nothing, and she could only hurt him. She bit her lip so hard it hurt.

"I—I like him a lot," Patti said. "But I haven't told him about the Huntington's. I just—can't seem to."

Serena whirled so that she faced her sister. "Patti, this time you've got to—it isn't fair."

"I know," Patti answered, shaking her head. "The first time I was too young to know the right thing. I was so crazy about him, Serena. You'll never know what I felt. I thought if I didn't have him, I'd die. So I lied. This time, I know better."

Serena winced at the irony of her sister's words: *you'll never know what I felt.* She knew now, all right. She knew only too well.

Patti paused. Her chin trembled. She ran a hand through her chopped hair and shrugged. "So I have to tell him—but I don't know how. I don't want to lose him. I—can't lose him. But what if—" She shook her head, unable to finish the sentence.

The fist clenched Serena's heart more tightly. "Oh, Patti," she said, shaking her head in despairing sympathy. "Patti."

Patti crossed her arms and looked away. Her shoulder twitched. Tears glinted in her eyes. "Serena," she said in a small voice, "I'm scared. For the first time in my life, I'm scared. Sometimes I understand where you're coming from after all these years."

Her voice broke and she turned her back so Serena wouldn't see her cry. Serena moved swiftly to her and took her into her arms. "I understand you better, too," she said, hugging her weeping sister.

And she did. If Serena had met Cal at seventeen instead of twenty-seven, she might have done what Patti did—simply seize life with both hands, blindly hoping it would work out.

"I'm scared, too," Serena whispered.

"I wouldn't change any of it," Patti said fiercely, "getting married, having the girls, none of it. But maybe I shouldn't have done it. Maybe I should never have loved anybody. *Was* I wrong? Have I done something terribly wrong? Just by loving? And wanting to love?" She laid her head helplessly against Serena's shoulder.

"Oh, Patti, don't ask *me* that," Serena said, trying to comfort her. "Everybody that faces this has to make their own decision. What would either of us do without the girls? Shh, shh, they'll hear. They don't know about it yet, do they? You've got to tell them. It's the only fair thing to do."

"I don't ever *want* them to know about it," Patti said with passion, drawing back and trying to dry her eyes. "I don't want them ever to *have* to know about it. I want them *spared* all this, dammit."

"But if we'd known ahead of time, how much better off we would have been," Serena offered. "Look at poor Mama—and Grandma—caught so off guard—"

Patti shook her head violently and fumbled in the pocket of the oversize, faded man's shirt she wore and found a fragment of a tissue. She tried, in vain, to mop her eyes and repair her face.

"Oh, here, let me," Serena said impatiently, wetting a clean dish towel and wiping Patti's tearstained face as if her sister were a child. She had never, in her life, known Patti to have a handkerchief when she needed one.

"Serena," Patti said, wiping away a sniff with her tatter of tissue, "I'm glad you're here, I really am. But why'd you come? Really?"

"I thought we needed to talk, just like this," Serena said, dabbing the cool towel against Patti's hot forehead. It was the truth, but only part of it.

I came because I fell into the same trap you did, Serena thought, looking at her sister's tired face. *I met a man and I fell in love with him. His name is Cal. And I ran away.*

But she looked at Patti and knew suddenly there was nowhere for them to run, not for either of them, nowhere at all.

If I really love him, Serena thought with unhappy determination, *I'll keep him away from all this. I won't let him be caught in it, too.*

The pregnant cat wound its way among Serena and Patti's feet, mewing, demanding to be noticed.

CHAPTER SEVEN

IN AMARILLO, Serena was worrying about life, death, love, right and wrong. She tried, for her sister's sake and her own, to stay calm. In Crystal Creek, Cal's cousin, Beverly, was worrying about etiquette. She was horribly distraught and might, it seemed, fall apart at any moment.

Tears trembled in Beverly's lovely eyes. Her mother, Carolyn, glowered at her, not in the least sympathetic.

"I'm sorry," Beverly said for what seemed the hundredth time. "I'm going to write notes of apology and send flowers to *everyone.*"

The lamplight glimmered on Carolyn's blond hair. Her jaw was set like a steel trap. She stood with her arms crossed, her feet slightly apart. It was her most dangerous stance. "Beverly, a note isn't going to undo what you've done. You can't buy your way out of this with flowers."

"But I didn't mean to do anything wrong," Beverly stammered. "It was an accident—it's not as if I had a—an evil intent."

"Oh, Beverly, really," Carolyn said, turning from her in contempt. She stared at the painting over the fireplace, but it was of Beverly, so she looked away, as if she could no longer bear to gaze upon her daughter in any form.

It had begun that morning when Beverly took an urgent phone call from Carolyn's cousin and accountant, Lori Porter. Lori was a pretty little woman in her forties with a lovely, smooth pageboy hairdo. She had gone home to her native San Antonio a few days before because her grandfather was ill.

Beverly knew little about that side of Lori's family and had stopped pretending to take an interest. Lori was usually cool to Beverly, cordial but distant as if she was slightly disapproving of Beverly.

Beverly had been surprised to hear Lori, always so self-possessed, sounding emotional and upset. She had also been surprised to learn she was still in San Antonio. Beverly had expected Lori to come walking in the door at any moment as scheduled, confident as usual.

Her voice full of suppressed tears, Lori had wanted to talk to Carolyn, but Carolyn was out with the county agent, inspecting a hay field that had been doing poorly. Beverly said she was perfectly capable of taking the message.

Lori, sounding numb and shaky, said her grandfather had seemed fine yesterday. Then, last evening, he'd had a second heart attack and died. Everyone had been stunned, including Lori. She hadn't even thought to call Carolyn to tell her she wouldn't be arriving as planned. She wouldn't be back in Crystal Creek for another four days.

"Lori, you just go right back to your family and your duties," Beverly had soothed her. "I'll tell

Mama, and it'll be *fine*. Don't you worry about a thing."

"Shouldn't you write this down, Beverly?" Lori had asked rather gingerly, but Beverly had waved away the idea. Goodness, did Lori think she couldn't carry the simplest little message?

Then, almost as soon as she hung up the phone after assuring Lori she'd tend to everything, it had rung again.

Snooky Everingham had phoned in absolute blind panic, *begging* Beverly to come to Austin immediately to fill in for a sick judge at the Miss Mall Merchandising beauty pageant. Snooky wailed that the pageant would be in total ruin without a judge of great knowledge and experience. If ever Snooky, who was an old, old friend, had needed Beverly, she needed her *now*.

It had all been urgent and dramatic, and Beverly had thrilled to the emergency call to duty. She'd had to rush through so many things—hair, makeup, choosing the right clothes—she had forgotten all else in the commotion.

She'd forgotten that she'd promised Dr. Nate Purdy that she would come to the hospital that afternoon to help the children make valentines. Rose was shorthanded, because of the flu that was making the rounds, and Nate had pestered Beverly until, at last, she'd reluctantly said yes.

But then, in the excitement of dashing to Snooky's aid, her promise to Nate vanished from her mind, conveniently and totally. Just as bad, she forgot to leave word for her mother that Lori would be delayed in San Antonio because her grandfather had died.

Instead Beverly had rushed off to Austin and thrown all her energy into being an astute, informed and fair judge. She also worked to give off an aura of glamour, as was her duty as a former Miss Texas. She was charming to everyone, as her station in life demanded her to be.

Afterward, Snooky had asked her back to Fair Acres, the Everingham mansion, to meet guests from California, including a young man named Lionel Sherwin, who was a television producer. Beverly, who loved the lore and glitter of show business with all her heart, agreed with enthusiasm.

It was not until much later, when she and Lionel had slipped off to have supper, that she realized with shock what she had done. She was *supposed* to have worked at the hospital all afternoon. Instead, she had been gallivanting all over Austin, not giving a single thought to anyone else.

Nate Purdy would be so disgusted he'd snatch her bald. Rose Purdy would be disappointed, which was even worse. As for the children, Beverly couldn't bear to think of them: she had failed them worst of all.

At almost the same sickening moment that she remembered her broken promise to Dr. Purdy, she also remembered that she hadn't told her mother of Lori's call. Carolyn would be livid. To have forgotten something as important as a death in Lori's family? It was crass, thoughtless, unforgivable.

Suddenly the elegant restaurant had seemed stifling to Beverly. She murmured something about a forgotten appointment and excused herself to go call her mother. There was no answer.

Beverly looked at her gold watch and felt sicker than before. It was eight-thirty, almost ten hours since Lori had phoned. Had Carolyn been waiting all day for Lori? Had she been nervous over what had happened to her? Had Nate or Rose phoned Carolyn, worried because Beverly wasn't at the hospital?

Oh, it was too terrible for words, Beverly thought, listening to the phone ring on and on. She had committed the ultimate sin: she had been *inconsiderate,* and she had done it twice in one day.

She made her way back to the table and told Lionel that she had to leave immediately, which irritated him very much.

Beverly was distraught, for she had somehow managed to offend yet another person. She had sped home as swiftly as she could. All the way she tried to convince herself that she was without real fault. She had not acted out of malice, only forgetfulness. It had been an accident, and she prayed that everyone would understand. She convinced herself that she would be forgiven.

But Carolyn was not in a forgiving mood. She'd waited for Lori until she'd grown so worried that she'd called San Antonio. With shock she'd learned of Lori's loss and that Beverly had forgotten to relay the news.

Then Rose Purdy had called, fretting that something terrible had happened to Beverly and harried because she needed help in the children's ward. Carolyn was forced to tell poor Rose that Beverly had gone, leaving only a hastily scribbled note about a beauty contest.

Now Beverly sat silently in miserable repentance, tears spilling over and running down her cheeks. Carolyn turned and looked at her. "Oh, stop that," she ordered. "What have you got to cry about? You spent all day having your fun. It's the rest of us who have something to cry about. You didn't have the common decency to think of poor Lori—or of Rose. First I worried myself sick over Lori, and then I was sick with shame over you."

Beverly looked at her mother. "It was an *accident.*" She dabbed at her eyes with her lace-edged handkerchief.

"Hush!" Carolyn marched over and took Beverly's chin in her hand. She tilted her daughter's face upward so that Beverly's unhappy gaze had to meet Carolyn's disapproving one. "You listen to me." Carolyn spoke with such passion that Beverly's tears immediately ceased and a look of alarm crossed her face.

"I said I was ashamed. I am," Carolyn said, blue-green eyes flashing. "But I worry, too. I can't understand what goes on in that mind of yours, Beverly. How could you let a *beauty contest* knock every thought of Lori out of your mind? How could it make you forget you'd *promised* Nate and Rose to help those poor, unfortunate children?"

"I—don't—know."

"What scares me is that maybe you *wanted* to forget," Carolyn went on relentlessly. "Nate says those children love you, but you act as if you don't care.

They just don't fit into the pleasant, carefree little world you want to hide in. Maybe Lori's grief doesn't fit, either. If there's a harsh truth anywhere out there, you refuse to face it. It's easier to forget—to run off to play.''

She forced Beverly to keep meeting her eyes. Carolyn's face lost its harsh cast, turned sorrowful instead. ''Part of it's my fault. And your father's. We knew you'd be the only child we'd ever have. We spoiled you. We overprotected you. But what did we create? Are you selfish?—or careless?—or are you scared? Can't you be honest with me? Can't you be honest with yourself?''

Beverly's face went blank at her mother's words, but an expression of anguish filled her eyes. She shook herself free from Carolyn's grasp and fled, weeping once more, into her room. Carolyn looked after her sadly and shook her head.

She walked to the fireplace and looked at the oil painting over the mantel. It was a portrait, and a very expensive one, of Beverly in her Miss America contest gown. Frank, bursting with pride, had commissioned it, even though Carolyn had privately thought it vulgar.

She leaned her elbow on the mantel and sadly studied her daughter's picture. Frank had been always been elated by the girl's beauty, her charming desire to please, her good grades, and Carolyn had been happy for his happiness. Now she wondered if they had failed Beverly by dwelling too often on her superficial gifts, by making her life too easy, by shielding her too much from all unpleasantness.

She closed her eyes and leaned her forehead wearily against her hand. Her thoughts drifted back to how she and her sister, Pauline, used to worry aloud, as mothers do, about their children.

Pauline, of course, had had three to worry about, and the one she fretted most over was Cal. Like Beverly, he seemed one to whom fate had given almost too much: a fine, strong body, a handsome face, a winning way, a carefree spirit. Nobody had ever been able to resist Cal or deny him anything.

And nobody had ever been able to see anything less than lovely about Beverly. But while Cal was squandering himself on rodeo, testing himself with senseless danger, wasting his life, Beverly went to the other extreme, avoiding unpleasantness altogether, refusing to test herself at all. Neither of them seemed to give a thought to tomorrow.

"I used to think," Pauline had once said, "that life would be easiest for Cal and Beverly. Now sometimes I think it's going to be hardest. It'll take them the longest to know what's important. Things come too easy to them."

Her eyes still closed, Carolyn shook her head helplessly. She still missed her sister deeply, and was almost as devoted to Pauline's children as her own. "I don't think raising children is difficult," Pauline had said once, laughing. "It's not one *bit* harder than walking a tightwire over a pitful of alligators."

Right. Carolyn smiled ruefully at the memory and opened her eyes. She straightened her back and stared again at the portrait of Beverly, who was almost impossibly beautiful in her blue gown.

"Honey," she said softly to the girl in the picture, "it isn't all silk and smiles. You're going to have to find out life isn't for sissies."

She went to Beverly's bedroom, quietly opened the door and looked inside. The small Tiffany lamp on the bedside table softly cast its jeweled light across Beverly's still form.

She had fallen asleep still clutching her handkerchief. Her blue silk suit was rumpled and unbuttoned, her golden hair in a wild spill against the lacy pillow sham. Her pale face was streaked with tears and ruined mascara. Her lips looked young and vulnerable. A ghost of a frown played on her sleeping brow, and her eyelids fluttered as if she were having an unhappy dream.

Carolyn reached to turn out the light, then stopped. Clenched in Beverly's other hand, pressed against her breast, was a small picture of her father, framed in antique silver. It usually sat on her night table, beside the Tiffany lamp. Tonight she clutched it in her sleep like a talisman against any evil that might befall her.

Carolyn's heart gave an unexpected wrench. Was that why Beverly let herself forget the children at the hospital? Because she would have to revisit the place where her father had died? Was that why she was able to forget Lori's sorrow? Because it reminded her too painfully of her own?

Carolyn stooped and let the lightest of kisses graze her sleeping daughter's cheek. *Oh, Beverly,* she thought with a pang, *I miss Daddy, too, but we have to go forward, love, we have to. Life goes on.*

* * *

CAL COULDN'T SLEEP. After his futile trip to La Herencia, he'd lain on the unmade bed in his motel room, reading the Woodie Guthrie book. By the time he finished it, he'd just as soon have been in hell.

In his mind, one by one, he'd watched the green-eyed children he'd thought he'd have by Serena disappear, never to be born, never to be named.

He missed the thought of them, but that was not what cut deepest; after all, he had hardly thought of children before he met her. What rankled worst was that he could have torn out his damned tongue for speaking to her of children at all. He might as well have struck her, and he hated himself for it.

He spent the night staring at the ceiling, sick with anger and emptiness and desolation, as he recalled passages from the book. His only comfort came from Tracey Cotter's words, *It's an old book. Things have changed... I don't think things are this bad anymore... she's looking at the worst-case scenario and prepared herself for it....*

He'd think of Serena and think of Woody Guthrie, then he'd grind his teeth and feel helpless and crazy, wanting to hit something.

He flexed his right hand, which was swollen and bruised from the night before when he'd punched the door of the van. He thought of shoving his fist into the mirror, just for the violence of it, the relief of blood-letting. But he didn't. It wouldn't help her. It would be childish, and she didn't need a man who acted like a child.

Finally, out of restlessness and despair, he'd got up and walked the empty streets of Wolverton. The long cold spell was holding, the night was bone-chilling, and overhead the stars shone like ice.

At last, an hour and a half later, in the deep darkness just before false dawn, he found himself standing before Serena's shop.

The wind rose, piercing his jacket and jeans. He didn't move on. He rocked back and forth slightly on his boot heels, his jaw set, staring at the darkened shop.

He imagined her there among the awls and needles and thread and glue, among the fragrant scraps of leather, the lasts hanging over her head like the feet of hundreds of puppets. He imagined her sure, slim hands cutting the leather, her smoky-green eyes steady in concentration, her beautiful mouth set as she worked, engrossed.

Serena, he thought, *Serena. Long-legged, faintly freckled, sweet-breasted, slim-waisted. Eyes of dusky green and hair like long black silk. Serena.*

Then he thought of Woody Guthrie and the photographs in the book. Guthrie at Serena's age was a wiry, vital little man, animated with creativity. Guthrie at thirty-seven was troubled, restless, gaunt and losing his grip. Guthrie at forty-four checked into the mental hospital for good. Pictures showed a man whose eyes reflected a terrifying vacancy. The body was there, but Woody Guthrie, singer, poet, musician, composer, was gone.

His voice and words had made him a legend, but he could no longer speak. His travels had made his name synonymous with freedom, but he could no longer move. He lived in the prison of his illness until he died at fifty-five.

He died as his mother had died before him, as his eldest daughter was to die after him. The daughter died at forty-one. The book ended there.

Go away, Cal. That was what Serena had meant the book to tell him. *Go away. Don't get caught in this. Forget me.*

He stared at the shop, standing silently before him in the darkness, and he knew he couldn't forget her.

It's an old book, Tracey had said. *Things have changed . . . I don't think things are this bad anymore.*

He stared into the blackness until his eyes smarted and his throat burned with tightness. He set his jaw and calculated. More than twenty-five years had passed since the book was written. Tracey *had* to be right.

After Guthrie's death, science had begun to study the disease in earnest. Now there were foundations and institutes that dealt with it; in Guthrie's day there had been nothing. Maybe the experts couldn't yet cure the disease, but in all this time, surely to God they'd found ways to alleviate it.

Tracey said she didn't think Serena kept up with medical news. Cal swallowed and nodded to himself. She didn't want to chance growing obsessed by the disease. She would try, as much as possible, not to think of it. But he had forced her to. Yes, he thought unhappily, he had forced it, all right.

He hunched his shoulders against the cold. He could understand her; doctors made him nervous himself.

He'd been afraid, more than once, that one would finally say, "Boy, you've got to quit that rodeoing." Sure, he thought, he could understand her avoiding doctors and such.

The wind dropped, leaving the world in an eerie silence. The only sound was the chains of the sign creaking as the swinging slowed. He shoved his numb hands more deeply into his pockets and swallowed again.

He could understand her not wanting to get her hopes up, either. Hell, that was only sensible, and she was a smart woman. He understood her need to be independent. He'd always been independent himself.

He shifted his weight from foot to foot, ignoring the cold and watching the first light of day edge the sky. Sometimes, after a bad fall, he'd think about the possibility that he might get seriously hurt one day. But he chose to take chances. It was different for Serena. She hadn't chosen her fate. She'd had no say in it at all.

He turned from La Herencia, and walked aimlessly west through the thinning darkness. He understood all the reasons she had for telling him to go away. He understood why she had turned her back on him. In her place, he might have done the same.

But he wasn't in her place, he was in his own. He just didn't know what in hell to do about it. He walked on until real morning finally came. Then he went back to the motel, showered, shaved, cleaned up and started setting up appointments with doctors.

Two DAYS LATER, unshowered and unshaven, badly in need of sleep, Cal drove the last fifteen miles home to the Double C.

Tracey had been right. Things were not as dark as the old book on Guthrie had painted them. Since Guthrie's death, twenty-five years of advances had been made against Huntington's. But the doctors were frank. Serena was not merely still at risk, she was at great risk.

One doctor warned Cal outright to walk away from her, live his life without her and count his blessings. Cal had refrained from hitting him in the mouth.

But another doctor, a woman, had assured him that the disease didn't have to be nearly as terrible as the Guthrie book described it. The disease was better understood and far more treatable than even ten years ago.

"Not all cases are as tragic as Guthrie's," the woman had said. "Some develop late and far more slowly. And how well a person does depends as much on attitude as anything."

Cal shook his head. The woman's words worried him. "Is her attitude bad for her? Is she too pessimistic?"

The woman sighed and looked at him sympathetically. She was older, gray-haired, and she had eyes that looked as if they'd seen everything. "No. Some people at risk deny the possibility the disease could ever get them. If it does, they're unprepared. They may be shattered. More often, people at risk fear they *will* get it. It's easy—maybe even typical—for them to envision the worst happening to them. Different people cope in different ways."

Cal was still troubled. Serena's way was to go alone wherever fate took her.

"You don't know what she's seen," the doctor said, her face more somber than before. "Or how her family handled it. She may have her reasons for being this way."

She might have her reasons, Cal thought grimly. She might truly believe she'd be happier without him. *But my God,* he thought, *wasn't she lonely? Wasn't she scared?* He was lonely and scared for her.

"Maybe," the woman suggested, watching his troubled face, "the kindest thing for you to do would be to let her cope in the way she knows best. You're not that deeply involved. Do as she asks. Let her alone."

Cal looked into the woman's eyes. She was trying to be helpful. He shook his head. "You don't understand," he'd said. He wasn't sure he understood it himself.

Now, in his van, he flexed the weary muscles of his shoulders. The hills beyond Austin were brown with February, hunched and ancient beneath the gray sky. Even in the last dregs of winter they had an austere beauty. The beauty, however, was lost on Cal.

He did not feel, as he usually did, the soothing familiarity that only the land of home can bring. He took no comfort in anything.

It was six o'clock in the morning, and he had been driving all night. Stubble shadowed his jaw, his back hurt, his ribs ached, and his whole body was stiff.

He'd drunk so much black coffee that he could feel it vibrating in his brain like the whine of a jet engine.

Usually when he got close enough to home to get the Crystal Creek station on the radio of his van, he grinned. This morning he did not smile. The corners of his mouth stayed grim, and his eyes narrowed, watching the curving road.

KRCW was playing all the wrong songs, a medley of George Strait's most mournful hits, the ones that made Cal think of Serena: "A Fire I Can't Put Out," "You're the Cloud I'm on When I'm High," and "Fool-Hearted Memory." Cal thought blackly that he'd like nothing better than to get drunk and punch out George Strait's lights.

When Strait began to moan about how he was down and out since his woman left him, Cal switched off the radio with a vicious flick. "Moron," he snarled to the ghost of Strait's voice, "what do you know?"

He slowed to let a deer bound across the highway and shook his head. He wasn't even sure why he was coming home. Lynn had told him Ken Slattery had found a roping horse that Cal might like and it was as good a reason as any, Cal supposed, with Sneezy lame and Grumpy laid up.

He'd decided against staying in Wolverton when he realized Serena meant exactly what Estaban and Tracey had said. She wasn't coming back while Cal was there, and that was that.

He'd taken the book back to Tracey yesterday, and thrown it on her desk. "Tell her it doesn't matter," he'd said. "I want to talk to her. I have to see her."

Tracey looked guilty, as if by talking to him she was collaborating with the enemy. "It matters to *her*," she said. "She wants you to move on. She'll stay away until you do. She means it."

"She *can't* stay away, dammit," Cal insisted. "She's got a business to run."

Tracey stared at him unhappily. "I know."

Cal straightened his spine and clenched his teeth. He didn't want to exile Serena from her home and her work. For one thing, she probably couldn't *afford* to stay away from work. He sighed harshly in frustration.

"All right," he said, bitterness in his voice. "Tell her I'm moving on. I'll leave tonight. She can come home. But she can't hide forever. I'll be back. She can count on it, sure as God made little green apples."

He'd spun on his boot heel and stalked out, temporarily beaten. He'd called home just so nobody would think anything was wrong, gotten word about the horse and decided he might as well go to the Double C as anyplace. He left Grumpy in the vet's care, got in the van and set off, his soul as heavy as if stones had been heaped on it, his heart full of darkness.

All night he'd driven across the February-bleak land, thinking of Serena. Then, ten miles from Crystal Creek, he glanced at himself in the rearview mirror and realized he looked like hell warmed over.

He supposed, listlessly, he should clean up. Lynn and Ty always teased him unmercifully about being vain. If he showed up looking as scraggly as a coyote, they'd know something was wrong.

He stopped at the Phillips station just outside Crystal Creek, washed as best he could, shaved with his battery razor and changed his shirt. "You still look like one sorry son of a bitch," he said to his reflection.

He got back in the van, determined to appear as normal as he could. He didn't intend to stop at the Double C for long. Just long enough to check out the new horse and be on his way.

When should he go back and try to see Serena again? Instinct told him that she needed time. Reason told him time might be the one thing they didn't have to spare.

He turned down the road to the Double C with a sense of grudging gratitude. He'd be glad to see somebody familiar, somebody he knew, even J.T. at his most militant. He was sick to death of living alone, without distraction from his own unhappy thoughts.

He managed, when he got out of the van, to square his shoulders and even swagger a bit as he crossed the lawn and took the back stairs two at a time. He knocked at the kitchen door, but didn't wait for an answer.

He stepped inside. Lettie Mae, the cook, turned, her brown eyes widening. Cal made himself grin his most dashing grin.

"Cal-vin!" Lettie Mae cried with a happy smile. "You rascal! What you doing here? You never told anybody you'd be here—"

Cal crossed the kitchen in three steps, picked up Lettie Mae and whirled her twice, which made her throw her arms around his neck and squeal for him to stop. He stopped, set her down and kissed her soft cheek. "Been too long since I've seen my best girl. How are you, Lettie Mae? Have you missed me, sugar?"

Lettie Mae beamed up at him. "Everybody misses you, you fool. How long you aim to stay? Don't tell me you finally gave up that old rodeo?"

"Not quite," Cal said easily. "Everybody home? Everybody up?"

"Tyler and Ruth have gone up to Arkansas to look at a winery," Lettie Mae said, affectionately straightening his shirt collar. "J.T. and Miss C. have gone to Dallas overnight. Why didn't you *tell* us you were comin', boy? They'd have stayed home for sure. You should *say*. And I'd make something special for you— that ol' sour-cream raisin pie you like. Why don't you give us warning, you scamp?"

"Everything you make is special, darlin'. Half the time I don't know where I'm going till I get there myself."

Lettie Mae laughed and shook her head. "Same old free spirit. My, my. Won't your little sister be glad to see you? I'll tell her, 'Calvin's home—let the good times roll.' I'm glad you're home. I can always use more smiles."

"What do you need more smiles for? You got a new boyfriend you want to knock dead?"

"Devil," Lettie Mae said with a chuckle. "I'll get Lynn. I think she's still in bed. I wanted her to sleep in. She's been workin' so hard. You tell her to slow down. She's got to have some time for play. You tell her that.

Sometimes I think you're the only one knows how to have fun in this family."

She bustled out of the kitchen, wiping her hands on her apron. The smile faded from Cal's face and moodily he turned to stare out the kitchen window at the brown rolling land, the gray sky above it. He heard Lettie Mae calling to Lynn, heard her repeating her joke about letting the good times roll.

He could still pretend to smile, pretend to tease, pretend to be full of careless cheer. But inside he felt hollow, lonesome and mean. He felt like anything except what Lettie Mae had called him, a free spirit.

Serena, he thought, her name twisting like a knife deep in his chest, *Serena.*

But then he heard the muffled beat of bare feet pounding toward the kitchen. The door burst open, and Lynn flew across the room into his arms.

He held her tight, his cheek against her sleep-tousled auburn hair. "Hey, little sister," he said affectionately. But oddly, there in his own home, Lynn in his arms, he felt lonelier than he'd ever felt in his life. But he grinned, for Lynn's sake.

Lettie Mae smiled from the doorway, content. Her happy, lighthearted boy was home again, the one that always brought sunshine with him and never kept sorrow company. She prayed that God would keep him that way. Of all J.T.'s children, heaven had smiled most brightly on this one, made him sunny. Cal was blessed. Sure enough.

IN AMARILLO, Serena had planned to wake early and drive back to Wolverton. Tracey had called last night to tell her that Cal said he was leaving. Yes, Tracey assured her solemnly, he'd seemed to mean it. And, she added without being asked, he'd seemed anything but happy.

Serena had said nothing. Twin impulses warred within her. Her rational self wanted Cal to go away forever, leaving her to her sane and careful life. Her emotional self wanted—she refused to put into words what her emotional self wanted. It was impossible.

She'd had trouble getting to sleep on Patti's lumpy sofa, and her dreams were uneasy, haunted by a tall cowboy with laughter in his eyes and honeyed words on his lips. He would vow to love her forever, promise never to leave her, and then he would vanish like smoke.

She awoke with a start at six in the morning, dimly aware that something was wrong. Her head was hazy from the nightmares.

She felt a peculiar weight on her feet, but did not think about it, too shaken by her dreams. She reached over and switched on the floor lamp. Then she looked down at the covers and screamed.

She leaped to her feet and backed across the cold floor. The cat, the ugly lop-eared cat, was on her bed, but to Serena's sleep-dazed eyes, something was strange about it.

Patti came running, sleepy-eyed, from her bedroom, and up the hall Serena heard the girls' door opening and drowsy mumbles of "What? What?"

"What is it?" Patti demanded, looking about wildly. "What's wrong?"

"The cat—fell apart," Serena cried, staring at the rumpled blankets on the sofa. The cat lay there, looking rather as if it had broken into several pieces, for three tiny bundles of live, damp, moving fur were ranged along its belly.

"What happened?" Dovey asked, stumbling into the living room, rubbing her eyes. Hope followed, yawning, looking more curious than alarmed.

"The cat," Serena repeated, still dazed by sleep and surprise. "It's come apart."

Patti began to laugh. She wore mismatched pajamas, her thick black hair stood out in different directions, and she laughed hysterically. "The cat—" she managed to gasp between laughs. "The cat had—kittens—on your bed."

She laughed so hard that she collapsed into the nearest armchair and buried her face in her hands.

Dovey brightened and ran to the couch, cooing. Hope looked at Serena's face, then at her mother giggling helplessly in the chair, and she, too, burst into laughter. She ran and threw herself into her mother's lap. Hope and Patti clung to each other, laughing until they cried.

"She—she—said—the cat—*fell apart*," Patti managed to sputter, then dissolved into giggles again.

"Her's a little mama, yes, her is," Dovey babytalked, scratching the lop-eared cat's chin in admiration. "Oh, look, Mama, one's all black except for its feet—*look*, Serena."

Serena, finally awake, her first shock fading, looked and smiled. The cat stared back regally, as if her newborn family had every right to share Serena's bed.

As for Patti's family, it was at its most ragtag and appealing. Patti hooted helplessly and hugged her laughing daughter.

Dovey, smiling and crooning to the cat and kittens, wore a nightgown three sizes too large and big pink curlers in her hair. She looked like a happy, maternal little Martian crouched there, admiring the kittens.

Serena's heart contracted so sharply it hurt. Patti's family was small—yet suddenly it seemed large, warm and marvelously complete.

As imperfect, inelegant, and vulnerable a little family as it was, it was a family. Its heart beat strongly and with its own unique character.

"Serena?" Dovey said, looking up at her with eyes much like her own, "you don't have a pet. Don't you want one? Look—the black one's got white boots— anybody who makes boots should have a cat with boots, especially if it's born right on you."

Dovey looked so gangly and silly and sweet and lovable by lamplight that Serena felt almost stricken. Suddenly, in the face of all of Patti's gambles, Serena's life seemed empty and orderly to a fault. But she still believed she was right. Somebody had to think of the future and its consequences. In this family, she was the one.

"No," Serena said, her voice as gentle as she could make it, "I don't think so. I'm too busy for a cat."

"But Serena," Dovey said earnestly, "you're always alone. Don't you want something to love? They're going to be beautiful cats—just bea-uu-tiful."

"No," Serena said, as quietly as before, "I've got you all. How could I need anything else to love?" But suddenly she remembered the touch of Cal's lips, the feel of his long body, the strength of his arms around her. She remembered it all and had to turn away so the others would not see the tears in her eyes.

CHAPTER EIGHT

THE ROPING HORSE that foreman Ken Slattery had spotted for Cal was a good one—if a little odd—a rawboned roan gelding with pale blue eyes. Cal had always had a taste for a horse that was slightly odd, and he bought it.

They hauled the roan home, and Cal was ready to take off for California, but Lynn begged him to stay a few days. To her surprise, he consented. He might as well work with the horse, he said laconically, and make sure the thing wouldn't humiliate him in public.

In truth, he wanted only to go back to Wolverton, not California. He'd already lost enough days—and enough money—this year that he knew he'd have to work like hell to have a shot at a title, and his heart wasn't in it. He spent all afternoon roping from the roan gelding, but he had a strange feeling his rodeo days were close to over.

He could return to Wolverton anytime to pick up Grumpy; his trailer held two horses. But how soon, he wondered, was too soon? And how was he going to see Serena when she didn't want to see him?

Before he cleaned up for supper, he sat on Grandpa Hank's front porch, his chaps and boots dusty, his hat pushed back on his head. He lounged on the top step, staring out at the hills. Hank sat, as always, in his rocker. They had made the usual small talk and then fallen into companionable silence.

It was Hank who broke the quiet. "All right, boy. What's the matter? You grin like a possum, but you've got the mopes, ain't you?"

Cal turned to look up at the old man, surprised. It always happened: just when he'd write Hank off as too far gone to look past his own moods, the old man would spy something nobody else noticed.

"Nothin' wrong with me, Grandpa," he lied blithely. "I've got the world by the tail."

Hank took out his bag of Bull Durham and his cigarette papers and rolled himself a smoke. "You always could lie like a rug if you chose," he said, striking a kitchen match on his thumbnail. "But you never fooled *me*. I had a feelin' you'd be home. That something was wrong. Had a feelin' in my bones."

Cal always pretended to mock Hank's peculiar "feelings" and premonitions, but in his marrow he half believed them. He grinned, trying to disarm the old man. "Your Indian blood talkin', Grandpa?"

"I might be part Indian, and I might not," said Hank, who would never say one way or the other. "All I know is I dreamed of you the other night."

Cal's grin faded. The last time Hank had dreamed of him, he'd been trampled and nearly had his back broken. "Don't dream of me," he said. "I don't want your hoodoo on me."

"T'weren't no hoodoo dream," Hank said, exhaling blue smoke. He pointed an arthritic finger at the lawn. "I dreamed you stood at the foot of these very stairs. You said, 'I finally brought your grandchildren to see you.' You stood there with two children, holding 'em by the hand. I opened my mouth to say, 'It's about time,' and the children plumb vanished. In the wink of an eye, they vanished. They was *gone*."

Cal felt as if death itself had clamped its cold hand on the back of his neck. He said nothing and thought of Serena. He remembered the night he'd had to stop thinking about their green-eyed children.

Hank went on, his voice quavering with irritation. "I said, 'Calvin, what have you done with them children?' And you looked me square in the eye and said, 'What children, Grandaddy? I don't have no children.' You went and robbed me of my own grandchildren. Now, what do you suppose that *means?*"

Cal stared out at the brown hills, feeling empty and mean again. "It means you shouldn't drink that damn cheap whiskey when your rheumatiz hits. It puts bees in your brainpan."

Hank drew meditatively on his cigarette. "You ever did have a sassy tongue. You're thinkin' of quittin' the rodeo, ain't you? I watched you ropin' out there. Your edge is gone. You don't care the way you used to."

Cal shrugged and pulled down his hat brim to shade his eyes. "So?" he challenged.

Hank cocked a tangled eyebrow. "So I hope you found something worth quittin' for."

Cal took a deep breath. He still felt cold inside from the old man's dream. Like Hank, he was superstitious. Like Hank, he had always followed his hunches. But this time, with Serena, his hunches had led him to the edge of an abyss that he couldn't get across. It yawned before him, bottomless and impassable.

"Grandpa," he said, grudging the words even as they came out of his mouth, "did you see those children's mama in your dream?"

"No."

Cal took off his Stetson and turned it in his hands, staring broodily at the dust in its creases. He said nothing.

"You at a fork in the road?" Hank asked, not unkindly. He tapped the ashes from his cigarette into his favorite ashtray.

Cal shrugged. He turned back to face the hills again. He remembered his mother's favorite verse: "I will lift up mine eyes unto the hills: from whence cometh my help!" Help wasn't really what he needed. What he needed were answers, but no matter how long he looked at the hills, no answers came.

Hank waited.

Cal slapped his hat against his thigh to knock the dust from it, then settled it on his head again.

Hank wouldn't understand about Serena. Like the whole family, he was a Texan, interested in bloodlines and breeding, ancestors and descendants. He was also an old man who wanted great-great-grandchildren, and Serena would not give him any. He was too old to remember what it was like to be in love, and he would caution Cal to be practical—as if practicality had ever had a damn thing to do with loving somebody. None of them would understand. He wished he'd moved on, not stayed here.

Hank shook his head and inhaled deeply on his bent cigarette. "'Man was born for trouble as the sparks fly upward,'" he rasped. "You're contemplatin' trouble, ain't you?" He shook his head again.

Cal said nothing. He tried to toss Hank a reassuring grin, but suddenly the old man looked every one of his ninety-nine years, shrunken and weary.

Hank shook his head. "You ain't climbin' down off one kind of buckin' horse just to climb up on a different sort, are you? You aren't plannin' something *foolish?* You're gonna keep takin' chances till all your chances run the hell out."

"Hell, Grandpa," Cal said moodily, "stop tryin' to read my thoughts, will you? I'm fine as frog hair."

"Boy, there is *something* on your mind, and I don't like it. I don't want to see you ruin your life."

Cal swore. "If I had a goddamn dime for every time somebody in this family told me that, I could buy Texas and New Mexico, too, and have enough left for a down payment on the moon."

"I reckon," Hank said sourly, "it's because you always seem so hell-bent on ruinin' your life. Has this got something to do with my dream? Why'd you ask if I'd seen a woman in it? For God's sake, this don't have nothin' to do with a woman, does it?"

"I don't choose to talk about it," Cal said with emphasis.

"You're the last man on earth to sit there sulled up like a sick dog over a woman. You could always have anyone you want. Just pick a nice, strong healthy one without these fool liberation ideas—one that'll stay home, raise your kids up the way a woman ought—"

"I said I don't want to talk about it," Cal snapped. "Drop it, okay?" He felt like taking off and starting back on the road right then. Hank would tell him what his whole family would tell him: leave her. It made him feel sick and more than a little vicious. The thought of Serena's green eyes went through him like a sword.

Lettie Mae appeared on the back porch of the ranch house and waved to them, calling, "Cal? Supper's almost ready. You bring Grandpa Hank over, will you, honey?"

Cal forced a smile and waved back. "Be there with bells on, sugar." His smile died as he turned back to his great-grandfather. "You took chances all your life," he said. "You took damn near every chance there was. If you could live it over, you'd take them all again. So don't lecture me. You've set a piss-poor example, Grandpa. I'm just like you, and you know it."

Hank blew out a stream of smoke on the evening air and ground out his cigarette. He set aside his ashtray and struggled to rise from his chair. He could not. "Now look what you done," he said querulously. "You've argufied me so much, you've made my pins go all a-wobble. I don't know why I try to give you advice—there never was a more thankless task. Help me out of this chair. I feel like a damn ant in a doodlebug trap."

Cal stood. An evening breeze had risen, riffling the worn leather of his chaps. He looked down at Hank, who was ineffectually trying to make his legs obey him. The anger faded from his face.

He leaned down and put his arm around the old man. "Don't say anything about this discussion to anybody else," he said to Hank. "This is between you and me, you hear?"

"Goes without sayin'," Hank agreed grumpily. "It goes no further'n you and me. Your business is your business, even if you are a damn fool."

He grunted slightly when Cal lifted him, and had to lean against him when he was on his feet. Cal kept his arm around the old man, supporting most of his weight.

"Hell," Hank said in disgust at his own frailty, "you done me good this time. Now I'm gonna have to lean on you. Get me movin'. My legs'll come back once I commence to movin'."

"Sure, Grandpa," Cal said. "We leaned on you often enough when we were sprats."

"You're sprats still," grumbled Hank, but he let Cal guide him down the stairs.

Hank was far too old to be surprised by much anymore, but as always he was surprised by the sureness and kindness of Cal's touch: the boy could drink and ride and raise hell with the best, but he had a quiet gentleness in him nobody would expect and few knew existed.

Suddenly Hank realized he was actually *scared* for the boy, scared by a premonition that Cal might be setting out on some damn fool road where he might be hurt beyond measure.

"I got a little patch of land," Hank said as he hobbled, borne up by Cal's strong arm. "You know—the land down by Pearsall. I always said there was oil on it. I've never knowed who to leave it to. Why don't you come home, drill on it? Forget about whatever's on your mind. Make yourself a millionaire—have any woman you want.''

Cal's grin was back in place. "Hell, Grandpa, I'm no oilman. That sorry land's waitin' for somebody who'll love it as much as you do. Thanks, but that's not me. You hang on to it.''

"I'm tryin' to offer you a *future,* boy," Hank said irritably. "To be frank, you don't appear to have much of one right now."

"It'll have to do," said Cal.

THE NEXT MORNING Cal worked again in a desultory way in the corral with the blue-eyed roan. Someone came walking up the long drive to the ranch house, and he recognized his cousin Beverly.

She wore blue jeans that looked as if they'd been sprayed on with an airbrush, tooled boots with gold bracelet chains and a blue suede jacket adrip with long fringes. Her lower lip looked pouty, even from a distance.

When she saw Cal, however, she gave him a brilliant smile and waved madly. He touched his hand to his hat brim in answering salute and nudged the horse toward the corral fence to meet her.

"Why, Calvin," Beverly called when she was within speaking distance. "I didn't know you were home. What a *divine* surprise. You haven't quit the rodeo, have you?"

"Nope. Came for a new horse."

"Well, I declare I've never seen a handsomer animal, and you do look fine yourself. Your poor back all healed?"

"Yeah," Cal lied. Sometimes Beverly really irritated him. His brother, Ty, said it was because Beverly was the only person in the family prettier than Cal. "Why're you on foot? The Cadillac break down?"

Beverly's beauty-queen smile faded. "As a matter of fact, it did, the mean thing. Right by your lane. Steam just came boiling out of the hood—like to have scared me to death. Is Lynn home? I need a ride into town."

"Lynn just left. She went to the vet's to get some kind of vaccine for that giraffe she wants to race." He nodded toward the near pasture where the long-legged racehorse grazed.

Beverly's eyes rolled heavenward. "I do believe I have the most horrid luck in the whole, entire universe. I *have* to go to town. Is Cynthia here? Ruth? Ty? Anybody?"

"Just Grandpa and me. You want to borrow my van?"

Beverly leaned against the fence and batted her eyelashes. "Why I couldn't drive your van, Calvin. It's got a shift. I just never mastered the intricacies of the shift. I wouldn't say *no*, though, if you were to offer to drive me. Besides, everybody thinks I'm nothing but an old maid, and it'd do my reputation wonders to be seen with a handsome thing like you. And you always were such a gentleman, once you grew up."

Cal groaned inwardly. He really was in no mood for Beverly. But she had him trapped like a rat. He knew better than to try to argue. If he didn't take her, she'd go to the house and nag Lettie Mae into driving her, and Lettie Mae hated to drive.

"Let me put the horse up," he said shortly.

"I'll just run up to the house and phone the garage about the Caddy," Beverly said, tossing her blond hair. "And Cal—if you want to take a shower before we go, I won't mind a bit."

"I wouldn't waste your precious time, Beverly, darlin'," he said sarcastically. He was damned if he'd take a shower just to ferry her around.

He was waiting for her when she came out of the house. She wrinkled her nose daintily when he gave her a hand up into the van. He shut her door, went to his own side and got into the driver's seat. "I could drive you home to get another car," he suggested, hoping to cut short their trip.

"No," Beverly said, settling into the seat and sorting and smoothing out her fringes, "Mama sold some cattle this morning, and I told her I'd take the money to the bank. She doesn't think I can do *anything* right lately. I'm not going to go back and tell her I didn't make it because the silly car broke. Then she *will* think I'm hopeless."

"Your mama's down on you?" he said out of the corner of his mouth. "How'd that happen? I thought you were everybody's angel-baby darlin'."

Beverly shrugged prettily. "It was just an accident, really. You'd think I'd caused the universe to end or something. Goodness."

He gave her a cool gaze. He remembered when they'd been little and he'd put woolly worms down her back. She'd scream and try to swat him on the head with her Barbie doll. He'd liked her better then.

"Oh, come on," he said. "I know you're dying to tell me your side."

Beverly needed little encouragement. She began to recite, in detail, the fiasco of going off to judge the beauty contest and forgetting to tell her mother about Lori Porter or to keep her promise to help in the children's ward.

The more she chattered of her silly troubles, the more irritated Cal became. If she faced one-thousandth of the problems Serena faced, she would run down the road as crazy as a cat with a firecracker tied to its tail.

"What do *you* think?" Beverly asked finally, obviously hoping he was on her side and would agree she'd committed no crime.

"I think we're at the bank," he muttered, parking in front of the library. The bank across the street, all steel and glass, glittered in the cold morning sunlight.

"Oh, look, there's that Billie Jo Dumont." Beverly nodded at a woman with red-gold hair and a fur jacket. Billie Jo was sashaying toward the law office where she worked.

"Can you believe Bubba Gibson is running around with her?" Beverly demanded. "Him with his sweet wife? He must be having a midlife crisis as big as a house."

"He's crazy," Cal said darkly, watching Billie Jo twitch her rear as she walked down the street. Bubba wasn't getting anything new with Billie Jo. Cal could personally testify to that. Now he looked after her as if she were an unsavory stranger. He remembered what it was like to hold Serena in his arms and a new ache of yearning shot through him.

He tried to shrug it aside, but couldn't. He opened the bank's door for Beverly and followed her inside. She stopped just beyond the door and laid her perfectly manicured hand on Cal's arm. "Why, look," she whispered. "Who's *that?*"

Cal's gaze followed hers to the teller's cage occupied by Mary Alice Priest. Mary Alice was Lynn and Beverly's age, but looked older. She was too thin even for Cal's taste in willowy women, and she had an anxious, shy air.

Cal had always felt sorry for Mary Alice and tried to be kind, but not too kind. Instinct told him she could mistake consideration for something more.

But now her usually nervous face was smiling and she looked almost pretty. The recipient of her smile was a man Cal had never seen before, and he was also the object of Beverly's pointed interest. He was fully as tall as Cal, six foot two, and his boots and long duster were worn but expensive. His white Stetson was tipped at a businesslike angle. He was good-looking in a hawklike way, with dark eyes, dark sideburns and a precisely trimmed dark mustache.

"My Gawd," Cal said in his most mocking drawl, "it's a dad-gum *stranger* in town, Miss Beverly. Dog my cats. And he's got a mustache. Must be an *evil* stranger."

"Oh, shush," Beverly said impatiently. "Mary Alice's face is lit up like a Christmas tree. I swear he's flirting with her. Maybe she's found herself a beau at last. Wouldn't that be nice?"

"Since I don't know him from Adam, it would be dumb of me to say, wouldn't it?"

"Oh, Calvin," Beverly said, biting her perfectly glossed lip, "you're so *contrary*. Be nice. I've been going through the very Slough of Despond. At least *you* could be nice."

"Slough of Despond," he repeated as sarcastically as possible, but she ignored him.

The stranger turned and headed toward the bank doors and them. He looked at Beverly with frank interest. Beverly smiled her prettiest noncommittal smile and he smiled back. Cal instinctively disliked the man and cast him a brief glance that told him so. The stranger's split-second return gaze at Cal was just as cold.

He passed them and was gone. Beverly stepped up to Mary Alice's window, shaking out her long blond hair. "Why, good *morning*, Mary Alice. Don't you look pretty today? I swear I do believe you've made a conquest. Who's that handsome man who was hanging on to your every word? Is he new in town? Surely I would have noticed such an attractive specimen."

Mary Alice blushed. Cal touched his hat in greeting and nodded to her. She blushed more deeply still.

"His name's Harte," Mary Alice said, looking down at the marble counter. "Luke Harte. He's— from Wyoming."

Mary Alice had pale ash-blond hair and pale gray eyes. Cal had always found something vaguely rabbity about her and felt sorry for her for blushing so easily.

"Well, *you* certainly seemed to have made an impression on him," Beverly gushed. "I hope he doesn't marry you and sweep you off somewhere, because you're our very favorite teller. Lori and Mama always say there's nobody more thorough than you. I brought some of those English peppermints for you. I know you like them so."

Beverly opened the leather purse that matched her boots and drew out a small tin of imported candies. She handed them to Mary Alice, who seemed deeply touched.

Beverly deposited the cattle sale money, keeping up a stream of chatter. "Now you hear me, Mary Alice," she said in parting, shaking a warning finger. "Don't you run off with that handsome stranger. What would this bank do without you?"

"Oh, Beverly," Mary Alice said in embarrassment, and blushed harder than before.

"Come on," Cal said between his teeth, "I want to get home in time for lunch."

He took Beverly's arm and led her firmly from the bank. "I swear, Cal," Beverly said, "you are a perfect grump today. Whatever *is* the matter with you?"

"I just thought you were laying it on a little thick in there, even for you. I don't have time to stand around waiting for you to win the Miss Congeniality contest."

"Cal!" Beverly said in wounded protest.

He threw open the door of the van for her. "Hush," he commanded. "You've got no call to take Mary Alice Priest peppermint candy and flatter her till she can't see straight. You talked like that man had proposed to her. She's *lonely,* Beverly. You ought not play such games with her head." He got in on his own side and slammed the door.

"Well," Beverly said with a sniff, "aren't you Mr. Consideration all of a sudden? Since when have you been so sensitive to the needs of women? This is a change, isn't it?"

He put the van into gear, backed out of the parking place with a savage squeal of tires and didn't answer her.

"Cal-*vin,*" Beverly said, sounding both angry and hurt, "you're in the vilest mood I've ever seen. What's the matter? Did you finally meet a girl you couldn't get? Now *that* would be something to laugh at."

Once more a knife seemed to twist in his chest, and once more he didn't trust himself to speak. He stared at the street and thought of Serena and felt turbulent and hollowed out.

"I told you my side of the story," Beverly said moodily. "Now I wish I hadn't. You're mad at me, too, aren't you? You think I set out to do some evil, terrible thing. And you don't even want me to have a chance to *redeem* myself."

"I have yet to meet a woman who redeemed herself passing out peppermints and BS. If you want to redeem yourself, why don't you go work in the children's ward like Nate Purdy wants?"

"Cal-*vin!*" True pain vibrated in Beverly's voice. "Why are you being so hateful? I told you, I don't *want* to work at that hospital. Nate Purdy practically *bullied* me into it."

Cal, his patience ripped to shreds, could stand no more. All his pain over Serena boiled to the surface. Without warning, he pulled the van off the road. They had just passed the boundary between Crystal Creek and the county, and he ground to a halt on the highway's graveled shoulder. He turned to Beverly, his teeth clenched in anger.

"Could you stop feeling sorry for yourself for one *minute?*" he asked. "Could you stop thinking about yourself for *one minute?* That's all you've talked about, all the way here and back."

"Cal—" Beverly looked truly frightened by his anger.

"You know your problem?" He shook his finger in her face. "You're nothing but surface. It's a mighty fine surface, Beverly, but it's all that's there. You're pretty and you smile all the time and you try to say all the right things. But hardly anybody has the slightest idea of who lives under that surface. Maybe even you don't know."

"Cal—" she said again and tried to back against the door, to widen the space between them.

"No," he said relentlessly, leaning closer. "You listen. I've seen you around kids. They *love* you. Know why? Because of that surface, Beverly. *Because* you're pretty and you always smile and say nice things. That's enough for little kids. They're dazzled. Why shouldn't they be? But you don't ever give anything deeper. Not even to a kid. Not even a *sick* kid, for God's sake."

"I don't want to be around sick people," Beverly said, tears brimming in her eyes. "Sick people *scare* me."

Her words made him so furious he wanted to shake her. He clenched his fists to keep from touching her because he knew if he did, he'd shake her until her teeth rattled. He swore violently. "Beverly, it's no damned sin to be sick. There's nothing criminal about being *sick.*"

He hit the steering wheel with his fist for emphasis, so hard it shook. "Sick people need happiness, too, dammit. Now here you are, a strong, healthy woman, and you *could* help, but you won't. All you'd have to do is walk into that ward and smile, even if you don't mean it. What's it to you? You've been smiling without meaning it all your life, dammit. Couldn't you do it once where it'd do some good for a change?"

A tear trembled free and inched down Beverly's cheek, ruining her powder. "Cal—why are you so *mad?*"

He hit the steering wheel again, so violently she winced. "I'm mad because you could walk in there, and those kids'd think a princess came to see them. But you won't. Sick people *scare* you. What are you scared of—caring about somebody else?"

"Yes," Beverly said, tears streaming down both cheeks now, "I *am*. I *am* scared of caring. Who wouldn't be? I don't *want* to care. It'll hurt."

Cal swore again. "It'll *hurt,*" he mocked. "God forbid Beverly Townsend should ever hurt. Let everybody else in the world get hurt, but not Beverly. No. Walk away and let everybody else suffer."

Beverly's breathing was labored and a sob strangled her voice. "You're not fair—you're not! What if I loved somebody and—and they died? How can you love somebody if they might die?"

"My God, Beverly," he said hopelessly, shaking his head. "How can you *not* love them if they need you? How can you not at least help them? I told you—all you have to do is smile. And say nice things. What's so hard?"

Beverly scrubbed at her streaming eyes, ruining her makeup. "You don't understand," she said, trying to choke back her sobs. "You don't know what it's like to care for somebody who might die."

He hit the steering wheel so viciously that the horn gave a frightened bleat. "I *do* know, dammit. Don't tell me I don't. I'm in love with a woman who might—" he paused, trying to find the right words, the most precise words "—might be terminally ill. She might die. I'm not going to stop loving her just because of that."

Now I've gone and done it, he thought, stunned. *Why'd I tell her, of all people? She'd never understand. Of all the people in the world, I had to tell her.* His anger evaporated, leaving him feeling drained and futile.

"Oh, Cal," Beverly said, reaching out to touch his arm. "I'm sorry—"

"Don't be sorry, *dammit.*" He shook her touch away.

"Now I understand why you're so unhappy," she said, drawing nearer. She wiped her eyes again. With her makeup smeared and her eyes naked, she looked like a kid to him. What was the matter with him? Beverly was his cousin—part of his family. It wasn't her fault that he couldn't get Serena out of his mind.

"Cal," she said timidly, "would you hold me? I'm so frightened. I don't think I've ever been this frightened before."

Wearily, almost tenderly, he took her into his arms. She laid her cheek against his shoulder like a child, and he could feel the tears on her face wetting his shirt.

"When we were little, growing up," she said, her voice muffled against his chest, "I thought everybody'd live forever—that nothing bad could ever happen to any of us. That we'd all be happy and safe forever. I believed it."

"I know." He patted her back awkwardly.

"And now—" She paused, searching for words. "I'm scared." Her voice was small. "Just plain scared."

"I know," he said and held her a little tighter. "I'm scared, too, sugar."

"Cal?"

"What?"

She drew back and looked up at him. Her hair was tumbled and her face was nearly naked. For the first time in years, she looked nearly pretty again to him. "Your girl? What will you do? Will you marry her anyway?"

He gently pushed her back to rest against her own seat, then let his hands drop from her and lie again on the steering wheel. He glanced out at the brown hills that crouched at the horizon. "She won't have me. Because of—you know. What might be wrong."

Shyly Beverly reached out and touched his arm again. This time he did not shake off her hand. "Cal," she said, "you're strong enough to handle it. Does she know that? You always have been strong. Not like me."

He shrugged and didn't look at her.

Her grip on his arm tightened. "You could make her happy. You always made people happy."

He managed a bitter, one-cornered smile.

"I—I was a little bit in love with you once," Beverly said. "Back when we were kids. Did you know?"

He nodded, the smile fading. "Yeah. I knew."

"And you were a little bit in love with me once, too, weren't you?" she asked. Her voice, usually so careful, sounded vulnerable and hesitant. "When I was fifteen and you were twenty. That summer for about a week. Weren't you?"

He smiled again. "No. Only four days. For four whole days, I kind of idealized you. Then Billie Jo Dumont got friendly, and I forgot about ideals. Just as well."

"It never would have worked between us, would it?" she asked, no bitterness in her voice. "We're too much alike in some things. It couldn't have worked."

"No. Besides, we're cousins. Our kids might have had two heads."

Once more his furtive smile died. He wished he hadn't mentioned children. He supposed that was why he'd gotten so angry at Beverly; because it was children she avoided helping. Every kid in the world seemed like a miracle to him now, and he was going to have to appreciate other people's for all they were worth.

"Cal?"

"Yeah?"

"You said she won't have you?"

"No. She won't even talk to me." He raised his hand and massaged his eyes tiredly.

"Look at me," she said softly. "Please. Look at me."

He lowered his hand and turned to her. He felt spent and his back was starting to ache. Once more he studied Beverly's face, almost bare except for the smudges of mascara. "Maybe you're not such a bad little filly," he said gruffly. "Just go help Nate with those kids, okay? You'll be good at it. Try it for me, okay? For one of the ten thousand boys who loved you once?"

She lifted her hand to touch his face, her fingertips resting on his cheek. "Cal, go back to her, wherever she is. Make her listen. You really do love her, don't you? I can tell. So go after her. You have to."

He shook his head in bemusement. "Beverly, you're probably the only person in the whole damned family who'd say that. Everybody else will say I'm a fool."

"Then don't listen to them," she said. "Go to her— I can see it in your look, how much you want her."

He turned from her, his eyes sad but his mouth turning up slightly. Her hand fell softly away from his face.

"Yeah," he said. "I know. There was never any question, I guess. Not really."

"Cal?"

"Yeah?"

"You and I've postponed growing up an awfully long time."

"I reckon," he said.

"You're a man, now. The boy in you is gone. I don't know where he went."

He was silent. He didn't know himself.

"Cal?" she said again, her voice small once more. "Could I kiss him goodbye? That boy?"

"No, Beverly," he said, cautioning her away, but it was too late. She had leaned forward and her lips touched his, briefly and softly. She tasted like tears and the last of childhood.

She drew back and smoothed her tousled hair. Her back straightened and she leaned back against the seat, every inch the beauty queen. She opened her purse and began to array her arsenal of makeup to make repairs.

"Now," she said with great dignity, "you may take me home."

CHAPTER NINE

CAL GOT BACK to the Double C shortly before noon. He loaded the roan into the horse trailer and hastily kissed Lynn and Lettie Mae goodbye. Both women were hurt at his sudden leaving and even more hurt that he refused to say where he was going or why. He had to employ most of his charm to get smiles on their faces as he made his escape.

He stopped at Hank's small stone house and shook hands with the old man. "From the look on your face, you're up to no good," Hank grumbled, staring up from his rocker. "Where you chasin' off to? Has this got to do with those chances you talked about takin'?"

"Grandpa, when the oil fields used to call you, did you stand around trying to explain? Or did you go?"

"I went," Hank said in disgust. "Which is why I'm now lame as an old cow and don't even live on land I call my own. All I got is scars on top of scars and a bunch of sassy grandchildren."

The mention of grandchildren sobered Cal. He didn't suppose he would ever have any. But he thought of what Beverly had said about Serena, and he grinned again. "If you could," he told Hank, "you'd be down drilling on Pearsall land, thinking you'll hit the next

Spindletop. You wouldn't change any of your life, and you know it."

Hank stared up at his great-grandson. Cal's boyishness seemed to have left him of late, and his height and strength suddenly made Hank feel old, wizened and weak. For the first time he wondered if he would actually make it to his hundredth birthday.

And for the first time, although the two men bore little physical resemblance, Hank looked at Cal and saw himself as he had been seventy years ago: a young devil with faith in luck and no faith at all in fear.

Those seventy years had taught him much. They taught him luck didn't hold and that life contained things the wise should fear. They taught him too much about the ways that fortune can lift a man high or hurl him low. And they'd taught him of loss, all too often.

He looked at Cal, and he sighed tiredly. He'd give a lot to know what Cal was up to. He'd give a lot to know, as frail as he felt today, if he'd ever see the boy again. Who knew when Cal might come home again? He had always been like the line from that old song—he'd come with the dust and go with the wind: there was no predicting.

Hank wondered what he should say to this young man, so like his old self, so sure no trouble was too great for him to triumph over it. What words should he give him, especially if they might, by chance, be the last words he would ever say to him? He said the only sensible thing he could think of. "Good luck," he said gruffly. "Good luck, boy."

"Thanks," Cal said, his grin fading into an affectionate, slightly melancholy smile. "Same to you, Grandpa."

Hank then waved Cal away as if he were a pesky fly. Cal looked down at him a moment longer, the smile still on his lips. Then he turned and left.

He climbed into his van and without further hesitation headed toward Wolverton and Serena.

CAL DROVE HARD and made Wolverton by ten o'clock that night. He'd never learned where Serena lived, so he tethered his roan horse at the rodeo grounds and headed across town for La Herencia. He aimed to sleep in the van in the parking lot so he could confront her first thing in the morning.

But the lights were on at La Herencia, her green Chevrolet was parked on the gravel, and his heart took a crazy square-dance step.

He'd thought of a hundred things to say to her, but they all fled his mind, disappearing like a flock of startled birds. He parked the van, went up the stairs and knocked at the door. When she answered it, he only stood, looking down at her, and he, to whom words had always come so easily, could not speak.

SERENA STARED up at him, startled yet secretly thrilled. Her face paled. She had wanted him to come back and yet she'd feared it, hadn't dared to hope for it.

Now he stood in the doorway, tall, lean-hipped and broad-shouldered, his handsome face unnaturally solemn and a small muscle jerking in his cheek.

He was hatless, his hair dark in the starless night. Although the night was cold, he wore no jacket, and the breeze fluttered his pale blue shirt against the flat hardness of his chest. He reached for the screened door that was still shut between them and opened it, stepping inside so that only a foot of space separated them.

Serena's heart beat faster. She held an awl in her right hand, and her dark pink sweater had a spot of glue over her breast. The air in the shop was warm and faintly fragrant with the scent of freshly cut leather, but she didn't notice. All that burned into her awareness was the tall man who had appeared, as if by magic, out of the night.

"What do you want?" she breathed.

"You," he said, his eyes never leaving hers.

A thousand possible futures flashed through her mind. She was afraid to examine any of them except the one in which she lived alone, safe from the danger of loving.

"You were supposed to go away," she said. A strange ache filled her chest, making it hard for her to breathe.

"I know. I couldn't."

She looked away from him, staring unseeing into a corner. "You shouldn't have come. We—don't have any future. I don't make that kind of commitment. I can't."

"Serena, look at me." His hand reached out and grasped her arm above the elbow. He drew her a fraction of an inch closer, but she refused to meet his eyes. The touch of his hand went through her like electricity, but she stared with dogged stubbornness into the corner she didn't really see.

"I can't promise what'll happen to me, either," he said. "But a person can't spend his whole life wondering what *might* happen. You've got to live life, not wait it out. We'll take it one day at a time and be thankful for that day."

She shook her head, her dark hair swinging. She bit her lip and wished her flesh wouldn't quake at his touch. "What happens if the days turn bad? You won't think about that. I do. I have to."

His other hand stroked her hair out of the way and settled on her shoulder. "Thinking about all the *ifs* in the world can kill a person, darlin'. You can't live in the future. You can only live now. Look at me. Please."

"No." She shook her head again, bit her lip harder.

"Are you afraid?"

"Yes."

"Don't be."

He put his hand beneath her chin and tipped her face up to his. "I can make you happy" he whispered. "But you have to let me. Let me."

"Cal," she said hopelessly, her senses in a wild tumble. She wanted to tell him it was crazy, that she couldn't and shouldn't feel as she did. But his mouth descended to capture hers, and his arm encircled her, pulling her against him. Her heart seemed to soar out of her body, as if it were trying to fly to find his, and she was left warm and melting and dizzy.

The awl dropped from her fingers to the floor. His mouth was so hot and sweet and hungry against her own that she thought she might die of it. His arms about her tightened, as if he could make their two bodies merge into one and they would never have to be separate again.

She was dimly aware that he used one booted heel to kick the door shut, and the sound of its closing sealed them away from the rest of the world.

Almost involuntarily she wound her arms around the strong column of his neck. Her lips parted to let his tongue enter, and when it did, she felt half-drunk, tasting him and being tasted. His mouth was demanding and giving at the same time; she felt ravished by the pleasure of his wild and expert touch.

A worn green couch stood against one wall, a sitting place for waiting customers or workers on a break. Serena gasped as Cal scooped her up into his arms as easily as if she were a child, never breaking his kiss.

Then he drew back momentarily and stared into her eyes. He grinned his beautiful white grin. Dazed, she could not help smiling back, besotted with happiness that he was there and she was in his arms.

"My God, you're beautiful when you smile," he said, shaking his head in wonder. "I love it when you smile."

He carried her across the room in three long swift strides and lowered her to the couch. Although she stretched out almost languidly, as if it were the most natural thing in the world to lie there, her heart hammered.

He lowered himself to sit beside her. He took her face between his hands and bent to kiss her again. "I want to do this right,'' he said against her lips. "To take you to the stars. Will you let me?''

"Yes,'' she said. "Yes.''

He kissed her mouth, the soft curve of her cheekbone, her eyelids, her temple, her ear. His lips traveled down the silky flesh of her throat. She could feel his breath warm through the fabric of her sweater, then hot against the aching thrust of her breasts. His hands moved to cradle the round warmth of their swell.

Then, somehow, his mouth was moist and hot against the tickling skin of her stomach and his hands were underneath her sweater, loosening her bra, cupping the soft weight of her breasts. He teased their peaks to points of sensual awareness, eased her sweater up, and taught one throbbing nipple, then the other, the secret pleasures of his mouth.

Serena's hand tightened on his hard shoulder, and her eyes shut tighter, because he made her feel such tides of desire, such waves of gladness she was faint with it.

She didn't protest when he drew her sweater off, gently stripped her bra away. She lay, half-naked, her long hair tangling on her white shoulders. He toyed with her hair, letting it run through his fingers, and he kissed her breasts again.

He unbuttoned his shirt and pulled it off, letting it fall to the floor beside her sweater. She felt the smooth, hard, naked sweep of his muscles beneath her hands.

"Look at me,'' he ordered gently. "Look at us.''

Her eyes fluttered open dreamily and she looked at his bare torso, gilded by the lamplight. He hadn't an ounce of excess flesh, and his arms were ropy with sinew and vein, his chest wide and his flat stomach sculpted with muscle. Even his scars seemed beautiful to her.

His skin was dark compared to hers, and her hand looked like a white flower resting on his biceps. She saw, with shy pleasure, how opposite they were, he all tanned and hard leanness, she softer, more delicate and rounded and fair. They seemed formed to fit together, two halves of a whole.

He shifted their positions, pulling her to sit with her back nestled against his chest. He put his arms around her from behind, drawing her hips back to rest between his thighs. He kissed the back of her neck, making her inhale sharply with pleasure. His hands moved to her bared breasts, caressing and stroking them, and his mouth played complicated games along her shoulders and against her nape.

The naked warmth of his chest cradled her back, and when his hand moved beneath the waistband of her jeans, she sighed with pleasure and turned to face him. He kissed her lips and pulled her closer.

"Cal," she whispered, worry suddenly clouding her face, "I don't want children. I can't take a chance—"

"Shh," he soothed. "I said I wanted to do this right. You won't have to worry. Come here." He drew her more intimately into the shelter of his arms. "Let me love you."

She did, and as he promised, he took her to the stars. Bursts of light seemed to blossom in her mind and body, brighter and brighter, until she became one with the light and the light was Cal.

Then he held her in his arms, and they slept till nearly dawn, when he nuzzled her awake again and once more they made love.

"IT WAS CRAZY," Serena said miserably the next morning over coffee and a doughnut. Last night she might have flown to the stars and joined them. This morning she felt she had crashed back to earth all too forcefully, dust to dust.

She hadn't intended for anything to happen between them, but she had been swept away. What was more, she knew she would be in his arms again tonight; she had to. But their helpless desire for each other seemed like a madness to her, one she desperately hoped would cure itself.

Cal stared at her over the rim of his coffee cup. He had shaved in the shop's small bathroom and had on a clean, dark-blue shirt. His eyes, as always, glittered with life, and a smile of gentle smugness played on his lips.

"It wasn't crazy," he said. "It's the first sane thing we've done since we met."

They sat in a small restaurant aromatic with the scent of morning coffee and baking cinnamon rolls.

"We're having an affair, that's all," she said, looking moodily at the vase with a yellow artificial rose that ornamented their table. "We're having an affair, and it can end at any time. No promises, no commitments. When you want to leave, you leave."

"I don't aim to leave," he said evenly.

She shrugged, ignoring his words. "It's like you said," she murmured. "We'll live it one day at a time. We don't even imagine this has a future."

His smile disappeared. "That's not what I said, and you know it."

"You'll have to move on. You've got rodeos to make."

"I'll let them pass. It's time I quit."

"You can't quit," she objected. "It's your life. It's how you make your living."

He laid his hand atop hers and she stiffened, fighting the powerful emotions that surged through her at his slightest touch. "Let me put money into your business," he said. "And set you up with Amarillo Tex. Let me throw in with you. It's what you need."

"No," she said firmly, forcing herself to draw her hand away. "We don't mix this up with business. What's between us is—is personal."

"Serena," he said in frustration, then paused. His brow furrowed and he shrugged. "I'm sorry. I shouldn't rush you."

She clenched her fist in her lap. He was so handsome and strong and kind he made her ache inside. When he made love to her, his touch had fired her with a sweet, haunting obsession. All the careful plans she'd made and kept for so many years threatened to topple down. She no longer felt in control of her life, and it terrified her.

"What's between us is only—physical," she said, trying to convince herself it was the truth. "We'll get tired of each other. Then it'll be over."

"I won't get tired of you. It won't be over. Even if I die it won't be over. If any part of me could live on, the part that loves you would. I know that as sure as I sit here."

He said it with such honesty and intensity, such a lack of affectation or drama that tears smarted her eyes. How could she protect herself from such a man? "Oh, Cal, don't *say* things like that. This is only about our bodies, not our souls."

"It's about our bodies *and* our souls. You know it, I know it."

"No," she said, shaking her head. "No." She thought of her father, slowly turning into a stranger who frightened and saddened her. What had happened to his soul? Had it been destroyed? Or only kidnapped from this world forever? She didn't know.

She remembered her grandfather, whom she had loved deeply. He had become erratic, his sanity eaten by disease. What of his soul? To where had it vanished?

Cal might swear he would love her forever, but he had not seen what she had seen; he had no way of understanding. "I don't want to talk about souls," she said, angry at the tears that swam in her eyes. "My soul's my own, dammit."

"Serena, don't cry." He reached under the table and his hand closed over her clenched fist. "Don't, sugar. Everything's going to be fine. You'll see." His hand tightened on hers.

Furiously she brushed the tears away. She wasn't like Patti; she would not take refuge in thoughtless optimism. "You have no *idea* if everything's going to be fine or not. None. Oh, I *hate* it when you make me emotional. I just *hate* it. I shouldn't even try to talk to you. It's impossible. I want to go home. I have to get ready for work. I'm already late.''

Once more she drew her hand from his. She stood and shrugged into her jacket. He rose, helping her, lifting her hair from beneath the collar and smoothing it over her shoulders. Then he bent and kissed her behind the ear.

She shuddered with a pleasure so sharp that it frightened her to feel it. ''Don't,'' she said, her voice low and shaking. ''This is a public place. Don't do things like that.''

''I can't help it,'' he said. He wiped her cheek, where the trace of a tear still lingered. ''Will you spend tonight with me?''

No, she should say, if she had a shred of reason left.

''Yes,'' she said, because she was unable to say otherwise. She looked up at him, trying as hard as she could not to love him.

His hand lingered on her cheek. ''I aim to get it yet,'' he said, smiling in a way that made her heart give a topsy-turvy roll.

''Get what?'' she asked.

''Your soul,'' he smiled. ''You'll see.''

It's not mine to give, Serena thought unhappily. *Fate might come along and rip it away from me at any time. I can't even promise it to myself. Why can't you understand?*

SOMEHOW Tracey realized that something had happened. This worried Serena. Perhaps her indiscretion was branded across her forehead in letters she alone could not see: This Woman Made Love With Wild Abandon Last Night.

She imagined even Jesus and Estaban looked at her slightly askance. When the men left for lunch, she stayed in the shop, stitching uppers, and Tracey remained at her desk. Neither of them spoke and the silence between them swelled, growing more strained.

At last Tracey came to the door and leaned against the frame, watching Serena. She held an apple in her hand. "Want half?"

"No thanks," Serena said, keeping her head down, trying to concentrate on the leather.

"He's back, isn't he?" Tracey said bluntly. "You've seen him."

Serena froze. She glanced up warily. "He's back. I saw him." She gave her attention back to the boot.

"You're not running away from him this time." It was a statement, not a question.

"No. This time I'm not running."

Tracey bit into the apple. The sun shone today, and a bright shaft of light fell through the window, making gold highlights glint in her short hair. "Does he still want to buy into the business?"

Serena hesitated. She pushed the boot aside and sat on a stool near one of the sewing machines. Tracey had every right to ask about the business, and besides that, she was Serena's best friend. If Serena was going to talk to anyone, it should be Tracey.

"He says he does. I won't let him. This is *our* business. What's between him and me—isn't business."

"Serena," Tracey said carefully. "I've been thinking. He made a good offer. It wouldn't hurt to consider it."

"No," Serena said more sharply than she meant to.

"Just let me say this," Tracey said, holding up her hand to halt Serena from interrupting her. "I know you worry about your family. About Patti and the girls. The more secure the business is, the better you're able to help them if they need help. That's all—it's something to think of."

"I've thought of it," Serena said moodily, and she had. She knew that on one level Tracey was right. Cal's offer made sense. The stronger the business grew, the more economic safety it provided if she had to come to the aid of Patti and Dovey and Hope.

Tracey sighed and set the apple down having taken only one bite from it. Her expression was both thoughtful and unhappy.

"Normally," Tracey said, crossing her arms, "I wouldn't interfere in your personal life. I respect your decisions. But I have to say that this man—well, it's obvious he cares a great deal for you. That he *sincerely* cares a great deal for you."

Serena locked her fingers together in her lap and stared at them stolidly. "He thinks so, that's all."

Tracey took a deep breath and went on. "All I'm saying is that if you were to rethink your position on getting married, I'd say more power to you. I've always admired you for being careful. But it's possible that a person can be too careful. . . ."

Serena's face went pale, and she shot Tracey an angry look. "A person like me *can't* be too careful," she said shortly. She stood and moved back to the work-table. "And don't talk about me getting married. He's someone I—I'm seeing, that's all. Until we get each other out of our systems."

"Serena," Tracey said, shaking her head, "that man isn't going to get you out of his system. And if this is someone you could—care for, I'd hate to see you pass the experience by, that's all. You deserve a life."

"I don't want to talk about it." Her voice sounded so tightly controlled it was almost strangled.

Tracey uncrossed her arms and held up her hands in a sign of surrender. "All right. I'm sorry to bring it up. It's just I can see that this is bothering you, and—"

"I said I *don't* want to talk about it."

Tracey exhaled in exasperation. "And I said I'm sorry. If you ever do want to talk, well, I'll be here. You know that."

Serena didn't answer. She stared unseeing down at her work. She was relieved when she heard Tracey move from the doorway and back to her desk. Serena kept her head bowed. When she thought of the other room, the blood rushed back to her cheeks as she remembered last night and making love to Cal on the couch.

Making love on the office couch, she thought in disgust. It sounded stupid, even sordid and common. Yet it had been none of those things; it had been something wonderful, almost transcendent.

She realized that with other men, she had merely had sex. With Cal she had truly made love. Their every move, their every touch had been infused not simply with desire—although the desire had been great, almost overwhelming—but with a glow of happiness, as well, a sheer joy that they were together.

She smoothed her hair back from her shoulders and bent more intently over her work. She forced her mind to turn hard, cynical. *He only wants me because he knows he can't have me. He's used to having women fall to their knees. He's a drifter. He's drifted for years, and he could never stay in one place, be true to one woman. He couldn't. He would tire of it and move on.*

She made a stupid mistake in her sewing and picked out the stitch. What she had told him was true: they must play out this affair not pretending it could last, not planning on any tomorrows.

Even if he did believe he loved her, that phantom of love would die once he understood the situation. She would have to make him see that.

Whether she loved him made no difference in the final scheme of things. No difference at all.

CAL SPENT THE DAY at loose ends. He groomed the blue-eyed roan and found a place to board it and work it. He'd put his money down and got two slots in next week's rodeo, one roping, one bareback bronc riding.

He didn't like the Wolverton Rodeo much, but he was not used to being idle, and he refused to seem like a slacker in Serena's eyes.

He visited Grumpy at the vet, who was puzzled by the big horse's injury. Grump was taking longer to heal than he should. Cal wondered darkly if he was going to have to turn the old boy out to pasture.

He sent Serena flowers from the florist. He decided that she was a quiet woman and maybe roses were too flashy. He looked at all the flowers in the display case and picked early-blooming irises because they reminded him of her, long-stemmed and delicate.

He sent a modest bouquet, making sure it came in a vase so she wouldn't end up sticking it in a boot. When the florist asked what he wanted put on the card, he shrugged. Serena didn't want declarations at this point, and there was no way he could say what was in his heart anyway. "Nothing," he said.

He got a hotel room, a good one, then spent the rest of the afternoon at the library, reading about neurological diseases. Wolverton's library left much to be desired, but he pored over everything he could find.

And he thought. When it came to women, Cal was a surprisingly good strategist. Surprisingly, for he had little need of strategy to make women fall in love with him. In his case, in fact, much of his strategy had been employed in keeping them *out* of love.

For years there had been girls like Billie Jo Dumont, who were fine to sleep with, but he surely didn't want them mooning about in love with him. He made it clear that they might have a fine time together in bed now and then, but he had no interest in making the arrangement permanent.

There was another sort of girl as well, the kind for whom he felt a certain odd protectiveness. Mary Alice Priest in Crystal Creek was one. Pretty little Lila Stang at the post office was another. They were nice women, the sort an honorable man wouldn't trifle with, and he dazzled them without meaning to. His job was to be friendly, make them feel good about themselves, but never to give them false hopes.

Serena, of course, was different, and he saw that she would be won slowly or not at all. He had frightened her away once and must be careful not to do it again.

Vainly, like a man too used to conquest, he'd thought the strength of his passion would be enough to make her his. But if passion wouldn't win her, patience would; he had to believe that.

Beverly said he could make Serena happy. That was what he intended to do: make her so happy that she could never even be able to think of life without him.

"WHERE ARE WE GOING?" Serena asked suspiciously. He had picked her up at the shop. This evening she had succumbed to vanity and worn her best plain boots, dark green slacks and a pale green blouse with arrows embroidered on the pockets.

Cal's jeans were faded but pressed to a razor crease, and his wine-colored shirt hugged his wide shoulders and narrow waist. February had turned suddenly warm, and he wore a light jacket of blue corduroy. He was heading out of Wolverton, and Serena had no idea of where he was taking her.

"Out to see my new horse," he said, flashing her a grin. "I thought you might like a ride. There's an old schoolhouse close by. They store hay in it, but it'd be a nice place to have a picnic. I stopped off and picked up some food." He pointed to the brown sack at the back of the van.

He could almost always make her smile, which struck her as dangerous, but her lips turned up in a shy, sideways curve. Only Cal would think of a picnic on a February night. But the thought of the horse took her aback slightly. "I'm not much of a rider. Not since I was a kid, really."

Her smile faded. Her grandfather had taught her to ride, and he had shown infinite patience and skill. A year later his patience wore thin, he was sharp-tongued and irritable with her, and his skill had dramatically faded. She hadn't known it had been the disease. None of them had known.

Cal reached over and took her hand. He did it with such easy confidence she could not help but respond, and let her fingers curl through his. "Your smile went away," he said, gripping her hand more intimately. "Where'd you go off to? The past or the future?"

She glanced at his profile, feeling a surge of affection for him, so strong it left her breathless. "The past."

He picked up her hand and kissed it, keeping his other hand on the wheel. "Don't go off like that without me. Take me with you or stay here." Gently he nipped the knuckle of her thumb, as if in warning.

"How can I take you with me?" she asked, smiling again.

"Talk to me. I can go with you if you talk."

Oh, heavens, she thought, shaking her head, if only he were right. If only when she went time-traveling into the past or future, she didn't have to go alone. If only she could share the burden; he made it sound simple and possible, but it wasn't, and he refused to understand.

She tried anyway. She tried because it was the only way to explain her fear and her reluctance about him, and to make him see things as he should.

She began softly, because she knew how harshly the story would end. "My grandfather taught me to ride. He bought me a pony. Its name was Harp." *There,* she thought fatefully. *That was easy enough to say. My grandfather bought me a pony. Its name was Harp.*

"Your grandfather, the stockman?"

She nodded, looking down at their linked hands, lying between them on the seat. Cal's thumb caressed her palm, tracing gentle arcs and tickling strokes across it.

"He tried to teach my sister, Patti, too, but she never had the patience. I loved riding, though—and the pony. We rode all the time."

He squeezed her hand. "And then he got sick? Your grandfather?" He didn't ask with pity in his voice, for which she was grateful. He asked matter-of-factly, calmly.

"Yes," she said, "he got sick." She took a deep breath, feeling tremulous. "You see, back then—it was a little town, a small-town doctor—nobody recognized what it was. My grandfather just got—different. His mind got *different.* And his body didn't quite obey him. It all kept getting worse. The doctors would call it by one name, then another. But never the right one. Until almost the end."

Cal nodded, his face solemn. He kept his eyes on the road, for which she was grateful. It would be harder to talk if he watched her. But he kept hold of her hand, firm hold.

"My grandmother put him in a private hospital for a while," Serena said, remembering. "But—she couldn't afford it. He'd never believed in insurance and they had hardly any. She lost everything before it was over. The stock. The ranch. The house."

"The pony?" he asked with the same calm.

She shrugged. She had cried bitterly over the pony's loss when she was a child. Now, in light of all that had happened since, it seemed of little consequence.

"The pony? Of course—he had to go. Everything did. But I missed my grandfather worse than any pony. He died in a charity hospital. It wasn't...a nice place. And right before he did, we found out what it was he really had. And that it could be hereditary."

He nodded quietly as he turned the van down a side road.

"It was only a year later that my father showed signs of the same thing," she said and swallowed hard.

"Look, Cal," she went on, glancing at his handsome profile again, praying he could understand. "We had so little by that time. My father had worked for my grandfather, but we were wiped out. He was a hand on another ranch. He didn't want to believe it was happening to him, too, not so soon. He wouldn't admit it. He wouldn't see a doctor."

"That's pretty much human nature," he said. "I never did meet a cowboy with much use for doctors."

"I know. But the disease—it went differently for him. My grandfather was forty-seven when it started. My father was only thirty-six. It happened relatively slowly to my grandfather. With my father, it was faster. Oh, how he changed—and he wouldn't get help. It broke my grandmother's heart. My mother's, too. She—divorced him finally. She couldn't forget him, but the only way she could survive was to divorce him. We moved up here.''

"Go on," he said, still watching the road. "Tell me what happened. All of it.''

She stared out the side window at the flat, brown fields. The moon had risen in a cloudless sky, and thousands of stars spangled the young face of night. She held on to his hand as if it were a lifeline. She had never told these things to anyone except Tracey.

"One reason we left was that people teased us— Patti and me—about our father. They said he was crazy, that it ran in the family. He—he'd loved my mother once. I think maybe he'd loved her to a fault. But the sickness made him change. He started being unfaithful. People talked about that, too. So we left. She couldn't watch it anymore.''

"What about you?" he asked, lacing his fingers more tightly through hers.

"Me? I was *scared*," she admitted. "And humiliated. And hurt. And confused. My grandmother wouldn't leave. She said, 'He has to have someplace to come home to.' She never forgave us for leaving. But her health was bad by then, and whenever anybody was in trouble, my father or my grandmother, it was my mother who had to go back and try to clean up the mess. And there was always trouble. Always.''

Her mind ran back unhappily over her father's last years. Calls from her grandmother, calls from the police, calls from this hospital or that. Between stays in the hospital, he was usually drunk. He'd apparently decided he'd rather have liquor kill him than the illness. He'd succeeded. He'd drowned in a drainage ditch outside of town one December night.

Serena told Cal that, too, sparing him nothing.

He never looked at her and he never let go of her hand. Instead, he stopped the van. For a terrifying minute, she thought her message had finally sunk in, that he was going to tell her to get out, and that he would drive on leaving her there, marooned and looking after him as he disappeared.

"What?" she said, confused by his action.

"Who wants to see an old roping horse in the dark?" he asked, drawing her into his arms. "I'll take you this weekend, in the daylight. Then we'll ride. Bareback. It'll give me an excuse to hold you."

"But why are you stopping?" she asked, looking up at his features, silvery in the moonlight that poured through the windows. "Why don't we just turn around?"

His hands flexed, kneading her shoulders. "I stopped to hold you. And to tell you two things. First, the past sounds like a sad place for you. You shouldn't go there alone. Always take me with you."

She was both deeply touched and frustrated. In one sense he had understood her almost too well; in another sense he had not understood at all.

"The other thing—" he said, lifting her chin so that she had to look into his eyes. Even in the darkness she could see the life in them, the clear, heart-shaking vitality that always electrified her. "The other thing is this. The past *is* the past, Serena. Those other folks got blindsided. Your grandfather never knew what hit him, nor did anyone else, not till it was too late. Your daddy knew but wouldn't admit it so there was no way to help him. Your grandmother and mama weren't prepared, either. They were all caught off guard. That was their tragedy as much as the sickness."

She looked away, shaken by his words. She stared at her hands, pale against the darkness of his jacket's shoulders. Her hands, she thought irrationally, looked right, resting there. "Cal, you just don't know—" she started to say, but he cut her off.

"I know you're different from them. You know and you're honest. And these times are different. Your whole family got caught up in something they never expected. How could they? But there's better medicine now, and doctors who know more, and counselors, and all sorts of ways to fight back."

"No," she said, shaking her head. She drew her hands away, folded them and buried them nervously in her lap. "No. It's not that easy."

He lifted her face to his again. "I never said it was easy," he murmured. "I would never be fool enough to say that. I only said it was different. That *we* know what we're getting into, and there's more help than there used to be and there may be more help still—"

"*I* know what it can do," she objected, powerless not to love the strength and tenderness in his face. "But you don't—not really. Why can't I make you understand—"

"Shh," he said, laying his finger on her lips. "I may never have to see it. And neither may you—not again. There's always that chance. Why don't you ever think about that chance?"

I do, but I don't dare count on it, she thought, losing herself in his eyes. *I do, but this is what I've always feared—that there'd be something to lose. Somebody to lose. Somebody—and it's you. You.*

His hand caressed her jaw with butterfly softness and he spoke gently. "I read—a doctor said, 'Every day can contain a whole life.' I've always believed that. I always lived that way. It's true. 'Every day can contain a whole life.' This day, too."

He kissed her so that she seemed to fall through the darkness, then fly toward the stars again. The touch of his hands on her face, his lips against hers filled her with exquisite sweetness and desire. The moment his mouth took hers, time lost both beginning and end and seemed endless, intense enough, indeed, to contain a lifetime.

"But this isn't the only reason I stopped," he said, drawing back and lacing his fingers through the silkiness of her hair. "I stopped because it's the tenth of February, and we're somewhere west of Wolverton, and the moon is nearly full."

"What?" Her lips trembled from the magic tingling his mouth had created upon her own.

"The moon is nearly full," he said softly, "and outside is a field of grass getting ready to turn green again because spring is coming, and I want to dance with you."

"What?" she repeated, not comprehending his words at all, only his nearness.

He reached over and switched on the tape deck on the dashboard. Music filled the van, and he pushed the button to roll down the windows. Then he opened the door, his hands sliding to Serena's waist, and drew her outside with him.

"Dance?" she asked, puzzled, yet oddly excited as well. "In a field? Why on earth?"

She saw the field beyond the road, slightly rolling, the brown grass stirring in the mild breeze.

"Because it's the tenth of February. We ought to celebrate that—and Wolverton—and the moon," he said. Without further ceremony, he picked her up, lifted her across the ditch that ran beside the road and deposited her in the field, safely on the other side of the barbed-wire fence.

He vaulted the fence, took both her hands in his and stood looking down at her. Music poured from the opened windows of the van and swept softly around them. It was country music, Serena thought a bit dazedly, George Strait or Clint Black or Garth Brooks; she couldn't quite tell.

She could only look up at Cal, who smiled down at her.

"What are we celebrating?" she said, letting him take her in his arms. "There's nothing special about February tenth."

He coiled one arm around her waist. His other hand grasped hers and pressed it against his chest. He began to move her to the music. "There's something special about every day, darlin'," he said.

CHAPTER TEN

SERENA FELT enchanted, waltzing in the moonlight. They whirled slowly and elaborately over the field, until she was breathless. Then he laughed, danced her to the fence with a Texas two-step and lifted her back over.

He vaulted the fence again, took her hand and led her back to the van. He drove to an old one-room schoolhouse he'd found earlier in the day. It was on the property of the man boarding the roan, Cal said, and he'd told Cal to feel free to inspect it.

They carried a blanket and the bag of groceries inside. The windows had long ago been broken, and part of the roof was gone, letting the moonlight pour onto the floor. Bales of hay were piled along the wall, and hay in thick wisps and clumps covered the floor.

When they entered, an owl flew out the hole in the roof, his great wings flapping. "His nest is up in the rafters," Cal said with satisfaction. "That means no mice."

Serena wasn't afraid of mice and had given them no thought. Instead she was amazed that a piano, an immense grand piano, weathered by wind and rain, stood in the center of the floor, its thick legs settled firmly in the hay.

"A schoolhouse full of hay—with a resident owl—*and* a grand piano?" She laughed.

"The old boy who owns the place says it has a history," Cal said, spreading the blanket on the floor. "It was a one-room schoolhouse, then a meeting house of some kind. He doesn't know how they got the piano in, but he never figured how to get it out. So you're in probably the only hay house in Texas with a grand piano. It even still plays—a little."

He turned to the piano and played nine or ten discordant bars of Jerry Lee Lewis's "Great Balls of Fire." The music, wild and primitive, hammered through the still air.

Serena looked at him openmouthed, still not having recovered from the sight of the piano.

"My mama taught me to play," he explained with a crooked smile. "Of course she didn't teach me to play *that.* In high school I could play part of it with the heels of my boots. You know, like Jerry Lee."

She smiled and shook her head. "Like the Killer? What a role model—I hope you never set a piano on fire."

"Only once," he said laconically. "But I wasn't myself at the time."

"Is this something I don't want to hear about?"

He reached into the grocery sack and took out a bottle of champagne. "Probably. It involves a honky-tonk in Bandera, a bottle of Jose Cuervo, and a really stupid bet about whether I could chugalug it and stay sane. I couldn't. Never again."

"A misspent youth?" she asked, watching how the moonlight made silver ripple in his dark hair.

"Pretty much," he admitted. He produced two champagne glasses, filled them with the sparkling wine and handed her one. "But I bet you were always a perfect lady." He clicked his glass against hers. "To your perfection."

"I was hardly perfect. But I never set any pianos on fire. Good grief, these glasses are real crystal, Cal. Do you always travel with crystal and champagne?"

"Only when I travel with you. Sit. I brought us bread and cheese and grapes and chocolates."

Serena settled crossed-legged on the blanket. Cal lounged across from her, his long legs stretched out. He broke a loaf of crusty French bread while she sliced the Edam and Gouda cheeses.

They ate, and drank champagne, and he told her funny stories about growing up in Crystal Creek. At last, she was lying back against his chest, his arm around her as he leaned against a bale of hay. He traced the line of her jaw with a stem of straw, and she smiled.

"No," she said, "I mean it. What *was* the happiest day of your childhood? Really?"

"And I told you," he said in her ear, "the day I could run faster than my brother could chase. That boy used to *whomp* me."

"And you, of course, were blameless," she teased, snuggling more tightly against him. The champagne made her feel tingly, as if she were all silvered inside as well as outside with moonlight.

"I was never blameless." He kissed her just beneath the ear and she shivered with pleasure, but her smile faded.

"Cal?"

"What?" He kissed the same spot again, and it seemed when he touched her, he made the moonlight shimmer.

"I don't think somebody like you is meant to settle down. You're a free spirit."

He wound his other arm around her, drawing her closer. "I've done my wandering. I'm the best sort for settling down you could find. There's nothing left to unsettle me. I've gotten all the craziness out of my system."

She shook her head in disbelief, gazing up at the space of sky showing through the broken roof. Clouds, edged with platinum, drifted by slowly. "No," she whispered.

His arms tightened around her. "Yes."

She lifted her hand to let it fall backward, resting on his arm. "You talked about children once."

"I talked about going to Mars once. When I was eight. I didn't go. I got over it." He kissed the side of her throat.

"That's different. You don't—a person doesn't just *get over* not having children. You'd always miss them. You'd always wonder what they'd be like. You'd always wish it was—different."

"Hush," he said, nuzzling the spot where her neck joined her shoulder. "You just told me I'd never settle down. Now you're trying to inflict a passel of children on me. Make sense."

"I am," she said, drawing away and turning so she could look into his face. She rested her fingertips against his chin. "You can't make a joke out of it. You said you wanted children. With me you'd never have them."

"Then that's the way it is, and I'd be a fool to fret over what I can't change, wouldn't I?" His hands were on her shoulders, and they tightened gently to emphasize his words.

She shook her head and let her forefinger trace the strong curve of his lower lip. "Cal, you sound so *logical.* It's not a matter of logic. It's—emotional. You can't think that way."

"I've thought that way all my life," he said, taking her hand and pressing it against his cheek. "A person changes what he can change, and he accepts what he can't. So we won't have children—lots of folks don't. It's a fact of life. I'm not going to get all bent out of shape about it. Neither should you. We accept it and go on."

She caressed the hard curve of his cheekbone with her thumb. "I wouldn't even adopt. If something happened to me—well, why should I put a child through that? I've been through it—no."

He shrugged almost carelessly. "I figured you'd feel like that. I thought it out on the way to Crystal Creek. I thought out a lot. It's all right. You've got your reasons. I understand."

"Cal," she said, her voice trembling, "you always say you understand, but you *can't.* I'm trying to be fair. I'm trying to be honest. To tell you again that there really *isn't* any future for us—and it hurts to pretend there could be—"

"Shh. You brought up the future. Not me. Come here."

He cradled her jaw in his hand and tilted her face up to his so that he could take her lips. He kissed her in the way that made her nearly faint with want and need of him.

"Cal," she managed to say, drawing away as much as he'd allow, "I never planned on having a future with anybody—"

"That's one of the things I'll work to change," he said. "It can be changed. And I'll change it."

He crushed her to him and kissed her again, deeply and with an almost ferocious possessiveness. Her mouth opened beneath his, and his tongue delved inside, playing against hers, thrusting and caressing. Joyously she accepted the intimacy, tasting him as he tasted her.

His hands described sensuous arcs against her back, pressing her more firmly against him even as he fondled her. His mouth moved down her throat, lipping and kissing it. Then his hands were on her upper arms and he was lowering her to the blanket and unbuttoning her blouse.

The blanket was soft beneath her and fragrant with hay. He knelt beside her, and she watched him silhouetted against the moonlit clouds as he opened her blouse and eased it from her shoulders. His fingers stripped her bra away, and the night air flooded coolly over her bared breasts. He stared down at her for a long moment, not touching her, just looking.

"Good *Lord,* you're beautiful," he said, his voice strained. "Are you too cold? Should I take you to the van? To my room?"

She shook her head. "No. I like being in the moonlight with you."

"Take my shirt off," he said, raising her to kneel facing him. He kissed her first on one naked shoulder, then the other. Her dark hair spilled across her breasts, almost hiding them, and he brushed it back, the better to see her. Her body shone white in the moonlight.

His right arm curled around her bare waist, his other hand tangled in her hair, and he let his eyes fall to watch her pale, trembling fingers as they unfastened the buttons of his shirt. Then he shrugged out of both his shirt and jacket.

He bent to kiss her full on the lips, leaning so that her breasts, the nipples erect and tingling, brushed the hard warmth of his chest. His hand slowly moved from her shoulders to frame her breasts, then, at last, to cup and caress them.

She gave a long, shuddering sigh and put her hands on the sinewy strength of his thighs. She closed her eyes and tilted her head backward, lost in the pleasure of touching him and being touched.

When his lips as well as his hands began to excite the aching swell of her breasts, she dropped her head to his naked shoulder, kissing its warmth again and again. He groaned and pulled her close to him, kissing her mouth more ravenously than before.

She wound her arms around his neck as once more he lowered her to the blanket. He stretched out against her, his body taut, one leg curling around hers to draw them closer to his.

He drew back, breathing hard, his lips still grazing hers. "Are you sure you're not cold?"

She was, slightly, but the contrast of the cool of the air mingling with the heat of his body intoxicated her. "Not when you touch me," she whispered, running her hands down the smooth, snaking muscles of his shoulders and arms. "Not when you kiss me."

"Then I'll touch you everywhere," he breathed. "I'll kiss you everywhere."

AFTERWARD they lay in each other's arms, wrapped in the blanket, their legs tangled warmly together. He dipped his head and kissed her breast again. His foot ran sinuously up her calf, then down. "Lordy," he said against her throat. "You make me crazier than the tequila in Bandera did."

She smiled, rubbing her cheek against his hair. "Is that supposed to be a compliment? Does it mean you'll set the piano on fire?"

He held her tighter, stroking her back and shoulders. "I'm surprised it didn't spontaneously combust. One of these days, I've got to try to get you into a bed to make love."

"I like it here," said Serena, kissing his chest, loving the warm, slightly salty taste of him. "With the moonlight for a roof and the hay for our bed. And a grand piano with our champagne glasses rolled under it."

"Our kind of place, huh?" He hugged her to him more tightly. He watched the moonlit clouds drifting above them, sailing across the space in the ruined roof.

Her body was cool and slender and fit perfectly into his arms, as if she had been formed for the express purpose of his holding her. Her legs were long, pale and flawless. Her whole body seemed flawless to him, so unlike his, which had been thrown, ripped, broken and abused so many times. His ribs were throbbing, but he hadn't noticed them before. She made pain go away. She made everything in the world go away except the two of them.

He'd never counted the number of women with whom he'd made love. Too many, he'd once cynically supposed, for sex to mean anything more than physical pleasure, sometimes intense, sometimes little more than a needed release.

He brushed his cheek against Serena's, ran his hand up and down her silky flank. She was different. When he made love to her he felt emotions, sensations he had never imagined a mere mortal could feel.

To caress her was like a drug, and once he started, he couldn't bear to stop. To be touched by her in turn was like catching fire, except it didn't hurt; it turned him into a blind and hungry flame, hungry only for her. And when he entered her, in the most intimate act of love, it was a little like dying, and a lot like turning into a god.

Only she had ever done that to him. He knew only she ever would.

"Cal?" she asked, nuzzling against him. "Do you suppose it was wrong to do it here? I mean it was a church once. Do you suppose it was sacrilege?"

He turned to her, taking her face between his hands. "He never said a church. Just a meeting house. And what happens between us isn't sacrilege. Heaven would approve. How could this be so good if it didn't?''

She laid her finger against his lips to silence him. "Don't say things like that. You might make what we've done even worse."

"Does it feel to you like we did anything wrong?" he asked. He laid his hand between her breasts, over her heart. "Does it feel wrong here?"

Her heart leaped beneath his touch. "No."

He took her hand and placed it over his own heart so that she could feel its hard, steady thud through the solid flesh of his chest. "It doesn't feel wrong here, either."

He kissed her. "I love you. Tell me that you love me."

She moved her hand and drew back from him, turning away. She pulled the blanket more tightly around herself and stared unhappily at the piano in the moonlight. "No. I can't say that. I don't want you to say it, either."

Beneath the blanket, he put his hand on her bare waist. He kissed her between her shoulder blades, a long, lingering kiss that made her quiver with desire and sorrow.

He kissed her up and down her spine, her nape, her shoulders. He ran his hands, gentle and knowing, over her body until she gave a ragged sigh and turned to him, knowing they were going to make love again, and it would be even more lovely and aching and intense than before.

"Some things," he said, bending to take her lips, "you don't need words to say."

THE NEXT FEW DAYS seemed to Serena to pass by in a sort of golden dream. She and Cal went bareback riding on the big roan, she sitting before him, his arm around her waist, his thighs tight against hers.

They cantered and galloped over the plains in a way she hadn't done since childhood. He was an excellent rider, moving with the horse as if he were one with it, and riding with him was like riding with the wind.

The next day he found a small college in a neighboring town that was holding a film festival. He took her to see Dustin Hoffman and Jon Voight in *Midnight Cowboy,* and its ending made her weep like a child. He held her, drying her tears and trying to soothe her with buttered popcorn.

Then he took her to see Rick Moranis in *The Little Shop of Horrors.* She laughed until her ribs hurt, and he held her and laughed with her. Afterward in the parking lot, he sang all of "The Dentist" song to her, making her dissolve into laughter again. He said he'd memorized it to torment his sister, who was upset that dentists had bought a share in the horse she was training.

They ate hot dogs in the park, they ate lobsters in the county's best restaurant. They tried making lasagna at Serena's apartment and ended up creating the largest indigestible lump of cheese and pasta in Texas. Serena had another laughing fit, and Cal sighed and sent out for a pizza.

They danced in one of Cal's beloved honky-tonks, doing the traditional Western dances like the cotton-eyed Joe and Texas two-step, all the glides and kicks and promenades. "You're a regular little goat-ropin' kicker," he teased her as they made their way around the floor. She hooked her thumb in the belt loop of his jeans and grinned up at him.

On Valentine's Day, Cal proposed an evening of feasting on the great Texan junk foods. They picnicked in his hotel room on frito pie, corn bread crumbled in buttermilk, Dr. Pepper, Moon pies, and frozen Snicker bars. Serena refused to try the pickled pig's feet or put salted peanuts into her Dr. Pepper. Cal accused her of being a wimp and a Yankee.

They watched the UT-Baylor basketball game on television and were pleased to discover that they both loved basketball, Serena almost fanatically. Cal grinned and nibbled her ear because she was the only girl he'd ever met who could name the entire starting lineup of Texas's 1979 nemesis, the Arkansas Razorbacks.

They also made love in bed, though it didn't seem to matter in whose bed, in his king-size one or her single one. Making love seemed as natural and necessary as breathing to them, but it was like breathing a rarified air, one that ran through their systems with the same intoxicating effect as enchanted wine.

Cal stopped speaking of marriage. He said he would wait until she was ready. As long as Serena didn't think of the future, she was blissfully happy. She knew she was in love, although she refused to say the words or even think them.

But she knew that being in love showed. At the shop she could feel Jesus and Estaban stealing furtive glances at her and smiling knowingly. Tracey said nothing but carried herself about with a self-satisfied air that said, I told you so.

On the street, she found herself smiling at strangers, and when she and Cal were together, strangers smiled at them, at the way they held hands and leaned toward each other and looked into each other's eyes.

Cal finished his roping event in record time at the Wolverton rodeo, and when he was done, he turned and waved his Stetson at Serena in the stands. Out of the thousands of people in the stands she was the only one he saw.

The other cowboys recognized his condition and had a hoot and holler over it.

"Boys, the honky-tonk devil's done retired. He's found the meadow muffin of his dreams."

"The ol' cutter? Cal? No way."

"Hey—miracles happen."

"I've seen her. She'll make your spurs jangle."

Cal only grinned. Later, behind the chutes, his saddle slung over his shoulder, his hat pushed back at a jaunty angle, he grinned more widely when he saw Serena making her way toward him. She looked radiant, and her answering smile made his heart soar like an eagle.

"You were fabulous." She smiled, throwing her arms around his neck and kissing his chin.

He slipped an arm around her and shrugged. "Well," he said with false modesty, "I suppose I was."

"How could you give up roping, really?"

"Quit while I'm ahead. It's not as if I haven't had my run at it. Besides, after twelve years, it's a mite repetitious."

He offered her his free arm and walked her to the side of the chutes so they could watch the roan work again. Cal had loaned it to a little cowboy from Splendora whose own horse had come up lame.

"I wouldn't mind if you gave up bronc riding," she said, caressing the muscles that played under his sleeve. "The bronc riding scares me. I don't know why you do it."

"Had to," he said easily, "to qualify for all-around. No, I won't miss broncs. Had too many dance on my spine. Hot damn! Look at that horse. He's made that kid one happy cowboy."

The roan had stopped on a dime, keeping the rope taut, backing up just so, helping the boy from Splendora make excellent time. Cal grinned in appreciation.

She looked up at him, her eyes shining. At that moment she was so in love with him that she could not have denied it if she'd wanted to. Lately he'd made her begin to believe that maybe there could be a future for them, that maybe some chances could be so wonderful, they were worth taking. He made her believe it now.

HER WORLD came tumbling down the next morning at work. Only she and Tracey were in the shop when the phone rang. Tracey answered. She listened for a moment, and her face grew first grave, then troubled.

"Serena," she called into the workroom, "it's for you. It's Patti."

Serena turned from the sewing machine and rose from her chair numbly. *Trouble,* she thought fatalistically. She could hear it clearly in Tracey's voice. *Patti was on the phone and there was trouble.*

Anxiety swarmed through her as she took the receiver. Tracey got up from the desk and tactfully left the room, closing the door behind her.

"Patti?"

"Serena? Oh, Serena!" Patti said. She was crying. Serena's blood froze. *Something terrible is happening,* she thought. A dark cloud formed on the horizon of her mind, growing swiftly, rushing toward her.

"Patti? What is it?" She pushed her hand through her hair, her whole body tense.

"Serena, I think I'm pregnant."

Serena felt as if she had been physically struck, knocked violently across the room. But she had not moved, she was motionless, almost paralyzed. *"What?"* she demanded, horrified.

"I think I'm pregnant," Patti repeated in the same tearful voice. "And Serena, if I am, there's no way I won't have this baby. No way. But I'm afraid to tell him—tell Jerry. What if he doesn't want it? And I've never told him about the Huntington's. What if he doesn't want *me?* What'll I tell the girls? How'll I keep working? What'll I do?"

Stunned, Serena raked her hand through her hair. She had to try to think clearly, but she could hardly think at all. Vaguely she remembered that Patti had seemed more nervous than usual last week, but Serena had been too caught up in her own troubles to notice. Now the fact hit her so hard she felt ill.

"Patti, if he doesn't want it—how can you support three kids? What kind of example is this for the girls? Now listen to me—"

"I said I'll *have* it," Patti practically screamed. She sounded at the edge of hysteria.

"Patti, calm down. Have you been to a doctor? Have you taken one of those home tests? That's what you've got to do right away. Find out for sure."

"No," Patti said flatly. "I won't. I'm too scared. Then it'll be final. It'll be real."

"Maybe you're scared for no reason," Serena argued desperately. "Listen, I'll come straight to Amarillo—I'll be with you."

"Serena," Patti said, her voice a whimper, "I'm scared of more than that. I'm scared I've got *it*. What killed Grandpa and Daddy. I—I—my hands keep shaking lately. My shoulder keeps j-jumping. This morning I dropped a bowl of cereal—it was like it *leaped* out of my hand—and my head feels funny. I don't want to see a doctor. I won't see a doctor. What if he says I have *it?* What'll I do? About Dovey and Hope? And the baby? I've got to have the baby, Serena. It might have a chance. What if it was the only one of us that has a chance?"

"Where are you?" Serena asked. *Think, think, think,* her mind commanded. "At work?"

"At home. I couldn't go to work. I don't want people to see my hands shake. I can't face Jerry. The girls are at school. Oh, Serena, what am I going to *do?*"

All life seemed to have flowed from Serena, as if Patti had opened a fatal wound. She felt empty, stricken, yet curiously calm. "Don't do a thing. You wait for me, do you hear? I can get there in a couple of hours. I'll take care of you. I'll figure out something. I'll handle everything."

It took a long time to talk Patti into a semblance of calm, and all the while Serena said the soothing words, her mind spun. In her worst nightmares she had never envisioned this scenario. It was as if her deepest fears had mated and produced a teeming litter of new fears, more threatening and venomous than the old ones.

Shock had done something eerie to her vision, and the room seemed to wink in and out of darkness. *The world's crashed down around me,* she thought, dazed. Until this moment, she had thought the words were a cliché. Now she understood: they described precisely how she felt, as if the world had somehow come undone and crashed down upon her.

She was terrified for Patti, for the girls, for all of them. What if Patti *was* ill? What if the disease had been lurking in her body all these years, and had finally come out of hiding? How would Patti, who had denied the very possibility all these years, deal with it? Would Jerry marry a woman so seriously afflicted? What would Pattie do about the baby if he did not want her?

Oh, God, thought Serena, *I was insane ever to think I could have a normal life. I was insane ever to think of a future with Cal. Insane.*

When she hung up the phone at last, she buried her face in her hands, trying to calm herself. She had no faith at all that Jerry, whom she had never met, would marry Patti. Perhaps Patti only imagined he was genuinely interested; perhaps it was only another symptom of her illness: how could Serena know anything for sure? Wasn't this how her life always had been, always would be?

If Patti was really ill, Serena would have to take care of her. And provide for the girls. Worse, if Patti had the disease, then Dovey and Hope were at risk, too, and that meant Serena not only had to guide them through their mother's sickness, but teach them how to live with the possibility of it in their own lives.

If anything happened to Dovey or Hope, there was only Serena to handle that, as well. On top of that, there might be a baby—a *baby*. How could Patti do such a thing? Serena would end up caring for all of them: Patti, Dovey, Hope and a baby, too. Oh, God, she thought, and the baby would be at risk, too. The whole thing was a nightmare, a curse that kept repeating and repeating itself.

She couldn't drag Cal into such a hopelessly tangled mess. He was still a young man, vital and full of careless cheer. Life should stretch before him full of happiness and possibility, not as an endless snake pit of responsibilities, other people's relatives, other men's children, another family's illnesses.

She let her hands drop to her sides, and stood, tearless, staring out the window without seeing. If nothing else, she thought emptily, Patti's call should reteach her the lesson she had so briefly, so carelessly forgotten: what happened to her father and grandfather could also happen to her, at any time.

Yes, she thought with bitterness, that would be the perfect icing on the cake, wouldn't it? The disease would get both of them, Patti and her, too. And then what would Cal have if he'd married her? Nothing but ashes and gall.

The door between the shop and office opened almost timidly. "Serena?" Tracey's eyes were haunted with apprehension.

"Patti—has problems," Serena said shortly, squaring her shoulders. "She thinks she might be sick. I have to go to her. I'm sorry."

A brief, ominous silence settled between them.

Then Tracey said, "Sick?" Fear crossed her face. She knew what Serena meant.

Serena nodded, trying to stay in control of herself. "She's afraid it's Huntington's. Well, you know Patti. The only way to get her to a doctor is drag her. Yours truly has to go drag." She took a deep breath. "We'll take this one step at a time. It may be nothing. Patti's always been the excitable one. Who knows?"

Serena hesitated. She wished she could tell Tracey about the baby, but she couldn't. Its existence was not yet a certainty, and she wouldn't discuss Patti's indiscretions; it would be disloyal.

Serena shrugged with a philosophic calm that was totally false. "So—if I'm going to Amarillo, I'd better get a wiggle on. Sorry, Trace. I'll be back as soon as I can."

"Oh, Serena, I *am* sorry," Tracey said, tears brimming in her amber eyes. "What about Cal? What should I tell him? Aren't you supposed to see him this afternoon?"

"Don't tell him anything," Serena said emphatically. "And don't tell him I'm at Patti's. I don't want his help on this. It's family business, not his."

"Serena," Tracey objected, "you can't treat him like that—just go off without saying anything."

"I'll treat him any way I like," she answered with a harshness that surprised even herself. "It's none of his business. I'll call him or something."

I'll call him and tell him it's over, she thought, her heart full of terror and bitterness. *This time I'll make him go away. I'll drive him away. I'll shame him if that's what it takes—I'll make him hate me if I have to.*

Tracey shook her head in disapproval. "I don't like the look on your face. You shouldn't let this change things between you and him. You—"

"Well, excuse my face," Serena said with asperity, "*and* the look on it. I've had a little bad news, my sister needs me, so if you don't mind, my face and I'll be on our way. As for Cal, I'll deal with him, and if you so much as *mention this* to him, I'll never forgive you. I'll dissolve this partnership so fast your head'll spin, and I'll never speak to you again. Have you got that?"

Tracey's expression was half angry, half wounded. "Yes," she said slowly. "I've got it."

"Good," Serena said and jerked her jacket from its hook on the wall. She thrust her arms into its sleeves, jammed her hat on her head, its brim low, and started out the door, her face taut with control.

"Serena!" Tracey's voice halted her. She turned and looked at Tracey, from whose face all anger had fled.

She looked sweet and kind and hopeful, all the things that she truly was and that Serena admired in her.

"I know it sounds stupid," Tracey said with an awkward shrug and a pained expression, "but good luck. Okay?" She tried to smile, but couldn't.

"Thank you," Serena said, her voice gentle again. "I'll stay in touch, Trace."

She left, pulling the door shut behind her, ran down the stairs and walked quickly across the parking lot. She figured she could be packed and out of Wolverton in forty-five minutes, driving toward Amarillo and away from Cal.

She did not know yet how she would tell him goodbye. First she had to tend to Patti and Patti's legion of problems. Then she must tell him goodbye, she realized. This time for good. This time forever.

Her life was too burdensome, too precarious to share. And what cut her most deeply was that she had known all along. Like a fool she had let herself fall in love with him anyway. Like a fool, a fool, a perfect fool.

"WHERE IS SHE?" Cal demanded. He had intercepted Tracey in the parking lot that evening at La Herencia. The sun almost down, but the air was still warm with the hint of coming spring.

Tracey tried to sidestep him, to escape to the safety of her car. On the phone she had barely been able to fend off his unrelenting questions. In person, she had no idea how to deal with him. She was determined not to betray Serena, even if she didn't agree with her.

Cal put his hand on Tracey's arm, gentle but inexorable, refusing to let her slip away. "Get in that car without saying where she is," he said, "and you'll drive down the street with me hanging on to your bumper—I swear it."

His eyes flashed with anger. Tracey was a small woman, far smaller than Serena, but beneath her elfin exterior lurked a stubbornness that had far exceeded Cal's patience. He glared at her, tightening his hold on her elbow.

"You *know* I don't mean her any harm. I'd sooner cut off my hand than hurt her. What's happened? Where'd she go? Why doesn't she want me to know? There's trouble, isn't there? Is something wrong? She isn't sick or something?"

Anger mixed with guilt in Tracey's face. "She's fine," she said, trying to jerk her arm away. "Don't use macho tactics on me. They won't work."

"Don't use female wiles on me," he said, gripping her more tightly. "They won't work, either. Cut the coyness. I want straight answers."

"Get your answers from Serena. My instructions are to stay out of this. She's my friend. My friend asked me not to talk. I'm not talking."

Ineffectually she pushed at his hand, stopping just short of swatting it.

"I'll get my answers from Serena. But first I have to find her. Where'd she go? Back to her sister's?"

Tracey stopped struggling. She stared up at Cal with what little dignity she could muster. "All you're getting out of me is my name, rank and serial number."

"That's it, isn't it?" he demanded from between his teeth. "She's at her sister's, isn't she? That's where she went before. In Amarillo. I know she's got a sister in Amarillo, so don't act like you never heard of her."

"No hablo inglés. Yo soy incomunicada."

Once again Cal was convinced that Tracey, determined though she was to conceal the truth, was ill-equipped to hide it. He could tell by her eyes and the set of her mouth that he had hit upon the correct answer.

Although his mind churned with apprehension, he tried to think clearly, logically.

He bent so that he could look Tracey in the eye. "She's at her sister's," he said with conviction. "Why? Is something wrong there, something she doesn't want me to know about?"

Tracey's face went so white that it scared him. He swore because suddenly he knew what she was hiding and why. He felt sick, as if a horse had thrown him and stepped on him, crushing something vital, tearing the air out of him.

He dropped his hand from her elbow. "Oh, God, that's it, isn't it?" Weariness and pain twisted his voice. "Her sister's sick, isn't she? They're afraid she's got it. What's she have—two kids?—girls, right?"

Tracey said nothing. She crossed her arms as if to ward off a sudden chill and stared up at him, her eyes looking unnaturally large and dark in her pale face. She didn't say anything, but she didn't have to. Cal knew for certain now.

"Are they sure? Or do they just think *maybe?*" he asked. His anger had evaporated, and he was truly sorry he had seized Tracey the way he had.

She shook her head and hugged herself more tightly. She looked away from him and bit her lip as she had been doing throughout their argument. She had worn all her lipstick off. She looked about eight years old to Cal, an unhappy and delicate child.

"I'm not supposed to talk to you about it," she said, huddling deeper into her jacket so that she looked even smaller.

"Look," he said. A muscle jerked in his cheek and he set his jaw against it. "Look, I just know her sister's name is Patti. Tell me her last name. That's all I ask."

"I can't," Tracey said, still staring off into the distance and biting her lip harder. The wind ruffled her hair into a waiflike disorder.

"Look," he repeated with feeling, "I *love* her."

Tracey nodded and swallowed.

"She shouldn't have to face this alone. I don't want her to face it alone. She must be scared."

Tracey shrugged helplessly. "I promised."

"This is going tear her into little pieces," Cal persisted. "It'll make her start seeing things differently. She may see them wrong. She was starting to say *yes* to life—maybe for the first time since she was a kid. I don't want her saying *no* again. It isn't right."

Tracey said nothing. Her mouth took on a hopeless curve that told him the situation was out of her control. She could do nothing.

He reached out and took her hand, a sort of desperate tenderness in his touch. She flinched but did not resist.

"Tracey," he said softly. "Tell me Patti's last name. Please. It won't be wrong of you. I promise."

She met his eyes at last, her mouth in the same unhappy line. "I won't betray her," she said, her voice shaky. "Life's done enough of that. I won't do it, too."

She drew her hand away, opened her car door and got in. She cast him a last, reproachful glance as she put the car into gear. Then she drove away and left him standing alone.

He watched after her, still feeling punch-drunk. He knew what it meant if Patti was sick. Serena would shut him out again, for God knew how long. Probably forever if she could. An empty sense of loss churned through him, swelling like distant thunder rolling nearer.

He looked up at the sky, which was turning dark. "I used to always think I was lucky," he whispered to the thickening night. "What happened? What the hell happened?"

Only the empty sigh of the wind answered him.

CHAPTER ELEVEN

I USED TO CONSIDER myself the luckiest person on earth, Beverly thought in perplexity. *What on earth happened?*

She pulled the Cadillac into the drive of the McKinney ranch. Evening was falling fast, and she saw Grandpa Hank sitting on the front porch of his little rock house, soaking up the last of the day's faint warmth.

She smiled gaily at him and wiggled her fingers in a wave of greeting. He either did not see her or pretended not to see her. With Hank, a person could never be sure. Beverly had been raised to respect her elders, but she sometimes thought that Hank went out of his way to be as unrespectable as he possibly could.

She saw Lynn come out of the little stone house, hand Hank a cup of coffee and sit beside him in the other of Hank's old sway-backed rockers.

Oh, poot, thought Beverly. She'd come to see Lynn, but now she'd have to cope with Hank, too. What she did not need in her life was another person who was frail and sickly. She wanted, for a change, a little sympathy for herself.

Lynn had said she was worried about Grandpa Hank lately, that since Cal left so suddenly, Hank just hadn't seemed to be himself. Beverly privately thought that Hank's not being himself would be an improvement, but was too polite to say so.

She got out of the Cadillac, her long blond hair fluttering in the breeze, and walked toward Hank's porch, determined to be as sweet as pie to the old man.

She had vowed to be as sweet as pie to *everyone* since the dreadful day of her shame and after her strange and emotional set-to with Cal the day after that.

Lori Porter and Carolyn were still cool to Beverly, but they would forgive her, slowly but surely. She was being so responsible and considerate around the ranch that Carolyn had finally shooed her out of the house tonight.

"Beverly, stop *fussing*," Carolyn had ordered. "Do you know the meaning of the word overcompensation? Let me be. Go see Lynn. Go see if anybody's heard from Cal. J.T.'s upset, Cal coming home and leaving so suddenly."

Beverly had bitten her tongue and not said anything about Cal. She knew he had gone back to Wolverton to try to win the girl he loved, which she considered very romantic and dramatic and certainly a lot more fun than she, Beverly, was having.

The scene with Cal had affected Beverly deeply for a few days. She'd even wondered vaguely if she'd actually been in love with Cal all these years and never admitted it. Stranger things had happened.

She envied the girl he loved and wished she was as lucky. Certainly no handsome devil was driving back and forth across Texas to woo Beverly.

Cal was lucky, too, she thought, to have someone to care about so much. Love had changed him, made him into somebody different, deeper, stronger.

It was partly for Cal's sake that she'd plunged into work at the hospital. Hadn't he asked her to do it for him? And hadn't she suddenly wanted to do something for him, to win his approval and respect and affection?

She *did* like children, and she *was* good with them; Cal was right. All she had to do was appear in the ward and look pretty and smile and say all the right things, and she'd see their faces brighten.

She did her very best. Last week she'd cut out two social lunches and her sorority alumnae meeting. Her effort and sacrifice should have made anyone happy, Beverly thought. If she did any more work she'd practically be Texas's answer to Mother Teresa.

But Dr. Purdy wasn't satisfied. He wanted more. He always wanted more from Beverly, and it wasn't fair. "I've got your body here," he'd said yesterday. "Now if I can get your mind and heart, I just might have something."

Beverly had been hurt and insulted. It was true she tried to keep a mental and emotional distance from the children, and that she stayed away from those with truly serious maladies. But that was only because she was more easily touched than Nate Purdy could ever guess.

Now he was asking her to do something almost impossible, and she resented it, and she wanted Lynn to commiserate with her. Around her own house or around Nate, she didn't dare complain. She was still on probation for her sins.

She climbed the stairs of Hank's porch and gave him her best smile. "Why, Grandpa Hank, what a pleasure to see you. Been enjoying the sunset? It was *fab-u-lous*. And you're looking fabulous yourself."

He really wasn't looking well, though, Beverly noted. He seemed shrunken to her, the fine bones of his face almost shining through his papery skin. Her eyes met Lynn's, and Lynn sent her a silent message: *He's lost strength. I don't like this.*

Hank's eyes, however, were as alert as ever. They flicked critically over Beverly. "A fab-u-lous sunset?" he asked sarcastically. "Glad you approved."

Lynn smiled. "Hi, Bev. What brings you out?"

Beverly sat on the porch railing, adjusting the fringes of her suede jacket and crossing her boots prettily. "Why, Mama just kicked me out of the house. I was trying to be helpful, but she seemed to think I was too helpful, if you know what I mean. How's everything?"

"Just fine," Lynn said brightly, reaching over to squeeze Hank's hand.

"It's not fine," Hank contradicted. He squinted malevolently at Beverly, then nodded at Lynn. "She's got dental problems."

"Dental problems?" Beverly said, as sympathetically as she could. But her heart sank. Was everyone in the world going to be a medical case?

Lynn gave Hank's hand a pat that was half affectionate, half disapproving. "He's teasing," she said, casting Hank a look of reproof. "I was just carrying on about those dentists. The ones who bought a share of Lightning. I just don't trust people who'd buy a horse without looking at it. What would a dentist know about training a horse?"

"Well, he'd probably know a great deal about its teeth," Beverly said helpfully. "And that's *something*. Have you met any of them yet?"

"No," Lynn admitted, "and I don't like the idea of absentee owners. You'd think they'd show more interest in this. It's probably only a tax write-off to them. I didn't put in all this time and effort to be somebody's tax write-off."

"Well, don't go borrowing trouble before you've got it," Beverly advised. "Who knows? One of them might be perfectly divine."

"A *dentist?*" Lynn said with scorn.

"I know some very lovely girls who've married dentists," Beverly said. "Miss Pennsylvania married a dentist."

"I will *never* marry a dentist." Lynn wrinkled her nose in distaste. "Ugh."

Beverly shrugged and played with her fringes. "Has anybody heard from Cal?" she asked casually. "Mama wanted to know."

Lynn looked guilty, and Hank tilted his head to peer at Beverly in the fading light. "We was just wonderin' the same about you," he rasped.

"Me?" Beverly said, unpleasantly surprised.

"You," Hank said. "You was the last to talk with him. You fetched him off to town. When he come back he couldn't get out of here fast enough. Something happened—what?"

"Wh-why, nothing," she stammered.

"You don't know why he shot out of here like a bat out of hell?" Hank asked, lowering a white eyebrow. He clearly didn't believe her.

"Indeed I don't," Beverly lied, losing herself once more in attentions to her fringe. "I was as surprised as anybody." She took a deep breath and sighed. "Mmm. Doesn't it feel like spring? I can almost smell the bluebonnets."

"I can almost smell a rat," Hank said, settling back in his chair. He made a weak impatient, waving gesture. "But I'm too tuckered to chase it. Why don't you women shoo? Come back when you want, to want to talk to a man like a man, man to man."

"What?" Beverly asked, perplexed. "I'm sure I don't know what you mean, Grandpa."

"You know exactly what I mean," Hank muttered tiredly, laying his head against the chair's headrest and turning his gaze from Beverly. "And I *ain't* your grandpa."

Oh, Beverly thought in frustration, he would be hateful just when she was trying her hardest to be sweet. And he would accuse her of withholding information when all she was trying to do was be loyal to Cal. She managed to smile at him. "Why, it's just that we *all* think of you as our grandpa—"

"Shoo," Hank said, flicking his fingers at her feebly.

"He wants a nap," Lynn said. "Let me walk him inside."

"Oh, I'll help you," Beverly said with a sigh. "You're too little to do it alone." She got one side of

Hank and helped hoist him to his feet. Lord knew she'd helped enough people in and out of beds this week.

They got Hank into his house and settled in his armchair with an afghan tucked around him. "I'll come back to check on you in about an hour, Grandpa," Lynn said. "You have a good nap."

Hank's eyes fluttered shut. "Shoo."

"My," said Beverly, as they descended the stairs and started toward the ranch house, "he doesn't seem a *bit* strong. Have you called Nate Purdy?"

Lynn shoved her hands into the pockets of her light jacket. "He was here this afternoon. Grandpa was as ornery as possible, of course. But Nate says it's only a touch of that flu going around. But at Grandpa's age it's scary. Sometimes I think maybe he won't make it to one hundred." She shook her head so that her auburn ponytail swung. "I hope he makes it. I really do." Lynn kicked at the brown grass disconsolately.

Beverly reached over and straightened Lynn's jacket collar, which was crooked. "Of *course* he'll make it, punkin. He's just having a sinking spell, that's all. Don't you worry. There's certainly nothing wrong with his mind."

Oh, heavens, Beverly thought in frustration, *I sound just the way I do at the hospital.*

But Lynn smiled up at her through the falling dusk. "Sorry. Things are just getting to me, you know? Grandpa this way. This crazy business with the dentists. And Cal going off with no explanation—after he said he'd stay."

Lynn kicked at the grass again and shook her head. "I just don't understand about Cal. Grandpa thinks it's about a woman—a woman who's maybe—I don't know how to say it—unsuitable. He's got it in his head that Cal might do something catastrophic."

She darted another look, a piercing one, at Beverly. "You don't know anything about this, do you? Grandpa says after Cal took you to town, he came back looking like he was aiming to go fight for the Alamo alone against Santa Anna. *Did* he say anything to you? *Did* something happen?"

Beverly tossed her hair in the breeze and took another deep breath. She smiled. "Now when did Cal ever tell *me* one single thing? He thinks my brains are feathers. All that happened was we saw Mary Alice Priest being flirted up by some scandalously handsome man with a mustache."

"That Luke Harte person," Lynn said, making a distasteful face. "He's looking for work. He asked Daddy, but Daddy wouldn't hire him. Daddy's worried about Cal, too. He's scared he's going to get really hurt rodeoing. That his luck can't last forever. And Grandpa's got him half-convinced that Cal's really tangled up with some woman who isn't right for him."

They had reached the back patio of the ranch house. The pool was still covered for winter, and the flagstones were bare. All the ornamental plants were gone until spring.

"Want to go in?" Lynn asked. "Ruth and Ty have gone to a dance, but Daddy and Cynthia are home. Or would you rather stay out here?"

"Let's stay out," Beverly said, her heart suddenly troubled. Cal was in love, deeply in love. Why was everyone suddenly thinking the woman was wrong before they were even sure she existed? Just because of some silly whim of Hank's? It hardly seemed fair when Cal loved the woman so much; it violated Beverly's sense of the romantic.

Cal had said the woman was at risk for a serious illness, and Beverly admired his bravery. What had he told her—that it was no crime, no sin to be sick? She had seen that lately, working in the hospital. She just wasn't able to face it as fearlessly as Cal. That was her problem.

She pulled out one of the wrought-iron chairs beside the patio table. She sat, carefully arranging her fringes. "Tell me," she said in her most innocent voice, "why everybody's so worried that Cal's involved with somebody who isn't *right?* Right in what way, exactly?"

Lynn sat on the table's edge and picked the design in its wrought iron. "I don't know. Just—not right, you know. Grandpa's got this hunch that Cal's got himself in a situation where he could get hurt. And it concerns a woman somehow."

"Oh, poot," Beverly said with a shake of her head. "Grandpa Hank's got a hunch that nobody ever really landed on the moon. That NASA made the whole thing up for television. He once told me that Eleanor Roosevelt and J. Edgar Hoover were the same person."

Lynn exploded into snickers.

"He did," Beverly said reprovingly. She shook her head in exasperation. "Now you're asking me to take him seriously when he has some *hunch* about a woman he's never met? I declare, you'd think Cal didn't have a brain in his head, when he probably knows more about women than the rest of the men in this family combined. Cal could have any woman he wants. I can't imagine him picking the wrong one—heavens."

Lynn sobered and pushed a stray tress of hair back into place. "You're right. Why do I always forget that under all that buffing and polishing you're really smart?"

"Because *everybody* forgets I'm smart," Beverly answered unhappily. Her grades in college had been nearly perfect. "I reckon I'm just not smart in ways that count."

"Oh, fiddle," said Lynn, dismissing the thought. "Don't talk like that. How's the hospital?"

Beverly suddenly found she was not as anxious to discuss her problems as she had thought. Compared to Cal's difficulty, or even Lynn's worry about Hank, her own troubles seemed less imposing than they had. "Oh, everything's fine," she said vaguely and smiled.

"Nate Purdy says you're a wonder, and that he has a boy he particularly wants you to work with—but you're resisting. Are you going to give up and do it? Nate almost always gets his way. If he didn't, he couldn't handle Grandpa."

Beverly tossed Lynn a disbelieving look. "Well, he doesn't tell *me* that I'm a wonder. He always seems to find me wanting. He says I don't put my heart in it. As if it wasn't hard enough to put my *body* into it, for land's sake. I've smiled until my jaw aches, I tell you. I've been such a bundle of cheer it's begun to depress me."

Lynn reached over and squeezed Beverly's soft hand with her callused one. "I'm sure you're a wonder. He probably just thinks you could be an even bigger one. But come on— Truth. Is your heart in it?"

She released Beverly's hand and Beverly self-consciously began to adjust her rings. "No," she said with perfect honesty. "I'm still afraid. Of getting involved. Of getting hurt. You know."

The wind seemed to rise a notch, and a chill suddenly nipped in the air. Both women thought of Beverly's father, Frank, dead two years ago in the hospital's emergency ward. Beverly hadn't been the same since.

"I know," Lynn said softly. "So…what about this child? A boy, Nate said. Why don't you want to work with him?"

Beverly sighed and stared off into the thickening shadows. "Oh, it's *so* depressing, Lynn. He's not a child, really. He's sixteen. He's been in and out of the hospital for a year and a half. Apparently he's seen me there. And now—" she shrugged, the words paining her "—well, now he's really, *really* sick, you know? And he told Nate he'd love for me to visit him. Maybe sort of make special visits. He's in a private room, not the ward."

Lynn flinched slightly. "He's not doing well?"

Beverly shook her head. "Oh, Lynn," she said miserably, "it sounds like he has a crush on me. Here he is, this poor sixteen-year-old kid, sick as can be, and he thinks he has a *crush* on me. Nate wants me to go in there and flirt him up and smile and be cheerful, but—''

She stopped and swallowed hard. She couldn't go on. Tears misted her blue eyes.

Lynn nodded. "I see. You don't have to explain."

Beverly threw out both hands in a helpless gesture. "I don't? Tell that to Nate Purdy. Better yet, tell it to the boy—Nate wants me to walk in there tomorrow, just as if nothing's wrong. 'I want you to make that kid feel like a million bucks,' he says. 'You can do it,' he says. Well, I'm a human person, not a light bulb he can switch off and on. Doesn't he realize *I* have feelings, too?''

The wind gusted slightly, rattling the bare branches of the forsythia bushes. "Have you ever told him how you feel?" Lynn asked, her voice gentle.

Beverly shook her head. "No. I can't. It's not fair for me to feel like this. Because being sick isn't a crime. It isn't a sin. But—I can't do it. I can't walk in that room and smile. I just *can't.*''

"Beverly," Lynn said as kindly as she could, "then just tell Nate. Be honest. That's all there is to it. I couldn't do it, either."

But nobody expects you to do it, Beverly wanted to cry. *Nobody's trying to make you do it or feel terrible.* Instead she just nodded and brushed the moisture from her eyes.

"I suppose," she said as gamely as she could. "Because I *can't* do it, Lynn. I just can't."

"Let's go inside," Lynn suggested, shivering in her jacket. "It's getting cold."

"No," Beverly said, shaking her head so that her long hair rippled. She didn't want J.T. or Cynthia to see her in her present mood. "I believe I'll go home and grovel. I think I've almost groveled my way back into Mama's good graces. Lori's still going to take some work."

She rose, and Lynn got up with her. Lynn put her hand companionably on the shoulder of Beverly's suede jacket. They walked in silence to the Cadillac. The stars were faint above them.

Beverly tried not to think about tomorrow and what Nate Purdy wanted her to do. Lynn was right. She should just explain and tell Nate she couldn't.

But she kept thinking of Cal. He was out there somewhere under those same pale stars, risking his heart in ways she didn't begin to dare. He wouldn't tell her to quit, she knew. He'd tell her to go ahead, to go to the boy, take a chance on breaking her heart.

But she wasn't like Cal. He was the gambler, the risk taker, the brave one, not she. Beverly was terrified to gamble with her feelings. What if she lost?

IT WAS THREE O'CLOCK in the morning. Tracey hesitated, then knocked on the door of the hotel room. The night clerk at the desk had given her a knowing smirk when she'd asked for Cal, as if there was only one reason a young woman would come to a hotel looking for a man at this time of night.

She knocked on the door with such resolution and such force that her knuckles burned. A few seconds of silence seemed to echo down the hall. Then the door swung open.

Tracey stared up at Cal and squared her jaw. He was shirtless and wore no belt with his low-slung faded jeans. His brown hair hung over his forehead and his eyes were shadowed. He looked like a man who had tried to sleep and could not.

His hazel eyes narrowed when he saw Tracey, and one brow went up in an unspoken question. Tracey glanced away from him, embarrassed by his half-naked body. He exuded sexuality without even trying to. It was no wonder that Serena had succumbed to him.

She spoke hastily, before she could change her mind. She kept her eyes trained on the rough texture of the plaster on the wall. "I came to tell you where she is," she said, her voice flat and determined. "You're right. She's with Patti. Patti's last name is Chadron. Her address is 2902 Sorrel Street. In Amarillo. I've written it down. Along with the phone number. Here. Take it."

She thrust a folded paper at him, still not looking at him. Cal took it, opened it, glanced at the name, address and phone number written there. He still said nothing.

Tracey glanced up at him. His face was stiff with control, but troubled. "I thought a long time about this," she said, biting her lip. "I couldn't sleep. And I came here because—" she hesitated, staring fixedly at the plaster again "—because I thought this was something that I should do face-to-face. She didn't want me to tell you. She said she wouldn't speak to me again if I did. That she'd dissolve our partnership. She probably will. Well, dammit, she can if she wants to. I just—I can't watch her do this to herself."

"Patti's sick, isn't she?" Cal asked. "How sick?"

Tracey shook her head and shrugged. "I don't know. I didn't get any details. But you're right. Serena thinks she has it. After she talked to her Patti looked like all the ghosts in hell had risen up."

"Come in," Cal said, reaching for her. His hand closed on her arm, and he drew her into the room. "Tell me everything you know. Everything."

Tracey swallowed harder, but allowed him to lead her inside. He closed the door, and she was glad when he reached for his shirt and put it on, buttoning it from the bottom.

He had a battered leather suitcase and he began to pack it even as he buttoned his shirt. Tracey stood watching, clenching and unclenching her hands nervously at her sides. "I don't know much more. She's dreaded this for years. You know that."

He nodded. "I know that."

"Patti's a little—scatterbrained, I guess. Serena's always been the responsible one. Maybe too responsible. Patti's tried—wanted to live a normal life. I don't think she ever accepted the possibility that something...might happen to her. Serena's always been the one who's done the worrying, made the provisions."

He nodded again, his face grim. "Two kids? Patti's got two kids?"

Tracey crossed her arms. "Yes. Girls. Eleven and twelve. And if anything ever happened to Patti, Serena's the only one they'd have. And Serena'd have to take care of Patti's medical expenses. It's a—a big responsibility. It's something she's always had to think about. Oh, Cal, she's been worrying about this since she was practically a *child*."

"Right. I understand that." He threw several books, thick ones on neurology, into the suitcase.

"What you've *got* to understand about Serena," Tracey said earnestly, "is she's *always* been the one in the family everybody's depended on to be sensible and take care of things—just her, alone."

Cal snapped the suitcase shut. "She doesn't have to do it alone anymore."

Tracey crossed her arms more tightly, as if protecting herself. "She—she's not used to depending on anyone else. She's extremely independent."

"So am I. I've just got to convince her we can be independent together."

He swung the suitcase off the bed and set it next to the door. He shoved his shirt into his jeans and threaded his belt through the loops. He buckled it and drew on his jacket, put on his Stetson and set it at a determined angle.

"She's *proud*," Tracey said, watching the strong and stubborn expression on his face. "She won't want you dragged into this mess. And to tell the truth, I think she's frightened. Maybe you love her the way she is now, but what if this—this *thing* should change her? She wouldn't want you to see that...."

"So? Love isn't for cowards. It's time somebody worried about her, for a change." He looked down at Tracey, his face grave. "Thanks for coming. I won't tell her it was you who told me. I'll make something up."

"It doesn't matter," Tracey said, lifting her chin. "I thought about it a long time. I know I made her a promise. But I kept thinking. And you know what I thought?"

Cal shook his head.

Tracey lifted her chin higher. "I've known her ten years. She's the best friend I have and the strongest person I know. But the first time—the *only* time—I've ever seen her truly happy is this past week. With you. You make her *happy.* That's why I came here."

For a moment his somberness lifted. He gave her a tired, crooked smile. He bent and kissed her cheek lightly. "Thank you, sugar. You're a good friend to her." He picked up the suitcase and opened the door for her.

She stepped out into the hall, and he followed her. She looked up at him, worried. "Cal?"

"What?"

"What will you say to her? How can you make her change her mind? I mean she's so determined to go it alone, with nobody's help—I don't know what you can say."

He shrugged, his shoulders wide in the leather jacket. He pulled his hat lower. "I reckon if I'm meant to have her, I'll find the right thing to say."

Find the right thing, Tracey thought. *Oh, please, find it.*

CHAPTER TWELVE

"SHE'S NOT PREGNANT," the doctor told Serena. She almost collapsed with relief.

Dr. Winston Marchand, general practitioner, was a stout, grizzled man in his early fifties, slightly taller than Serena and built like a bear. He exuded an air of grumpy dependability and common sense. At that moment Serena felt he had handed her back at least a bit of her sanity.

She sighed and put her face in her hands.

"What she *is,*" Marchand said, shaking his graying head, "is bawling her head off in my examining room. I gave her a tranquilizer. When it takes effect, you can take her home."

Serena straightened in her chair and gazed across the desk at Marchand. She was deeply relieved that no baby was on the way, but there were still other frightening questions to be answered about Patti. She had to face their answers. She took a deep breath. "What about her health?" she asked, meeting his eyes steadily. "Her shaking? The twitch in her shoulder?"

Marchand tapped his fingers on the desk and studied Serena with gruff kindness. "I'm not an expert. But I called in Dr. Bradford to look at her. He's one of the clinic's neurologists. He says he sees no sign of any real deterioration—there are fifty other causes for a case of shakes besides Huntington's. Our consensus is she's overstressed. She doesn't feel in charge of her life, and she's repressed so many fears for so long it's finally caught up with her. I recommend—and I can't recommend it too strongly—that she see a psychologist on a regular basis. The interior of your sister's head, to be frank, is not an orderly place."

Serena almost managed to smile. For the second time that morning, Marchand seemed like a delivering angel to her.

"This condition, the Huntington's—" he said "—the possibility that you both could inherit it—creates stress for both of you, of course. I assume *you* have talked to a psychologist somewhere along the way. You strike me as far better adjusted to the situation. Frightened—but better adjusted."

She nodded. "I could never make Patti go. She never wanted to admit anything could be wrong."

"Well, she'll go now," growled Marchand, "or she'll answer to me. I'll give you a prescription for medication for her. In my opinion—and Dr. Bradford's—she's having anxiety attacks. The business with her shoulder is simply a muscle spasm, we think, related to her general nervousness. And perhaps a touch of overactive thyroid. But I want her to check with Bradford again for more thorough testing. We can't be too careful."

Serena nodded, feeling strangely empty. Although Marchand's words had eased her mind and subdued her fears, a strange sensation of dullness and helplessness still gripped her. *Reprieve,* she thought. *We've been reprieved one more time. Safe again. But for how long?*

"I'm also writing her a prescription for birth control pills," Marchand rumbled. "In her state she has no business getting pregnant—none. That's partly what put her in this state, and that's why she's bawling—I gave her a good talking to. A *damned* good one, if I do say so. Now—what about you?"

Serena blinked in surprise, her hands tightening on the arms of the metal chair. "Me?"

"You," he said with a nod. "You still look green around the gills from all this. Are *you* all right?"

"Fine," she said with conviction she didn't feel. "It was a crisis, but—we seem to have weathered it. We'll just get along with our lives now. Business as usual."

"Your sister says you're the responsible one in the outfit," Marchand said with a wry slant to his mouth. "That's easy to see. But you can't spend your life taking care of her messes, you know. She's got to do some of it for herself. There's such a thing as being *too* responsible. You do take time to have a life of your own, I assume."

Serena said nothing for a moment. Her body tensed slightly. She forced a smile. A life of her own. She could only have a life alone, the way she had before she met Cal. She must learn to live that way again, deadened against her own feelings and desires. "I have a perfectly satisfactory life," she lied.

"Not married?" he asked, nodding at her left hand with its bare ring finger.

Her false smile faded from her lips. She thought of Cal again, and something seemed to die within her.

She and Patti might, mercifully, be reprieved, but she still took the incident as a warning: she could not be so arrogant as to think she might live a normal life like other people. She could not have Cal, and she had been a fool to think so.

"Not married," she said as evenly as she could.

Marchand studied her again, but what he was thinking, she could not tell. "I see," he said. "Your choice, I take it?"

"My choice. Yes." She nodded. "That's the way I want it."

He shrugged and wrote out the prescriptions. "It's your life," he said.

"I FEEL *TERRIBLE* about this," Patti wailed, once they were in Serena's car. "I put you through all this— dragged you away from your work—made you go through this sheer *hell* with me—"

She sounded as if she were going to weep again, in spite of the tranquilizer. "Patti," Serena said firmly, her hands tightening on the wheel, "get *hold* of yourself. I can't take any more dramatics, any more scenes. Please!"

"I don't blame you for resenting me," Patti answered, tears gleaming in her eyes and her chin trembling. "You *should* resent me. The doctor's right—I need my head examined. He's probably lying about me being well—this is the start—I'm losing my grip."

"Patti," Serena said, trying to muster patience from somewhere, anywhere, "I *don't* resent you. The doctor doesn't think you're crazy—just irresponsible. What you have to do is get your life—and your mind—in order. He doesn't think you're sick, but he's right. You've avoided thinking about this for years, and now it's hit you all at once. You're worn out and one of the things wearing you out is *you*. You've got to take control of your life."

Patti sniffled and wiped away a tear. "I've missed two days of work. And what about Jerry? How can I tell him about this thing? What if he decides he doesn't really care about me?"

"If he doesn't care about you, you should be glad to be *rid* of him, for God's sake," Serena exploded. "If you've got to have a man, find one that *does* care. You've got two children to take care of—and how on *earth* you could ever get yourself in a situation where you might have been pregnant—"

"Serena, please don't talk like that," Patti begged. "You don't know what it's like to love somebody, to need somebody. You don't want to be married—but I do—and maybe you don't ever think about children, but I love mine, and I wish I had more—"

"I *do* know what it's like to need somebody," Serena retorted angrily. "I *do* think about having children. I love the girls, too, but—"

"But you think they never should have been born, don't you?" Patti challenged, tears filling her eyes again. "Is that it? Is that why you're so relieved I'm not pregnant? You don't think I should have ever had children at all? Is that what it comes down to? Do you think none of us should ever have been born? You or me or Daddy, even?"

An ache started pounding through Serena's head, driving into it as sharply as a nail. "I never said that," she argued. "Of course, I don't wish the girls weren't ever born—that's unthinkable. I love them. As for you and me and Daddy, it's a little late to worry about that, isn't it?"

"I don't know if you remember Daddy as well as I do," Patti said, biting her lip. "If you remember him when he was well. He was so sweet and so funny—the best daddy in the world, I thought. Well, I wouldn't have traded him for anybody, and I'm just glad we had him while we did. His life had some wonderful times in it—it wasn't all bad. And you know Mama never really loved anybody else but him. He was the love of her life."

"I know." Serena bit off the words. Her head ached harder. She had thought a good deal about her father and mother lately. She remembered them kissing and hugging all the time when she was small. They had seemed deeply and truly in love. Then the kissing and hugging had stopped as her father changed. Her mother had never been able to love another man, and she had grown into a badly embittered woman. Whether she would have been better off not loving so much, or not loving at all, Serena could not, for the life of her, say. It was one of a thousand questions too tangled for her to answer.

"I believe it's better to love and lose, than never love at all," Patti said stubbornly. "I believe in love, that's what. And you don't."

"I believe in living a sensible life," Serena said without emotion. She was suddenly too weary to disagree with Patti. It was as if Patti had used up all Serena's emotions and left her so empty she almost echoed inside. She sighed, struggling to keep her exhausted mind on the problems at hand. "You've *got* to have an honest talk with this Jerry person. Immediately. Good grief, you nearly had a *child* by him. I still can't believe it."

"Well, I'm not pregnant—so stop throwing it up to me, *please,*" Patti said.

Serena sighed. Patti wasn't pregnant—this week. Who knew what might happen next week? Patti wouldn't change her ways overnight. Who knew if she would even change at all?

And although Patti didn't seem seriously ill—now— Serena had no idea what tomorrow might bring, and she was weary to death with worrying about it, trying to prepare for it, trying to be strong for all of them, all of the time.

"You were lucky this time," Serena said, shaking her head and feeling more empty than before. "Maybe next time you won't be. You've *got* to straighten things out. If not for your sake, for the girls'."

"I'm *going* to," Patti promised, almost petulantly. "I'm going to try. I've just been terribly upset, that's all. I mean I thought I was seriously *sick.* I'd think you, of all people, would understand."

They had reached Patti's house. Serena parked in the drive. Suddenly she was swept by a ghostly wave of terror, remembering how frightened she'd been for Patti, how lucky they really were. She felt more exhausted than before. "I do understand," she said softly. She reached over and hugged her sister.

Patti clung to her a moment. "I was so scared."

"I know." Serena patted her back. "I know."

Patti sighed and straightened up. She looked at herself in the rearview mirror. "I'm a *mess*. I'm going in and wash my hair."

"Do it this afternoon. First have lunch," Serena said. "No wonder you're run-down—you eat like a bird. You have to start taking care of yourself."

Patti frowned. "Somebody just drove up. In front of the house. In a van. It looks like—a cowboy. Why would a cowboy stop here?"

Serena's heart froze in midbeat, then began to hammer so hard it tore at her chest. Her gaze followed Patti's, and she saw the familiar gray van, the tall man with the black Stetson getting out.

"Why, he's handsome," Patti said, frowning harder. "He's very, very handsome—he's looking this way. At *us*. Do you know him?"

Cal crossed the curb and came walking purposefully toward them, his hands in the pockets of his jacket, his Stetson pulled down. His boots gleamed in the thin sunshine. Serena's breath crowded in her throat, leaving her lungs empty and panicking for air.

"I know him," she said tonelessly. "I—I have to talk to him. Patti—let me do this alone. Just go in the house, please."

Patti looked at her sister, then at Cal as he approached. "Serena, why's he here? Don't tell me you're involved with somebody. Are you? And you haven't told me?"

"Please, Patti, go. Just let me have five minutes to myself, all right?" Serena breathed. Her heart knocking crazily, she got out of the car herself and went to meet Cal. She was vaguely conscious of Patti making her way into the house, slowly and with many curious backward glances.

Serena felt odd, not quite real. Her knees didn't want to support her, and the emptiness that had filled her before somehow grew until she felt almost drowned in it. She was frightened, but Cal looked solemn and handsome and fearless under the blue-gray noonday sky, his eyes steady on hers.

He can't be here, she thought, slightly dazed. *He can't. And I can't let him stay, can't ask him in the house even. It's going to end here and now, break apart and be over now. Now.*

"I was here earlier," he said. "You were gone. Was that your sister?"

She nodded numbly. She had her hands jammed into her jacket pockets, and she stood as straight as she could, trying to lock her knees so they wouldn't drift from beneath her. "How'd you find me? Did Tracey tell? I told her not to."

"Never mind how I found you. Why'd you go off without saying anything? Aren't you going to ask me in? Introduce me to your sister?"

"No," she said sharply, trying to keep her expression blank and controlled. "I left because I had to. I was going to write you."

He sighed harshly, looking her up and down. When his eyes rested on her face again, the intensity in them shook her. There was, as always, so much *life* glinting in his eyes, she thought. She felt more alive herself, just looking into them. At the same time they made her fear she would never be truly alive again.

"Well," he said, an unhappy sarcasm in his tone, "now you don't have to write. You can tell me what you have to say."

She turned, unable to meet his disconcerting gaze. She didn't like the expression on his face. It hurt her that he wasn't smiling and that the fault was hers. She loved his smile and hated that she was the one who had killed it. She stared across Patti's tattered little yard, guilty and unhappy.

"All I have to say is goodbye," she said, taking a deep breath. The air caught in her chest, making it hurt harder. "Goodbye. It's over. I don't want to see you again. It'd be easiest if you'd just go away."

"Easiest on which of us?" His voice was bitter.

"Both of us," she said and stared down at the ground.

He came up behind her and put his hands on her shoulders. "Don't," she said with a shudder. "Don't touch me. I shouldn't have gotten involved with you. It was a mistake. Please. Just go."

"I have to touch you. I was born to touch you. I can't just go. Turn around and look at me. You're afraid to look at me, aren't you?"

She shook her head hopelessly, willing her knees to stay steady and hold her. His hands upon her made her almost faint. His touch had always been her undoing. She could not let it be so again.

"Don't put me through this," she said, her voice shaking. "I've been through enough in the past twenty-four hours. Don't do this to me. It would truly be kindest of you—just to walk away and not turn back. Please."

"Serena," he breathed. One hand raised to the back of her neck. He pushed her long hair aside and kissed her nape. "I'm not the sort who walks away," he said, his breath hot against her skin. "Not when it comes to you. No. Not you."

She closed her eyes, cursing her body because it had started to tremble. "Cal," she said biting her lip, "I can't do this. You don't understand. I'll be honest. Patti called. She thought she was sick—that it had started—the thing that killed our father. And she thought she was pregnant—by a man who might not even want to marry her. I mean—*pregnant?* And in the starting stages of a terminal disease? With two kids already? And if she has it, it puts her girls at risk— they'd each have a fifty-fifty chance to get it. And Cal, *I* could get it. Four people at risk? And then another one—a baby, too? Who knows? With Patti, there might be something like that yet. Now you tell me, how do we build a future with all that staring us in the face? We can't."

"We can. We build it strong, so it lasts. We build it so strong it's like it's made out of stone. But it's made out of love. And nothing will tear it down. Nothing. Serena, turn to me. Look at me."

Wearily she shook her head again, her eyes still closed. She trembled harder than before. "Cal, I don't have anything left to give you. I'm—used up. She's not pregnant, thank God. And the doctor doesn't think she's seriously ill, but she *does* need help. How do I know? She really might do something to mess up her life—or she might really get sick. Who knows what can happen?"

"You're shaking," he said, and forced her to turn to face him. "Honey, don't you see you can't keep on with this alone? You can't. I'll stand by you."

She looked up at him sadly. "You always say that. You never understand—"

He gripped her tightly by the upper arms and for the first time anger flashed deep in his hazel eyes. "No. You're the one who never understands. Sometimes I think maybe you get off on being the strong one—it's a power trip. You don't want to think anybody else can be as strong as you—or as brave. You want to think only you are tough enough to face it and take it. My God, do you think I'm *weak?* Do you think I can love you and then be a goddamn coward about it? You run off like you're protecting me from something. I tell you. It's insulting. It's *damned* insulting, in fact."

She blinked up at him in shock, profoundly surprised by his words.

"In case you haven't noticed," he said, one brow arching and the crook of his mouth scornful, "I'm not the sort of man afraid to take chances. I make my living taking chances. Now if any man on earth is equipped to handle this situation of yours, I reckon that man is me."

She opened her mouth to contradict him, but he gripped her tighter, drawing her nearer and bending closer. The twist of his mouth grew more contemptuous.

"What else you never realize is that you *need* me. You're always saying, 'don't think about the future'—but the truth is you never stop thinking about it. I'm the one in this pair that knows how to live each day as it comes. Me. I know how to live and squeeze every last sweet drop of life out a day. I was *born* knowing it. But I keep having to teach you. You're so hardheaded I suppose I'll have to teach you again every day of my life. Because you always want to run off and get stuck in that damned future of yours."

"Th-that's not true," she stammered, fighting the idea not because it was false, but because it was so true that it hurt.

"And the bottom line is this, Serena. It's true— something *might* happen to Patti—or you—but something might happen to anybody. I could walk down the street and a damn meteor from outer space could fall on me and smash me flat. I might get run over by a chicken truck from Arkansas. I could fall down the steps of the LBJ library, roll out the door and drown in the reflecting pool. Or so might you, for that matter. The truth is that everybody in the world's at risk, and your family has a bad corner on it, but it doesn't have the only corner. Life is a mighty chancy business, so to live it—you take chances. That's how it is."

She stared up at him, fascinated by the fire and strange anger in him.

"One last thing," he said from between his teeth. "You think you're brave, not wanting to share any of this. But you're not. You're a coward. You're so afraid that something might go wrong in that future of yours, that you're *scared* to admit you care. You love me, but you've never once had the courage to say it. Serena, could you finally look past the fear, and say what's in your heart? If you're so damned brave, couldn't you be brave enough to share your life with somebody else? My God, look at you," he said, shaking his head, "you're shivering like a little rabbit. Does it really frighten you that much, the thought of sharing? Do *I* scare you that much?"

Tears welled into her eyes, blinding her. "Yes! It does—because what if there's not that much to share? What if we had one good year, and then things changed—I changed—and that's all we could ever have—"

"If all we could have was one good year, wouldn't we be fools not to take it? Wouldn't one good year for you and me be better than twenty good years for most people? A hundred years? Because what you and I have is—not like what happens to most people, Serena. I believe that. What you and I have is almost like a blessing. A man doesn't turn his back on a blessing. He takes it and he treasures it. Every moment that it's his."

"Cal," she began, then paused, biting her lip. "Oh, Cal."

His hands slid to her waist. "Don't shiver. I can keep you warm," he said. "And don't be scared to lean on me." He drew her to him, wrapping his arms around her. "Maybe you need leaning lessons, too. Probably do, probably do. Come here."

He nuzzled his mouth against her ear, kissed her neck, her ear, the silky line of her jaw.

Her hands rose to rest first on his shoulders, then slide around his neck. She laid her face against the warm, reassuring hardness of his chest. She leaned against him. It felt good. It felt right.

"Say it," he whispered in her ear, then kissed her neck again. "Say it."

"I love you," she murmured against his chest. She felt the strong pulsing of his heart like a caress against her cheek. The words tasted like a strange, rare wine in her mouth, so she said them again. "I love you."

She drew back then so she could look into his face and say it. He smiled. She loved it when he smiled. "Oh, Cal," she said, smiling too, but tears shimmering in her eyes, "I do love you. I do—I do."

He bent and kissed her. She felt almost faint with rapture as his lips took hers. He hugged her so tightly she couldn't breathe and her ribs hurt, but she didn't care.

"Serena," Cal said raggedly, taking her face between his hands, "I believe you've got no choice. You have to take me in the house and introduce me to your sister. Otherwise, I'm going to ravish you at high noon on this lawn in Amarillo, which won't be seemly."

She grinned at him and slid her arm around his waist. She hooked her thumb in his belt loop, the way she had when they danced. They kept stopping to kiss, but she finally led him inside.

HANK HAD BEEN DOZING in his armchair. He awoke with a such a violent start that he swore softly to himself. "Damn!" he said.

"Grandpa?" Lynn said. She had just stopped by his house to look in on him. "Are you all right?"

She sat down on the edge of the chair and studied him. He looked stronger than he had yesterday, and his eyes, though still blinking back sleep, were bright.

He shook his head and ran one gnarled hand through his hair. His wrinkled brow furrowed more deeply. "I had me a dream," he muttered, remembering. "No—two dreams. It was peculiar. I had a good dream and a bad one."

Lynn settled her hand on his shoulder affectionately. She was glad to see that he truly did seem livelier today, his movements stronger and surer. "What was the good dream?"

He settled back against the chair and seemed to gaze off at some horizon invisible to Lynn. "I dreamed about Cal again," Hank said. He thought about his dream and nodded once. "And I ain't gonna worry about him no more. It come to me, almost like a vision. I seen your great-grandma. I seen Mary, standin' there as clear as day."

Hank slipped Lynn a sideways glance, for Lynn, with her auburn hair and feisty ways, reminded him greatly of Mary. He smiled crookedly to himself. "She shook her finger at me."

He shook his own finger to show Mary's gesture to Lynn. "And she looked at me real stern, and she said, 'Henry'—that's how I always knew when she meant business—she'd call me Henry—'Henry,' she said, 'that boy was not born to be sad. His life may be different from other people's. But it's fine. He'll be all right.' Now I don't know how, I don't know why, but I think she's right. I feel it."

Lynn smiled, half skeptical, half reassuring. As always, she almost believed him. "Well, Cal's going to go his own way whether we worry about him or not. It's his nature."

Hank gave her a cool, measuring glance. "Indeed it is. But I ain't gonna worry about him no more. I have better things to worry about."

Lynn laughed again, humoring him. "Like what? What're you going to pick on next? Me and my horses? Tyler and his wine? What?"

Hank stared off at his private horizon again, shaking his head. "My other dream, that's what. I never had such a nightmare. It affrights me still."

"Hmm," Lynn mused, picking up his hand and lacing her fingers though his. "It *must* have been something to discombobulate you, of all people. What was it?"

Hank scowled and reached for his cigarette makings with his free hand. It was as if what he had to say was too horrible to utter without the support of tobacco.

He shook his head again. "It's too terrible for to say it out loud." He flicked the match into flame and lit his cigarette.

"Oh, come on, Grandpa," Lynn said. "Don't be superstitious. Tell."

"You don't want to hear it," Hank said ominously.

"I'm not afraid of an old dream. Tell."

"All right," Hank said and sighed. "I'll tell you, but it's *mighty* terrible. I dreamed you fell in love with—a city man—" he paused for effect "—and he was—*a tooth-dentist.*"

"What?" shrieked Lynn. She dropped his hand and sprang away from him as if stung. She put her hands on her hips in indignation. "A dentist? You did not. You made that up—just to tease me—didn't you?"

Hank inhaled deeply. "Maybe I did," he said with a mysterious smile, "and maybe I didn't."

Lynn glowered at him. Beverly was right. There was no putting stock in Grandpa Hank's dreams or feelings at all. "I'm insulted," she said, and she was.

Hank reached out and gave her sleeve a playful tug. "Oh, hush. I'm funnin' you. I never dreamed of no tooth dentist. I dreamed I sat on a scorpion. Now you get that look off your face. Tell me what's happened to that silly Beverly. What's she up to today?"

Lynn's displeasure fell away as quickly as it had flared into life. If Hank was well enough to spring such a joke on her, he was indeed in fine fettle again. But she didn't smile. The thought of Beverly made a cloud of emotion pass across her face. She was worried for her friend.

"I don't know what Beverly's doing today—exactly," she said.

BEVERLY STOOD in the staff lounge of the Crystal Creek Community Hospital, nursing a cup of decaffeinated coffee and staring resentfully at Dr. Nate Purdy.

She wore a pleated white wool skirt and her loveliest blue sweater. Her blond hair was heaped atop her head with studied casualness and spilled down in pretty tendrils past her ears to tickle her neck.

Her makeup was perfect, as usual, and she had worn most of her best daytime jewelry, just to cheer herself up and give her confidence. She had on her diamond stud earrings, her gold chain with the sorority charm drop, her fourteen-carat beaded gold necklace, her best gold ring, her gold Rolex and three golden bangle bracelets.

"Beverly," Nate Purdy said, shaking his head, "if you had on any more gold, you'd look like something out of King Tut's tomb. How do you walk and not *clank?*"

Beverly felt insulted, but she swallowed her anger, allowing herself only the smallest, most ladylike pout. "If I walk in here, at your request, to help you," she said sweetly, "it doesn't seem to behoove you to comment on whether I *clank*. Now just tell me what you and Rose want me to do today. What *I'd* like is to read stories to those little girls again."

Nate sighed. "What I'd like is for you not to blind the interns with your finery or make my nurses sick with envy. This is a hospital—you don't have to dress in the crown jewels."

"Well," Beverly said, pushing back a stray curl, "I'm only trying to look nice. I swear, you criticize everything I do. Now, do you mind if I just go do what I came to do? Which is—I hope—to read stories."

Nate's weathered foxlike face grew suddenly somber. He leaned one hand against the wall. His stethoscope gleamed against his conservative gray sport jacket. "Beverly, to be honest, I *do* criticize you too much," he admitted, sounding tired. "Rose gives me hell about it all the time. Maybe I'm not fair to you. I don't know."

He shook his head again and stared at the coffee machine. He was silent for a moment, as if searching for the right words. At last he spoke.

"I've known you since you were born," he said slowly. "Right here in this hospital. Your daddy stood there, looking at you through the glass, and he said, 'Look at that face. She's going to be a beauty queen.' I thought the world of your daddy, Beverly, but I wished he'd had higher ambitions for you. You've got talent. And I don't mean with that damned—excuse me—with that ventriloquist's dummy."

Beverly looked at him, her surprise mingling with affront, but she kept her face politely blank.

Nate sighed harshly. He didn't look at Beverly, only kept staring at the coffee machine. "You know," he said gruffly, "that Rose and I never had children. Couldn't. In a sense, these are our children, the kids in this hospital. In another sense, you're our children—all you bodacious kids I've brought into the world. And you know what they say about criticizing your kids, Beverly?"

"No," she said softly, her heart suddenly contracting in apprehension.

He met her eyes. "They say parents are sometimes hardest on the kids they expect the most from. And somehow, for some reason I can't explain even to myself, I've always expected a lot from you. Maybe because if we'd had a daughter, I'd have wanted her like you. Beautiful like Rose, blond like Rose, smart like Rose, good with children—like Rose."

Beverly swallowed. Never before had Nate Purdy said anything to her of such a personal or emotional nature. She was troubled by it and wanted him to stop. "Well, that's very sweet of you—" she started to say, but Nate cut her off impatiently.

"Now don't sweet-talk me, Beverly," he ordered. "I've something to say, so let me say it. It's all well and good, I suppose, that you got your gowns and your crowns and your titles. But a woman doesn't make a *life* out of that, you understand me? These past two years, I've watched you. You have an air of emptiness about you, a sense of being wasted and not understanding why."

Beverly bit her lip and tried to interrupt him, to contradict him, but he silenced her with the wave of one lean hand. "No," he said flatly. "Hear me out. What you get from life, Beverly, is exactly the same as what you give. Always has been. Always will be."

Beverly was growing more and more uncomfortable. She was used to having her face and body judged. But lately people had been judging her soul, and it made her feel naked and somehow incomplete. Once more she tried to protest.

But once more Nate cut her off. "No. You could give a lot, Beverly, if only you would. I said you have a gift. You do. You can light up a room when you want to, especially for these kids. I just don't know how to make you want to share that gift—not as much as it's needed."

A lump formed and tightened in Beverly's throat, and she blinked against the threat of tears. "I *am* trying to share," she said, defending herself. "Haven't I been here more and more lately? Haven't I helped

Rose as much as I can? What do I have to do to make you happy with me?''

Nate sighed more harshly than before and turned toward the window, staring out. "I don't know, Beverly. But first thing, I'd like you to see that boy. The one who's so seriously sick—you know that. I think maybe I'd like to see you do it as much for your sake as for his.''

"Look," Beverly said, stretching her hands out helplessly, "I'm being honest. He's just—too sick. The children that are just here for a little while, well, I can handle that. Don't ask me for something I *can't* do.''

He turned to face her, his expression implacable. "Beverly, look me in the eye. These are the very first eyes that ever saw you as a human being on this planet. I delivered that boy down the hall, too. Now he's sick as a kid can be, and I don't know if I can make him well. All I know is his face shines when he talks about you—like he's describing a princess. Call it a crush, call it infatuation—call it whatever you want. But, my God, he's only *sixteen*. Do you know how happy you could make him? Do you know how few possibilities for happiness he has at this point?''

Beverly clenched her hands together and stared down at the tiles of the floor. She was suddenly almost as frightened as when her father was sick. It made her feel hollow and trembly and sad and weak inside.

Nate came up to her and put his hand on her shoulder. "He's sixteen years old, Beverly. But he's human and a little bit in love with you. He might never reach seventeen. Now—look me in the eye and say you won't go to him, talk to him, flirt with him, make him happy. You tell me that. And you tell me that your daddy wouldn't want you to do it.''

Beverly's perfectly made-up mouth began to tremble. The tears welled up again. She stared into Nate's solemn, challenging eyes.

"Don't cry, Beverly," he said, squeezing her shoulder. "You'll ruin your makeup. I want you to smile instead. I want you to walk into that boy's room and smile for all you're worth. Will you do it?''

She blinked back the tears by a ferocious act of will. A small but fierce war, one private and intense, took place in her chest. But she held her head high. She remembered her father telling her that she was the stuff of which winners were made. She remembered Cal saying she could do this job, asking her to do it for him.

"I'll try," she said in a voice that didn't sound at all to her like a winner's.

"I knew you would," Nate said with satisfaction. "Come on. I'll walk you to his room. His name's Garry, and he likes football and cars and science fiction. He's not looking great right now—his weight's way down—but just remember, inside that pale, skinny frame, he's just a kid with feelings, okay?''

Beverly nodded, more unsure of herself than before. Nate walked her down the long hall, keeping his hand on her shoulder. She heard the faint echo of her high heels ringing against the tile.

Nate stopped beside a door. Beverly could hear a television set droning within. "I'll introduce you," he said gruffly. He gave her shoulder a final squeeze, then stepped inside the door. "Hello, Garry," he said heartily. "Just stopped to say hi. And introduce you to somebody. I believe you've seen Beverly Townsend before. The former Miss Texas?"

Beverly, her heart feeling like a terrified humming-bird trapped inside her chest, followed Nate into the room. She saw an incredibly thin and pale boy resting against the pillow. His face was gaunter than Grandpa Hank's, and his arms seemed like matchsticks. But his brown eyes widened and brightened when he saw Beverly, and a look of true wonder crossed his face.

He gulped, and he didn't seem able to speak.

For a moment, neither could Beverly. She had never seen a human being so thin or so waxen. Yet, slowly, miraculously, a shy smile began to form on his mouth.

"Lawsy," he said in a shaky little voice, "Miss *Texas.*"

"She stopped by to talk to you," Nate said. "I'll leave you two alone. See you later, Garry. Behave yourself."

Then Nate was gone and she was alone with the boy, who looked at her as if she could not possibly be real or be there with him in his room.

She took a deep breath and so did he.

"Miss Texas," he repeated, as she stepped to his bedside. "Wow. Oh, wow."

You can do it, Nate Purdy had said.

You can do it, her father had always told her.

Do it—for me, Cal had said.

So she cocked her head prettily, and she reached deep down inside herself, looking for a way to make this boy the happiest sixteen-year-old in Crystal Creek.

"Hello, handsome," Beverly said and took his hand. "Do you suppose you could have a little time for me?"

And she smiled. She gave him the most brilliant and charming smile she had. It was just for him, and it lit up the room.

IT WAS NIGHTTIME in Wolverton, and it was Cal's last rodeo ride, he knew. He hadn't expected it to be at a flashy, artificial place like the Wolverton Arena, but that didn't matter. What was over, was over.

He'd had them announce on the PA system that it was his last ride: he wanted Serena to know he meant it, that it was official.

He was only sorry he'd drawn that mean little bronc that had nearly killed him once, Judas, the horse nobody had ridden all season. He wished he hadn't because he knew the horse made Serena nervous.

He pushed his hat down more firmly on his brow and settled onto Judas's back. The horse danced, and Cal gripped the handhold in his fingerless leather glove with the rosined palm.

Judas reared in the chute, his hooves striking out. "Whoa!" yelled one of the cowboys manning the gate. "This is one evil devil! Damn!"

Cal set his jaw and focused his concentration. Judas moved restlessly beneath him and he clamped his thighs more tightly against the horse's flanks, set his heels to spur him when they came out of the chute. He inhaled deeply. "Luck, be a lady," he said under his breath.

"Pull the gate," he said aloud with a curt nod.

The metal gate swung away with lightning speed, and Judas exploded into the arena, bucking like a maniac. He arced so high into the air that the crowd gasped, and hit the dirt so hard the earth shuddered. Cal felt the jolt to the top of his head, but he spurred to make the bronc fight him even harder.

No sooner had the horse's hooves crashed into the ground than he was airborne again, twisting and snaking so crazily through the air that Cal couldn't help himself, he grinned and give a whoop.

The bronc came down a second time with such a crash he had no breath left to whoop. Judas put his head down and began an insane series of spinning, sideways leaps that nearly hurled him against the fence. Then he pitched high into the air again, kicking out his back legs so wildly that he stumbled when he came down, threatening to roll with Cal.

But the horse recovered, and Cal stuck with him, though the damned thing had shaken him to his teeth, and he heard the blessed sound of the buzzer and knew he'd made it, and then the pickup man was neck and neck with him and he reached out and got off that crazed piece of horseflesh, which was still bucking around as if possessed by all the devils of hell.

Vaguely Cal heard the applause, and he didn't bother looking up at the judges' scores when the scoreboard lights flashed; he knew he'd been nearly perfect, and he didn't have to see it in numbers. He grinned and picked up his hat, which had fallen.

He whacked it against the seat of his jeans to knock the dust from it and limped back toward the chutes. He was glad it was his last ride. It had been a hell of a good one, but his back felt like all the vertebrae had come unhooked.

The breeze was high but warm tonight and flapped the stiff leather of his chaps. He made his way behind the chutes, jammed his hat back on and looked around for Serena.

She came, more running than walking, making her way through the knots of cowboys and horses that milled behind the scenes. She wore her sage-green outfit, the one he liked best because it matched her eyes and because she'd worn it the first time he saw her.

They came together and he took her into his arms, grinning down at her. "Am I good or what?" he asked.

She hugged him as hard as she could. "Perfect," she said smiling up at him. Her smile was brilliant, but there were tears in her eyes. "What a finale! Are you sure you can really walk away from all this? That you really want it to end?"

"Yep," he said, touching her face. "I've got new things to begin. Besides, I want to walk away from it while I still can. That sucker rearranged my spine. I can do without that. Let's get out of here. I need to walk."

He slipped one arm around her waist and started to walk her to the parking lot. She put her arm around him, too, hooking her thumb in his belt loop, as was becoming her habit. They walked slowly, he limping slightly. She leaned her head against his shoulder.

"You are perfect, you know," she said fondly, looking up at the stars. "You can even handle my sister. I couldn't believe it."

His arm tightened around her and hers about him. She should have expected it, she supposed. He had charmed Patti completely. Not only had he charmed her, he had, by the strength of that charm, taken charge of her.

When Patti said she wasn't hungry, Cal somehow got her to eat. When Patti said she was afraid to tell Jerry about the family illness, Cal said he'd be glad to talk to Jerry, too. "We're all in this together, aren't we?" he asked. And when Patti voiced fears about seeing the psychologist, Cal assuaged them smoothly and far better than Serena ever could have.

Serena had quickly realized that Patti liked Cal and almost desperately wanted his approval. It was if a load of stones had been lifted from Serena's shoulders. She knew that with Cal around, Patti would be far easier to handle.

But even now a shadow of her old doubts came back, haunting her happiness. Shouldn't such a perfect man want more from life than her? Shouldn't he want children, to carry on his name and his values? What could he want with someone such as she? Wouldn't he grow dissatisfied with her?

"You're perfect," she repeated moodily, glancing at his profile. It was gilded by the lights outside the Wolverton Arena, and his hat was pulled down at a rakish angle. "I look at you and think hundreds of women must want you."

He shrugged, as if it didn't matter.

"So," she said slowly, wishing she didn't have to ask, "answer one question for me."

He stopped. They were beside the huge flower beds that flanked the arena's side entrances. At this season of the year there were no bedding plants set out, and the rosebushes were still hidden by hoods of yellow plastic. Ornamental crushed rock covered the beds.

He looked down at her, touched her face again. "What?"

"With all those women after you, what on earth do you see in me?"

He sighed. He took her face between both his hands. "Sugar, I'm far from perfect. As for those other women, they only think they want me. You need me. And I need you."

She blinked up at him in confusion. She didn't want pity to play any part in his emotion for her, none. "I need you?" she asked and swallowed hard. "What for?"

"On a purely practical basis, you need me at La Herencia. But mostly you need me to keep you from asking dumb questions like that one," he said, shaking his head. "And I need you for this—" he bent and kissed her "—and this—" He took her lips again, longer this time, and with even more tenderness and passion.

"And I need you for celebrations, like now," he said, saying the words softly against her lips. He kissed her a third time, so gently that she shivered. "Dance with me," he said.

"Here?" she asked in surprise, but he was already taking her into his arms. "Now? This is a garden-to-be."

"Here. Now." Slowly, hypnotically he began to whirl her over the rock of the flower beds, his booted feet moving with astonishing grace. "Everywhere. Always," he said. "But especially here and now."

She laughed and would have protested, but he kissed her again, never missing a beat of the phantom waltz to which he whirled her. When he at last drew back, she was breathless.

"It was my last ride," he said. "It was a good one, and it was for you. Let's celebrate."

He whirled her more slowly and sensuously and rhythmically. On they danced in the garden-to-be, his spurs jingling and the moonlight spilling down like silver. He pulled her more tightly into his arms and looked down into her eyes, studying her face with love.

She smiled up at him, and he smiled to see her smile.

If you enjoyed
AMARILLO BY MORNING

don't miss

WHITE LIGHTNING
by Sharon Brondos

the fourth installment of the
Crystal Creek series
coming to you in June

Lynn McKinney knows Lightning can outrun any
horse in the field—all he needs is time and training and
her in the saddle. But Sam Russell, dentist and part
owner of Lightning doesn't see things her way. He
knows nothing about horses except that this one was
supposed to turn a fast profit. Seems the jockey and
the dentist are headed for a showdown...till their
interest in Lightning is overshadowed by their interest
in each other.

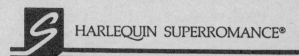

HARLEQUIN SUPERROMANCE®

HARLEQUIN SUPERROMANCE NOVELS
WANTS TO INTRODUCE YOU TO A DARING
NEW CONCEPT IN ROMANCE...

WOMEN WHO DARE!
Bright, bold, beautiful...
Brave and caring, strong and passionate...
They're women who know their own minds
and will dare anything...
for love!

One title per month in 1993, written by popular Superromance
authors, will highlight our special heroines as they face unusual,
challenging and sometimes dangerous situations.

Love blooms next month with:
#553 LATE BLOOMER by Peg Sutherland
Available in June wherever Harlequin Superromance novels are sold.

Fifty red-blooded, white-hot, true-blue hunks from every State in the Union!

Beginning in May, look for MEN MADE IN AMERICA! Written by some of our most popular authors, these stories feature fifty of the strongest, sexiest men, each from a different state in the union!

Two titles available every other month at your favorite retail outlet.

In May, look for:

FULL HOUSE by Jackie Weger (Alabama)
BORROWED DREAMS by Debbie Macomber (Alaska)

In July, look for:

CALL IT DESTINY by Jayne Ann Krentz (Arizona)
ANOTHER KIND OF LOVE by Mary Lynn Baxter (Arkansas)

You won't be able to resist MEN MADE IN AMERICA!

BE PART OF CRYSTAL CREEK
WITH THIS FABULOUS FREE GIFT!

The attractive Crystal Creek cowboy boot brooch—beautifully crafted and finished in a lovely silver tone—is the perfect accessory to any outfit!

As you share the passions and influence of the people of Crystal Creek ... and experience the excitement of hot Texas nights, smooth Texas charm and dangerously sexy cowboys—you need to collect only three proofs-of-purchase for the Crystal Creek cowboy boot brooch to become YOURS ... *ABSOLUTELY FREE!*

HOW TO CLAIM YOUR ATTRACTIVE CRYSTAL CREEK COWBOY BOOT BROOCH ... To receive your free gift, complete the Collector Card—located in the insert in this book—according to the directions on it. If you prefer not to use the Collector Card, or if it is missing, when you've collected three Proofs from three books, write your name and address on a blank piece of paper, place in an envelope with $1.95 (Postage and Handling) and mail to:

IN THE U.S.A.:
HARLEQUIN CRYSTAL CREEK PROMOTION
P.O. BOX 9071
BUFFALO, NY 14269-9071

IN CANADA:
HARLEQUIN CRYSTAL CREEK PROMOTION
P.O. BOX 604
FORT ERIE, ONTARIO L2A 5X3

Below you'll find a proof-of-purchase. You'll find one in the back pages of every Crystal Creek novel ... every month!

PREMIUM OFFER TERMS

Requests must be received no later than March 31, 1994. Only original proofs of purchase accepted. Limit: (1) one gift per name, family, group, organization. Cowboy boot brooch may differ slightly from photo. Please allow 6 to 8 weeks for receipt of gift. Offer good while quantities of gifts last. In the event an ordered gift is no longer available, you will receive a free, previously unpublished Harlequin book for every proof-of-purchase you have submitted with your request plus a refund of the postage and handling charge you have included. Offer good in the U.S.A. and Canada only.

Here's a proof of purchase—start collecting Today!

ONE
PROOF-OF-PURCHASE

088-KAW

Crystal Creek

CCPOPR